Dedicated to my husband, Dean, the man I fall in love with every day:

"For you see, each day I love you more—

Today more than yesterday and less than tomorrow."

–Rosemonde Gerard

ACKNOWLEDGMENTS

This novel began with a tube of chocolate-flavored lip balm. Yes, the incident described in chapter one really did occur. My husband really did say he thought he smelled brake fluid. We laugh about it now, but that night as we drove home from the holiday party, I remembered when we first met and the glow of young love. Years of struggling on one income while raising three children and build a house had siphoned the romance. *Before I die I want to fall in love again,* I thought as I stared out the window into the winter night.

The years between that night and today have brought many changes—empty nest, grandchildren, finishing the house in time to start remodeling. In that time, I've learned that marriages *can* be restored, love renewed, and passion rekindled.

A wise pastor once said that marriage is not fifty-fifty—each half must give 100-percent to make it work.

I'm blessed to have a husband who gives 100-percent, who is the embodiment of 1 Corinthians 13. It is to Dean, my husband of nearly forty-one years, goes the first thank you: Thank you, Dean, for putting up with me, for allowing me to write about our struggles so other couples could learn from them and work on making their marriages all they can be. Thank you for giving me the time to write and for believing in me.

Thank you, also, to the first readers of this novel who critiqued it as I wrote it, the "Novel Buds": Virelle Kidder ("Cookie"), Melanie Rigney ("Joy"), and Christa Parrish ("Ace"). A big thank you goes to my editor at Helping Hands Press, Marsha Hubler, whose suggestions helped to hone and polish the manuscript.

And a hearty thank you goes to my brother, Pete Maddock, and my best friend, Sharon, for believing in me, even when I didn't.

And to God, who has blessed me with the opportunities to do what I love.

Oh, yes—thank you to whoever gave me that tube of chocolate lip balm to begin with—you don't know what you started!

CHAPTER ONE

Before I die, I want to fall in love again.

That from a fifty-four-year-old grandmother with a thirty-two-year marriage, which, thanks to her big mouth, is now on the rocks. Which is why I'm sitting in a motel room, trying to figure out what I'm going to do, where I'm going to go. I'm certainly not going back home.

I probably shouldn't have said anything, but, darn it, I was mad. Can't the man say I look nice—ever ? So I'm not the slim, young, sexy thing Brian met in the Holiday Inn lounge when he was twenty-three and I'd just turned twenty-one. He carries a picture of me in his wallet, taken the day we got engaged, which was thirty-three years, three kids, and eighty pounds ago. Long, silky auburn hair cascaded over bare shoulders. I clasped a soft white crocheted shawl over a shimmery emerald green halter dress. The "I'm-worth-it" look was all over my face.

I suppose he thinks if I don't look like that, I don't look good.

Anyway, last night was our one big date of the year—his company's holiday party. Last year I'd felt fat and ugly. So I read up on what type of clothing looks good with my body shape ("O" meaning voluptuous with a full figure, but my volupt is down near my waist). Then I went shopping. I found just the right top to match my black velvet skirt: black velvet with three-quarter-length sleeves, a scoop neckline, and silver sparklies all over. The hemline was diagonal, ending below my hip, leaving me with no lines at obvious flaws on the body, which, in my case, is my whole middle as well as my thighs, calves, arms, and cheeks.

I dug out the dangly, diamond-like earrings I bought our daughter Jasmine for one of her proms and wore black hose with black heels. "Your hose should match your shoes," my fashion book stated.

For once my hair didn't fall flat. I slathered in extra mousse and took the time to curl it, now short and layered, as

I blew it dry. It may be short—Brian doesn't like short hair—but I'm proud to say it's still the same color—naturally. Except for about five gray hairs that I pluck. One of the few blessings, looks-wise, I've retained over the years.

I chose green eye shadow to match my eyes instead of the bland flesh colors I'd been wearing, then I brushed on sparkly face powder to give my face a "translucent glow." I looked good for "voluptuous with a full figure."

Brian was parked in his recliner in the game room watching a football game when I descended the open stairway, feeling like Scarlett O'Hara. Wordlessly he aimed the remote at the television, got up, and walked to the door. I forgot my cell phone, so he went upstairs to my study to get it—but not before giving me that "we're going to be late again" look. While he was upstairs, I slipped into my "bear" coat. I call it that because Brian once said all that fake fur makes me look like a bear. Which is the closest thing to a compliment he's paid me in a long time. When he came back down, I jammed the phone in my too-small purse, pulled on my gloves, and we left.

He looked good. He always does. Even when he comes home in that ugly brown shirt he often wears to work. Brown does nothing for his twinkling blue eyes—the eyes I fell in love with and that don't twinkle much anymore.

He's only an inch shorter than he was when we met. He's six feet tall now, still a foot taller than me. He says it's posture, but I know better. Sure he slouches, but all that weight in the middle pulls his shoulders down. His wavy black hair is getting thin on top, but is still thick enough in the back to run my fingers through. Wisps of gray at the temples give him a dignified look.

He was wearing his dark green tweed jacket with navy slacks, a white, long-sleeved shirt, and a dark tie that pulled all the colors together. I like him better in his camel hair coat and dark blue shirt, but I didn't say anything. And he wore the light brown, square-toed Dingo boots that he's been wearing for twenty years. He can't find another pair exactly like those, so he refuses to replace them.

He didn't tell me I looked nice. Not then. Not on the forty-five-minute drive to the Holiday Inn, which, by the way, was the same one where we met. Not during the entire evening.

It was the usual evening. Eat...then sit and watch everybody else dancing and having fun. We used to dance a lot in the early years. He used to sing to me too.

"I never liked the way you danced," he told me sometime between the first and second babies. "But I never wanted to say anything to you." So I told him I didn't like the way he sang either.

While Brian made his rounds—he's the owner of the company and likes to go around and greet everyone—I sat there alone, watching people ten, twenty years older than me shimmying and twisting and not caring what anyone else thought. If I wasn't wearing those stupid heels, I would have joined them.

I drank diet soda and ice water and ate veggies and smiled. But I was hurting inside. I wanted to dance. I wanted my husband to tell me I looked beautiful. I wanted him to look at me like he did when that picture was taken.

We have this thing—one slow dance a year. I was determined I wasn't going to dance if he grabbed my hand and said his customary, "Well, we might as well get it over with."

He did. And I said, "No—if that's how you ask a woman to dance. What's wrong with, 'Will you dance with me?'"

So I sat there through that slow set then watched the others doing the electric slide. The band was a lip-sync group that did songs from the fifties, sixties, seventies, and eighties. Brought back a lot of memories. Like falling in love. Like being treated like I was the queen of someone's life. *Being in love was great*, I thought, recalling my college beau, who became my fiancé, then my ex-fiancé. Then I remembered the tall, handsome Italian boy I dated in high school. How would those loves have weathered the years? Would either one of them have taken me for granted?

Funny the things you think about when you're feeling neglected and unloved and unappreciated and ugly and fat.

Brian finally asked me the right way, but his words lacked the sincerity—the romance—I hungered for. I followed him out to the parquet dance floor. The song was "Unchained Melody"—our song—or it used to be anyway. But either he didn't remember or wasn't listening, because he pulled me to him and bent his head to mine—but said nothing. And so we "danced," taking little steps from side to side so we wouldn't bump into other couples. I put my head on his shoulder, nuzzling my nose in the crook of his neck to get a whiff of his cologne—Brut— the same kind he's worn for as long as I've known him. I never tired of it.

But emotionally I felt nothing. The truth of the matter is I haven't felt love for him for a long time now. Nobody knows.

I probably could have talked to my sister about it, but she died suddenly two years ago. The emotions came roaring back then. I screamed. I cried. I sat on the couch and shook. I was so cold. She was only fifty-four. I'm fifty-four—fifty-five in eleven months.

What pushed me over the edge last night was something little, probably stupid, but, darn it, can't the man say anything complimentary?

We were on our way home. My lips were chapped from this cold I've had, so I pulled out some lip balm from my purse. I have two kinds: the regular, medicated kind and a chocolate-flavored kind. I love chocolate. Anyway, I smeared some of the regular kind on then covered it with the chocolate-flavored. I figure if I can't eat chocolate, I could smell it.

"Did you just open something?" he asked, sniffing the cool air in the car.

"Why?" I asked.

"I just smelled something different, like brake fluid, and I wanted to make sure nothing is wrong with the car."

Brake fluid. And here I showered with raspberry shower gel then slathered on body lotion, half sun-ripened raspberry moisture lotion and half skin-firming lotion. I don't like the raspberry lotion by itself. It makes me smell like cotton candy. So I mix them together. Even my deodorant is raspberry.

But he smells brake fluid.

I simmered the whole, quiet, way home. By the time we pulled up to our two-story log house, I was spoiling for a fight. We don't argue much because he never fights back. I remember one time I was so mad at him, I followed him to his woodshop and yelled at him there. But he just ignored me. So I figured why bother.

But last night I bothered. Last night I didn't care if he ignored me. I was going to say what's been on my mind for a long time.

"Why can't you ever tell me I look nice anymore?"

He slipped off his jacket and dropped it on the bed.

"Even if I don't, can't you lie, just a little? What would it hurt?"

I stood there in that stupid bear coat, clutching my purse, knowing that this conversation, like all conversations between us anymore, was going nowhere.

"Tell me I look beautiful," I pleaded. "To you I should be."

He shrugged—a slight lift of his shoulders that said, "So what?"

I hated when he did that.

"We've been married thirty-two years, and you still don't know me, do you?" I said, slipping out of my coat and draping it on a coat hanger.

He pulled off his tie and tossed it on the jacket.

"I need to hear 'I love you' every day...." I kicked off my shoes.

He stopped unbuttoning his shirt and stared at me. "You know I love you, so why should I have to say it?"

"I need to know you still think I'm beautiful."

He looked away and sighed that long-suffering sigh I hate as much as I hate the way he sneezes.

"After all these years, you still don't understand me. You still don't understand my needs. Whenever I try to tell you, you treat me like you do any other problem you're faced with: You ignore it and hope it'll go away."

The anger drained, but in its place a well of sadness, of regret, opened up.

"I don't love you anymore," I surprised myself by saying. "I think my love died of neglect."

"I don't neglect you," he answered. "I built this house for you—while working a full-time, twelve-hour-a day job, if you remember. Whatever you wanted, you got. And I never say anything when you run up the credit card bills."

"Yes, you've provided my *physical* needs," I shot back, "but you're clueless when it comes to meeting my emotional needs. I wanted to dance so badly tonight. I want to have fun. You never want to have fun. You won't even play board games with me.

"Yes, you work long hours," I continued, "then come home, eat, and work some more until nine or so. By then I'm too tired to even carry on a conversation, so I go to bed, and you fall asleep in front of the TV. I lay there, thinking how lonely I am. How empty and cold the bed is."

I stared at him, the sadness in me growing.

"Maybe I married the wrong person."

I slept alone. He fell asleep on the love seat with the TV on. No, I take that back. I didn't sleep at all. I lay awake all night, thinking of how much my life had become a rut. Knowing that in the morning, he'd act like nothing was wrong. He's like that. Most of the time I'm glad to be forgiven for words spoken in haste.

But not last night. I knew I didn't want a lackluster marriage anymore. I didn't want a marriage in name only. I wanted to be in love with my husband. And I wasn't. Our love had wilted in the busyness of life.

I want it back. I want to fall in love again. I want to experience that head-over-heels, swept-off-my-feet, I'm-crazy-about-you-feeling one more time. Before I die.

And that's why I left. Packed up what I could fit in my Explorer while Brian took his customary Sunday afternoon walk in the woods, and I left.

*****

I go to the big front window looking out at the motel parking lot and pull the drapes shut. It's evening now, and the early winter darkness makes it seem like the middle of the night. I feel the fatigue then.

Pulling my flannel pajamas from my suitcase, I head for the bathroom. After a long, hot shower, I brush my teeth, smooth age-fighting moisturizer over my face, then pull the covers down on the queen-size bed and slip in between the cool sheets.

Reaching up to turn the switch on the wall light, I glance down at my cell phone on the nightstand. I have a message.

But tonight I don't care. I turn off the light and pull the covers over my head.

Tomorrow I'll decide what to do with the rest of my life.

CHAPTER TWO

"Linda Sue, how are you?"

I recognized the deep bass voice singing my usual Monday morning greeting as I stepped to my office door, juggling a steaming sixteen-ounce stainless steel coffee mug, my filled-to-the-gills purse, overstuffed music bag, and my mail. I turned to the tall, teddy-bear-like man opening the door of the office next to mine and put on my biggest smile.

"Good morning, Wil," I said.

Professor Wilson Benedict and I taught music theory at the local community college. While I also gave piano lessons, Wil gave lessons in just about any instrument available and directed the community orchestra. He was the only one—besides my dear departed father and occasionally Brian—who ever used my middle name.

"Got those finals graded yet?" he asked, leaning against the dark pine door. He was wearing blue jeans and a black-and-gold Pittsburgh Steelers sweatshirt. The semester had ended the previous Friday, so we could dress more casually than when classes were in session. Wisps of his unruly salt-and-pepper black hair, straight as a poker, escaped from under his Pirates baseball hat.

"Are you kidding?" I grinned and rolled my eyes. "You know me—always right up to deadline. I'll be done by Friday."

I turned to my door and tried to force the wrong key in the keyhole, dropping my mail and spilling my coffee. My music bag straps slipped off my shoulder and landed in the crook of my elbow, which couldn't handle the weight. With a jerk, the heavy canvas sack slid the rest of the way down my arm and overturned on the floor. Papers I'd graded over the weekend—before the ill-fated holiday party—scattered.

"Having some problems?" Wil set his briefcase on the carpeted hallway floor and stepped toward me. Bending over, he began retrieving the papers as I stood there, feeling klutzy and stupid.

"Just a little tired," I said, finding the right key and inserting it. "That and I'm still a little shaky from my near-death experience a few minutes ago."

Wil straightened up and tucked the papers and mail in my music bag.

"Near-death experience, huh?" He arched his eyebrows and grinned, knowing how I liked to embellish a good story.

"Some idiot driving a Humvee way too fast almost ran me down in the parking lot. I had to jump to get out of his way. People who drive those things think they can do anything, go as fast as they want—but, hey," I said, pushing my door open, "I don't want to hold you up. Thanks for the help."

"Don't mention it." He held the music bag and watched me curiously. Could he see the dark rings under my eyes?

I'd smeared on extra concealer so I wouldn't look like a raccoon and put on my reading glasses, which were good for hiding bags and circles and wrinkles.

"I guess you haven't seen the memo," he said.

"What memo?"

"The one that should have been in with your mail. Hold on." He pulled the music bag handles over his shoulder, strode over to his briefcase, clicked it open, and plucked a sheet from the top folder.

"Here," he said, holding the sheet to catch the light from the wall sconce beside my door and adjusting his glasses. "All employees of the Glenwood College of the Arts are required to attend a mandatory meeting on Monday, December 14th, at 9:30 a.m. in the conference room." He glanced up at me for emphasis and continued. "All must attend. No exceptions."

"Do you have any idea what it's about?" I asked, puzzled as to why the powers that be would call a mandatory meeting during crunch week.

"There's a rumor that the college has been sold to a developer."

"What on earth for?"

"Supposedly he wants to build a retirement village."

"That's insane," I said. "What would they do with the college? They can't just shut it down."

Our building was the oldest structure on campus, built in 1910 as a high school. When a new high school was built in 1960, a group of arts-minded businessmen bought the old campus, along with several surrounding acres, and founded the college.

"I agree," Wil said. "Old things that have weathered the good times and bad, that have endured and stood the test of time, just can't be replaced. But you know the mindset these days. It's progress, progress, progress, with little thought to the history that's being destroyed. Besides, enrollment for next semester dropped again, so perhaps...."

He followed me into my office. Setting the music bag on my desk, he turned to me.

"Well, I know you have a busy morning ahead, so I won't keep you." He glanced at the wall clock above my piano. "I'll see you at the meeting."

"Thanks," I called after him as he left.

"Oh, by the way," he said, popping his head back in the door. "Nice shoes."

I glanced down at my feet—and groaned. I was wearing two different styles of sneakers. In my haste this morning—and probably because I was out of sync getting ready in a motel room instead of home—I'd put on a blue walking sneaker on one foot and a white running shoe on the other.

Placing the mug on the workstation, I dropped my purse on the desk then pushed the on button on my computer. While it booted up, I hung my jacket on the coat tree beside the door and plopped in my desk chair.

I scanned the room, feeling satisfied. I loved my job. Teaching was my passion as much as making music. In the early days, Brian and I sang together and to each other, often writing our own love songs. Then the kids came along. I hadn't written a song in ten years. Even when the last one left for college four years ago, the music hadn't returned.

Taking a sip of my hazelnut brew, I swiveled the chair to face the window overlooking the courtyard. Skeleton branches of the giant oak tree right outside my window sashayed in the wind. The sky was overcast, the clouds low and heavy and as gray as I was feeling. I arched my back to stretch out the kinks. Sleep had eluded me. I didn't know if it was my hips and legs protesting the unfamiliar mattress, my arm reaching over to find the other side of the bed empty, my brain beginning to absorb what I'd done, or all three.

Not good moving weather. I had to find a place to live before I maxed out my credit cards on motel bills and restaurant meals. Whatever was I thinking? I stared at the snowflakes beginning to swirl in the wind. I should have stayed and told him to leave. But he probably would have ignored me.

Reaching over my desk, I pulled the day's edition of *The Glenwood Gazette* from my music bag and opened to the classifieds. I scanned the "Apartments for Rent" column quickly. Nothing. I wanted something big enough to have a music studio. So I moved over to the "Houses for Rent" section, found something that sounded nice, and nearly got my socks shocked off.

"Seven hundred dollars a month!" I gasped. The last time we paid rent it was $175 a month for the entire second floor of a large house. But that was, what, twenty-six years ago? I planned to support myself on what I made at the college. But seven hundred bucks a month, plus utilities, plus a security deposit? And where would I get furniture and appliances? I guess I'd been spoiled without a mortgage. Brian was a carpenter-turned-contractor and had built our house on the pay-as-we-build plan. Our house was free and clear.

A muffled ringing interrupted my search. I stared at my desk. Where was the phone? Ah, under the music bag. I shoved the bag aside and lifted the receiver.

"Linda Laverly," I answered.

It was a student wanting to schedule a final she'd missed because of a funeral. I checked my appointment book. I didn't know why. It was finals grading week. Nothing was scheduled except that stupid meeting. We set up the makeup test for right after lunch.

"Thanks, Mrs. Laverly," she said. "See you this afternoon."

MRS. Laverly, I thought, hanging up. *If Brian and I divorce, I won't be a "Mrs." anymore. And I absolutely hate "Ms." I'm not a "Miss" any longer. So what will I be?*

As I pondered this new development, my cell phone rang. My, I was popular this morning. I dug it out of my purse and looked at the caller ID. Jasmine. Daddy's girl. Who probably called last night and got the whole story from Brian. Who wouldn't—never in a million years—take my side on anything.

I flipped open the phone. *Well,* I thought. *Time to face the music.*

CHAPTER THREE

"Mom?" Jasmine's voice came across clear and strong.

"To what do I owe this Monday morning call?" I asked, feigning innocence. "What's going on? Daddy was so upset last night he could hardly talk."

"What did he say?" It wasn't like Brian to talk about anything unpleasant. Outside, the wind howled, whistling a mournful tune in the crevices of the old building.

"Not much. I could tell something was wrong as soon as he answered the phone. I did all the talking, as usual. When I asked for you, he broke down."

"Oh?" I pushed my errant bangs behind my ears.

"He said you left him."

I took a deep breath. "Yes, I did."

Silence. I stared outside. The snow-sleet-rain mixture crashing against my window panes full force blurred my vision of bare branches whipping back and forth in the wind. Or was it my eyes?

"Why?" Jasmine asked.

How do you tell your twenty-seven-year-old daughter, still in the love-conquers-all phase of her marriage, that love dies? I was young and idealistic once, too. I had dreams. Big dreams. Maybe I read too many romance novels. Real life turned out to be not so sparkly and romantic.

"Is there someone else?"

"No," I said. "There's no one else."

I suddenly remembered the man in the yellow Humvee. He was zipping through the parking lot, way too fast for the slippery pavement, probably not paying attention to where he was going. I was picking my way across the icy blacktop, head down against the wind. I didn't hear anything but the sleet hitting my jacket until he blasted his horn and swerved to the right. I jerked my head up—and gazed into the grayest eyes I'd ever seen.

"Then why?" Jasmine's voice broke into my reverie.

I wondered how you make a healthy, beautiful young woman oozing with vitality understand that there comes a day when your hormones dry up and your own body becomes a stranger. That passion ebbs. How do you explain the longing in a woman's heart when she's fifty-something? On the outside her skin is more wrinkled, her eyesight blurrier, her hearing fuzzier, her hair thinner and grayer, but on the inside she still sees herself as the girl in the picture her husband carries in his wallet.

You can't.

"Jasmine," I sighed, "it's a long story, and I really don't want to get into it now."

"Is this a temporary thing, or—"

"I don't know. I don't think so." Feeling uncomfortable with the direction the conversation was taking and the emotions stirred up when I thought of Humvee Man, I pulled a stack of papers from my music bag, dumped them on my desk, and began rooting through them, one-handedly sorting the exam papers from the mail. I glanced up at the clock. The urgent, everyone-must-attend staff meeting was in fifteen minutes. "How could you just leave him like that?"

He left me long before I left him, I wanted to say. Physical separation I could stand. It was the emotional one that drove me out.

"Jasmine—" I began, arranging the piles of exam papers on my desk in order of class.

"Mom, think about what you're doing. It's almost Christmas. Can't you go back and work things out?"

The papers were somewhat sorted. I needed to hang up and get to the meeting. Maybe if I jingled my keys close to the phone, Jasmine would get the hint. I sifted through the papers on my desk. No keys. I picked up the music bag and shook it, listening for the tell-tale jingle. Nothing. Where were my keys?

"Well, can't you?" Jasmine asked.

"Can't I what?"

"Haven't you heard a word I've said?" She sounded exasperated. Good. After all these years, the shoe was on the other foot.

"I. Said." She punctuated each syllable, like I was hard of hearing, "Can't you go back home and work things out?"

I suppressed a groan. "No, Jasmine, I can't."

She was silent for a few seconds, which, for Jasmine, was unusual.

"You can't or won't?" She paused. "You're throwing away a—how many years have you and Dad been married? Thirty-three?"

"Thirty-two."

"You're throwing away a thirty-two-year marriage and for what? And what about your family? Your granddaughter? Your kids? Do you think this isn't going to hurt us just because we're all grown up now? Seems to me you're just thinking of yourself."

What did I do with my keys? I rummaged through the papers, scattering them across the top of my desk. So much for organization. I looked in and under my purse, then emptied my music bag. No keys.

Jasmine raved on.

Wil, my life saver, popped his head in the door. Just a minute, I mouthed to him, holding up a finger. I wondered if he noticed it was shaking.

"Jasmine," I said, trying to keep the tremor out of my voice, "I have to go."

"Sure you do. You just want to avoid talking about it."

"This is neither the time nor the place. Look, I have a meeting in five minutes. I'll talk to you later. Promise."

I snapped the phone shut before she had a chance to utter another syllable.

Wil just stood there, eyebrows raised.

"Don't ask," I said.

"I won't." He smiled. "Ready?"

"Yes." I stood, but my knees felt like they were made of gelatin. "No." I eased back down into the chair.

"Why don't you go without me?" I suggested. "I'll be down in a minute or two."

Wil shook his head. "I can wait. Besides, you look like death warmed over."

"Thanks, Wil," I said with a shaky laugh. "You always make me feel so good about myself!"

Grabbing my coffee mug, I took a sip then plucked a pen from my desktop and pulled a spiral-bound notebook from my top drawer.

"Let's go." I sounded braver than I felt.

He opened the door for me.

"Wait," I said, patting my pockets. "My keys."

Wil grinned and held up his hand. There, hanging from his hooked index finger, were the missing keys.

"You left them in the keyhole," he said. "You were on the phone, and I didn't want to interrupt."

At the elevator, Wil pushed the down button, and we waited wordlessly, watching the red up arrow until the down arrow turned green. The elevator dinged, and the doors swooshed open. Wil stepped back and motioned for me to go before him. But…I stood frozen to the spot. There, standing in the elevator, was Humvee Man—wearing nothing but red and green boxer shorts.

CHAPTER FOUR

"Thomas!" Wil's voice thundered behind me. "You crazy man, what do you think you're doing?"

My cheeks flamed, and it wasn't a hot flash. Thomas, to his credit—or, should I say, shame—acted as though it were perfectly normal to stand nearly naked in a public elevator.

"Good to see you, too, Bro," Thomas said to Wil, eyeing me from head to foot and flashing perfect, white teeth. The elevator doors rumbled, closing, but Wil shoved them back open and stepped in.

"Come on, Linda," Wil said, pushing the button for the first floor. "It's safe. This—" he tilted his head towards Humvee Man—"is just my insane baby brother. Thomas, meet Linda Laverly."

I stepped into the elevator and nodded curtly to Thomas, trying to keep my eyes on his face and not on his muscular, tanned torso. The doors slid shut.

"So, Thomas," Wil said, "would you care to explain why you're wearing nothing but Rudolph-the-Red-Nosed Reindeer boxer shorts? I know it's Christmas and all, but you're not in sunny California now, you know."

Pointing to a heap of what appeared to be brown fur at his feet, Thomas grinned.

"I planned to don my reindeer costume and surprise you. It's not my fault the men's room on the first floor was closed for cleaning."

"So you used the elevator as a dressing room." Wil chuckled and rolled his eyes. "I'll hand it to you, Thomas, you certainly are creative."

"Where there's a will, there's a way, as they say. Lulu, do you teach here too?"

Those cool gray eyes pierced my soul, and my fifty-four-year-old heart picked up pace. I wanted to appear suave, cool, sure of myself, sophisticated. But instead I stood there, stupidly mute, feeling like a country bumpkin with rumpled jeans and windblown hair.

"Yes. And it's *Linda*."

Great answer, Linda. You meet a guy that gets your pulse racing—and you can't come up with anything better?

The elevator dinged and the doors swooshed open. Wil and I stepped out.

"Here." Wil tossed his keys to Thomas. "Coffee in my office. You can get dressed there. I'll be back as soon as our meeting's over. Half hour maybe. And don't give any more ladies a near-cardiac arrest. Although you should be okay. Everyone in the building will be at the meeting."

"Gotcha, Big Brother," Thomas said. "Oh, and Lana?"

I turned around to face him.

He grinned wickedly. "Nice shoes."

The elevator doors slid shut.

"I pity his wife," I told Wil. "Does he embarrass her often?"

"Wife?" Wil shook his head. "Thomas isn't married. Good thing. He's too much of a free spirit to stay in one place for long."

"Oh," I said, flustered. "Where does he live?"

"I haven't the slightest idea. He retired early after a successful career as an investment manager. He flits around as the spirit moves him. Here we are."

He opened the door to the conference room for me. I stepped in and glanced around, surprised. The room was full. The twenty-foot mahogany conference table, partially covered with a white linen tablecloth, had been shoved against a wall, and rows of plastic white folding chairs had been placed in front of the podium. Riley—that's Dr. Stephen Riley, our campus dean—fiddled with the microphone, as a low hum of conversation blanketed the room.

I smelled coffee. Following my nose, I saw two large, shiny coffee urns and several trays of doughnuts on the table.

On my way over to the goodies, I saw Sam, our building janitor. I once introduced him to one of my classes as our "maintenance engineer." Sam would have none of that. "Honey," he boomed, his voice echoing down the hall. "I'm the *janitor*!" Anything I needed done, he did—and I didn't have to wait a week or more like I had with the other janitor.

I strode over to Sam, who was eyeing the doughnuts.

"Good morning, Sam," I said, filling my mug with steaming coffee. "How's Goldie?"

"Mornin', Lin." Sam selected a glazed doughnut. "She had chemo Friday, so she's feeling a little under the weather. Hey, thanks for the card. It really cheered her up."

"You're welcome," I said, swirling sweetener and creamer into the mixture for just the right shade of mud. "I wish there was more I could do."

Goldie had been diagnosed with breast cancer earlier in the year. It had spread to her lymph nodes, so a radical mastectomy wasn't enough. I'd always envied Sam and Goldie. They moved through life together seamlessly, like two birds in flight. Not like me and Brian.

"Attention, everyone," Riley's voice cut into my thoughts. "Please take your seats." I plucked a chocolate doughnut from the tray and headed for the chairs. Wil waved me over to an empty seat beside him. The murmur of conversation died down as Riley cleared his throat and began.

"I realize this isn't the best time to call a meeting, but there simply isn't a good time for what I have to say."

He scanned the room.

"As you know, we lost most of our investments in the recent RonDel scandal. The board of trustees tried unsuccessfully to secure a loan to continue operating. After much discussion, the board, in an emergency meeting Friday night, voted—unanimously—to accept Rosenfield & Sons' offer to buy the campus."

The total silence amazed me. Even after all the rumors, we were taken by surprise.

"We'll complete the spring semester, but with a skeleton staff, based on seniority. After that, the Glenwood College of the Arts will close its doors."

Glenwood College closed down? It couldn't be! I'd put my heart and soul into this job. The lump in my throat wasn't the dry donut. My mind went back to my office, where notes from students were pinned proudly on my bulletin board, where my "Teacher of the Year" plaque hung on the wall beside the "Heart of Gold" award I'd been given by the student body. No! This couldn't be happening! This was who

I was? I'd never find another position, another campus like this one.

Brian will know what to do. Then I remembered. There was no Brian anymore.

How was I going to support myself? I wouldn't be teaching the spring semester. I didn't have seniority status. One more paycheck. I pushed down the fear mushrooming inside of me. *Now what?*

Questions punctuated the room.

"What about our contract?"

"Can we collect our retirement?"

"How much did they get for it?"

"People, people!" Riley held up his hands. "There is still much to be determined. Those of you who are leaving will receive your final paycheck on the thirtieth."

"What about a severance package?" someone called out.

Riley shook his head.

"Once outstanding bills are paid and furniture auctioned off, there won't be much left over. I'm sorry."

At this point Riley nodded to the back of the room, and a fleet of secretaries began distributing booklets. *All You Ever Wanted to Know about Being Canned, But Were Afraid to Ask,* I thought, plucking one from the pile being passed down our row.

"Dr. Riley." Sam's voice cut into the din. "My wife is undergoing treatment for cancer. What about our medical benefits?"

Riley, obviously uncomfortable, shifted his weight from one foot to the other. His bald head shone under the recessed ceiling light right above him.

"Yes, uh, we knew that would come up, so we asked Nancy Haiggie, our HR rep, to be here to answer your questions."

I noticed Nancy, all prim and prissy and platinum, standing like a loyal soldier behind Riley. *I'll bet SHE gets to stay.*

"But I asked *you*, Dr. Riley," Sam said.

"Yes, well, obviously the board will not pay the premium for January, so your medical benefits will expire at the end of this month. You may choose to continue coverage at your own expense. And don't forget COBRA. I believe all the information is in your packets."

"But how am I gonna pay for it?" Sam said. "Premiums are high, and no one will cover my Goldie now."

Riley's face showed no emotion, no sympathy, no understanding. At that moment I almost hated him, but it wasn't his fault. He was just the messenger. Then whose fault was it? The board for investing in junk bonds? Unscrupulous investment managers? A greedy developer? The poor economy? The lack of interest in the fine arts? Or employees who had asked for too much in our last contract?

Riley was saying something about the office hours and how the administration and board would help us in any way they could in the transition, and here was dear Nancy to answer your questions, blah, blah, blah. But the words weren't getting past my buzzing ears.

I stood and looked down at Wil.

"I need to get out of here," I said.

I marched out of that din and down the hall to the elevator. I was pushing the up button when reality really hit me: I was now homeless *and* jobless. The doors rumbled open, and there stood Thomas, completely dressed now, grinning at me.

"Going up?"

No, I wanted to say, *I'm going down—down, down, down.* Instead I gave him a lame nod as we exchanged places.

"Hey," he said, his hand keeping the door open, "What are you doing for dinner?"

What indeed.

CHAPTER FIVE

"I, uh, hadn't thought that far yet," I stammered.

There was a lot about which I "hadn't thought that far yet." My life was quickly becoming one big mess. All because Brian didn't compliment me Saturday night. Was I, as my kids would say, being a butthead? Or maybe God was punishing me for leaving Brian. Or for skipping church Sunday.

"Well?"

My heart did a little flip-flop as I took in the man standing before me. He appeared to be about my age. No flab. He wore his jeans well—not too tight, not too loose. A cobalt blue cable knit sweater gave his gray eyes a hint of blue. Soft curls the color of sunshine caressed his ears and kissed the collar of his matching turtleneck. He was a bit shorter than Brian, I guessed around five-foot-ten or eleven.

"Move fast, don't you?" I said, trying to appear more confident than I felt.

"Dating is like shopping," he said. A wily smile punctuated with a dimple in his chin made him look like mischievous angel. "I've learned to grab what I want when I see it."

I nodded. How many times had I put off getting something I wanted? It was never there when I went back. *But I'm not a hot item on the "just released" table*, I thought. *No, more like a forgotten one hanging from the clearance rack.*

"Is that a 'yes'?"

I shook my head. "Thanks for asking, Thomas, but I can't tonight."

"Maybe another time?"

It depends how long a divorce takes, I thought, startling myself. Now I was moving too fast.

"We'll see," I said. "Well, Thomas, it's been nice chatting with you, but I've got a ton of work to do, so if you'll excuse me—"

His hand slid off the door. "See you around, Laura."

"It's *Linda*," I said firmly. "L-I-N-D-A. Linda."

"Linda," he said, grinning and winking at me. "I'll be sure to remember that."

Back in my office, I locked the door and plopped on the piano bench. Sliding the cover back, I stretched my fingers over the keys. An indefinable longing seized me. Closing my eyes, I began to play, softly at first. I started with songs from the time Brian and I first met and fell in love then played the song I wrote for our wedding. Then I played every song I wrote until the time the music in me died.

I played my pain, my loneliness, my fear, my anger. I played my dwindling hopes and my dying dreams. I played my disappointing past and my uncertain future. *Pianissimo* became *fortissimo*. I played, my fingers dancing on the ivory like an angry ballerina, until, in a crashing crescendo, I played myself empty.

A sharp knock jerked me out of my music world.

"Just a minute," I called, sliding off the bench and glancing up at the clock. Eleven-thirty! I opened the door. Wil stood there, holding my coffee mug.

"You left this downstairs."

"Thanks, Wil." I took the mug. "Did Riley have anything more to say?"

"Not really."

I wanted to tell him about Brian and me. I needed to talk to someone. And Wil was like a big brother. He'd understand. He wouldn't judge me or tell me I was making a big mistake.

"Do you have a few minutes?" I asked.

He looked at me for a second before nodding and stepping into my office. We sat on the two well-worn pine chairs in front of my desk.

I took a deep breath. "I left Brian."

He gave me a quizzical look. "Why?"

"It's a long story."

"I didn't even know things were bad, let alone that bad."

"Well, I didn't, either, until Saturday night."

"What happened Saturday night?"

"Let's just say I realized I didn't love him anymore, and I didn't want a fake marriage. I mean, look at you and Trish.

You two act like a couple of lovebirds. How long have you been married?"

A soft smile lit up his face. "Forty years."

"And you still treat her like she's the most important person in your life."

"She is."

"It isn't—wasn't—that way with Brian and me. I thought after Danny left for college and the nest was empty, we'd finally have time for each other. But it didn't happen that way."

"Oh?"

"You remember Brian started his own construction business when I got this job? I had my degree—finally—and was bringing in a regular paycheck, and with two of the three kids on their own and the third on a scholarship, he felt the time had come."

Wil nodded.

"So, of course," I continued, "he had to put even more time into building up his business, and ten-hour days five days a week became fourteen-hour days, six days a week. Sometimes seven. When he was home, he was playing catch-up with the work that needed done around the house and had no time—or energy—left over for me."

"Some men show their love by being good providers," Wil said.

"Well, I need more."

"I see. Have you talked to anyone else about this?"

"Who? My sister's dead. Aunt Retta's out gallivanting again."

"What about your friend—what's her name? You know, the one who was maid of honor at your wedding. Connie?"

"Kelly." I shook my head. "For some reason, I just don't feel comfortable talking to Kelly about Brian anymore."

"Is there no one else? Surely an outgoing person like you has loads of friends."

I mentally scanned my friends list then shook my head.

"I guess I've been too busy over the past few years with school and teaching to cultivate any friendships, other than the ones I have here."

"What about your pastor?"

I snorted. "Pastor Frank? You've got to be kidding! He's about as approachable as Big Foot."

"Do you have a counseling service at your church?"

"In name only—look, I don't want to talk about my church." I stood. "I just wanted you to know about Brian and me. I know I've been acting goofy today—well, goofier than normal. Now you know why."

Wil gave me a sad smile and stood. "Where are you staying? With family?"

I shook my head. "At the Holiday Inn Express until I can find a place to rent."

He whistled. "That can get expensive."

"I know. I was planning to support myself on what I made from this job." I fought the rising panic. "But I guess that's not going to happen."

"Unemployment benefits will be only a small percentage of your salary. You could give private piano lessons," he said. "Any chance of reconciliation? You two could get counseling—outside of your church, that is."

"I already suggested that last year. Brian was too busy. Said he didn't see why I thought we needed it."

"Maybe now he'll change his mind."

I shook my head. "It's too late. Even if he did change his mind—which I highly doubt—I'm through. Finished. Kaput."

Wil glanced at his watch.

"It's almost lunchtime. Why don't you join Thomas and me for lunch? We're going for Chinese."

I loved Chinese. But Brian turned his nose up every time I suggested it.

"Sounds great," I said.

So I went to lunch with Wil and Thomas and ate Chinese and laughed myself to tears at Thomas's dry wit and endless funny stories.

As we were riding back in Thomas's Humvee, Wil turned to me.

"I've got it!"

"What?"

"Where you can live."

Thomas's cool gray eyes met mine in the rearview mirror. "You're homeless?"

"You know Jordan Thames, don't you?" Wil asked me.

"The sculptor?"

He nodded. "He and his family are leaving for Africa after the first of the year, and he's looking for a house-sitter."

Until he became a famous, commissioned sculptor, Jordan Thames had been on the faculty at Glenwood. He, his wife, Glenda, and four kids lived about fifteen miles north of the college, in a historic stone house once owned by John B. McCormick, whose work on the turbine engine brought him both fame and pain. Jordan took frequent jaunts to all parts of the globe to observe firsthand the species he'd be sculpting for his next project, often taking his family with him for extended periods of time.

"How long are they planning to be gone?" I asked.

"A year."

Finally something was looking up on this horrible, absolutely worst day of my entire life.

CHAPTER SIX

On the way to the McCormick House that evening, Wil filled me in on its history. The two-story farmhouse, built in 1820, was on the National Register of Historic Sites because it was where John B. McCormick lived after he got fed up with the betrayals and lawsuits.

"What lawsuits?" I asked. History was never my strong point.

"McCormick perfected the design of the water turbine, but he was double-crossed repeatedly throughout his thirty-year career."

As we rounded a curve, a three-story circular stone tower with stone parapets, illuminated by floodlights, came into view. I gasped.

"Look at that tower! I thought it was a farmhouse," I said, having misgivings about staying here for a year by myself. "It looks more like a castle!"

"You'll be fine." Wil pulled up to the front, where a cement sidewalk, recently shoveled, led from a low stone wall to the house. Standing between two stone pillars on either side of the sidewalk, I took in the sprawling porch, which extended across the entire front and wrapped around past the stone tower. Pine boughs, tied together with red velvet ribbon, hung on the white columns supporting the porch roof. A garland of greenery intertwined with strings of white lights wrapped around the handrails. Candles lit up every window on the first and second floors, as well as the ones in the dormers. Evergreen wreaths trimmed with red velvet bows hung on the outside of each window.

"How many rooms did you say this monstrosity has?" I asked Wil, who took my elbow and directed me up the wooden porch steps.

"I didn't," he said. "I'll leave that for Glenda."

The front door opened and there stood Glenda, looking casual and elegant in jeans and a red cashmere sweater. Gold hoop earrings accented her short strawberry blonde hair.

"Wil, Linda, welcome to the McCormick House," she said, with a warm smile. "Come on in. Don't worry about your shoes."

Glenda took our jackets and hung them with a half dozen others on a rack mounted on the wall beside the door. A braided rug covered the hardwood floor, darkened with age. Wall sconces cast a warm glow in the foyer.

We joined Jordan in the living room, where he and the kids were sorting through boxes of Christmas tree decorations. A partially decorated Blue Spruce stood in the center of the room. Two German Shepherds nosed through the boxes until they noticed us. Then they came bounding, tails wagging, wet noses in our palms, yelping with joy.

"Jonathan! David! Come! Heel!" The dogs galloped to Glenda's side and sat obediently. "Good boys! Down! Now stay!"

"These," she said, pointing to the pair, "will be your guardian angels."

"Their ferocity just fills me with fear," I said, laughing.

"Don't let their friendliness fool you," she said, serious. "You came in with me. But just let someone knock at the door, and their ruckus is enough to wake the dead. Any noise they hear that isn't usual will get them barking. And they'll hear sounds you won't. Trust me. They are excellent guard dogs, not to mention their canny knack for sniffing out the bad characters who show up."

"Wil, Linda! Welcome to our humble abode!" Jordan's booming voice echoed in the high-ceilinged room. He picked his way through the scattered ornaments, tangled strings of lights, and boxes of tinsel to pump Wil's hand heartily and crush me in a bear hug.

"Humble, my eye," I said, hugging him back. "It's a good thing you make all those millions with your sculptures, because you'd never be able to afford this place otherwise. I'd hate to have your heating bill."

"Actually, Linda, you'd kill to get our heating bill," Jordan said. "We have a gas well on the property, so we get free gas."

Good, I thought, with a sigh of relief. *I won't be cold.*

The grand tour took an hour, with Glenda and Jordan alternately relating stories of John B. McCormick and the house he bought to hide from the world. Afterward we sat at the big oak table in the kitchen, sipping hot chocolate, while Jordan and Glenda gave me the specifics of my house-sitting assignment, should I choose to accept it.

"The groundskeeper will take care of the outside work," Glenda said. "The upstairs rooms will be closed off, but you'll have access to the entire first floor."

"Which is more than what I'll need," I noted.

"All the bills, including the utilities, will be paid by our accountant," Glenda said, "so all you'll be responsible for are your groceries, and any long distance charges on the phone bill. And will two hundred dollars a week for house-sitting be sufficient?"

Two hundred dollars per week of income versus seven hundred dollars per month, plus expenses, to rent? I didn't have to think twice.

"You're my hero," I told Wil on the way home. "Thanks so much."

Wil glanced over at me. "I don't know, Linda Sue. I hope this gives you some time alone to think about things. Maybe, with a little time and distance, you and Brian could work things out."

I didn't know what to say. I'd prayed for years for God to rekindle the romance, the passion we once felt for each other, that we would fall in love all over again. But it hadn't happened.

I stared out the window. It had started snowing again.

"When are they leaving?" he asked.

"January 15—that's a Friday. I'll move in Saturday."

"Where are you going to stay until then?"

"I can't afford to stay in the motel for a month." I hated what I was about to say, but it was the only affordable alternative. I guess I'll go home for the time being. It'll be easier on the family, because I'll be home for Christmas."

"What about Brian? Will he think that you're coming back to stay?"

"I hope not. I'll just have to make it clear that the arrangement is only temporary."

"Brian's a good man, Linda."

We rode the rest of the way in silence, Wil maneuvering the slippery roads and me trying to decide how to maneuver my slippery situation. Finally we turned into the Holiday Inn parking lot. I reached for my purse and pulled out my key card. Wil stopped under the portico.

"You're a sweetheart," I said, pulling the door handle. "I really appreciate all your help."

Wil reached over and put his hand on my arm.

"Linda?"

I looked at him.

"Be careful."

"I will. I have my boots on."

"No, I mean be careful with Thomas. He's my brother, and I love him dearly, but he's not the answer for you."

I shut the door and walked into the motel, wondering what Brian's reaction would be when I showed up at home.

"Well," I muttered as I stepped into my room. "Tomorrow we'll see."

CHAPTER SEVEN

"What's Kelly doing here?" I wondered aloud as I turned into the driveway. Then it hit me: We were supposed to meet at the house after work yesterday, then go out for our annual Christmas dinner. I'd forgotten all about it.

"Oh, rats!" I muttered, pulling into my space in the garage.

Kelly was my closest friend. She took me under her wing when I moved from Pittsburgh right out of college. She was the one who introduced me to Brian. She and Brian had been high school sweethearts, but that was over, she told me, long before I came on the scene.

I pulled my suitcase out of the backseat and wondered why she hadn't called me. She would have shown up to an empty house, since Brian was supposed to work late all week. I let myself in through the basement door.

Christmas music filled the house. I dropped my things on the carpet in the game room, warmed by a cozy fire crackling in the stone fireplace. A scented candle flickered on the coffee table. The spicy-sweet aroma of spaghetti sauce wafted down from the kitchen and mingled with the scent of burning logs. Did I smell garlic bread baking?

Slipping out of my sneakers, I headed up the stairs. Kelly's back was to me as she stood at the kitchen sink, her dyed blond tresses woven in a French braid. Lettuce leaves glistened in my crystal salad bowl on the counter to her left, and on the right an array of salad vegetables waited their turn under the faucet. Her willowy frame shook slightly as she peeled a cucumber.

To my left, in the dining room, a pumpkin pie sat on the table, set with my blue carnation dishes—my *good* dishes. The ones I got from my mother as a wedding present and that I used only on holidays. My red pillar Christmas candle glowed on a white lace tablecloth, its flame mirrored in the glass of the bow window.

I leaned against the wall, speechless. She was in my kitchen, acting for all the world like she belonged there. Outside the patio doors, a snow squall raced before an angry wind. It was only 6:30, but it seemed as though it was the middle of the night.

"Linda!" The paring knife clattered to the floor. "What are you doing here? I thought—" Her face blanched then blushed a shade that put the Christmas reds to shame. I almost felt sorry for her, but then anger surged, like dry kindling when it first catches fire.

"What am *I* doing here? This is *my* home, you know." Dropping the day's newspaper on the counter, I pulled out one of the counter stools and sat at the breakfast bar. I was amazed at how calm I felt now that the initial shock had worn off. But then, given what I'd been through in the past few days, maybe I was just getting used to being shocked. Or maybe my anger at finding my best friend in my kitchen making supper for *my* husband in my absence gave me more courage than I normally had.

"But I thought...Brian told me you left him," she stammered. She bent down to pick up the knife, and, as she did, her scarlet sweater slid up her back, and a black lace strap peeked out above her tight—and I mean tight—jeans.

"How does that explain what you are doing in *my* kitchen, making dinner? Smells good, by the way. Am I invited? Never mind. I'll set myself a place." I got up and pulled another setting from the hutch.

"Linda, I know how this must look to you."

If you only knew, I thought, putting my setting in its usual place at the head of the table opposite Brian's and moving hers to a side seat. I could have just put the extra setting on the side, but I didn't want to eat from dishes she touched. I plucked the wine glasses from the table and put them back in the hutch.

"I mean..." She paused, as though trying to figure out what to say that would defuse the situation. "I came by yesterday and no one was home. I waited for half an hour."

Fifteen minutes is more like it, I thought, sliding onto the stool again.

"Then I tried to call you, but your phone must have been turned off. Brian pulled up about the time I was leaving. I asked where you were, and, one look at his face, and I knew something was wrong. He invited me in, and I made coffee. He told me the whole story. Oh, Linda!" She rushed across the kitchen and put her arms around me. *Now I know how Jesus felt when Judas kissed him*, I thought.

"I'm so sorry!" she gushed.

I'll bet you are.

She sat on the stool next to mine and faced me, looking like a concerned physician with her sickly patient. I sniffed. Perfume, too.

"Tell me, what happened?" she asked.

Like I'm going to confide in you now. "I'm just not in the mood to talk right now, Kelly. Why don't you tell me what you're doing here?"

Strains of "Do You Hear What I Hear?" rose above the sound of sleet hitting the windows.

"I'm cooking supper for Brian."

"I can see that," I said. "Why?"

"Because I feel sorry for him! You should have seen him last night! He was falling apart. I just wanted to cheer him up."

The cozy dinner table, the candles, the fire in the fireplace. The perfume, the sexy underwear. She wanted to cheer him up, all right.

"Don't you think you're overdoing it a bit?" I said. The timer on the range sounded. Kelly slid off the stool and drained the spaghetti noodles.

"How long has it been since your divorce?" I asked. "Six months?"

"Eight. But it's not that."

"No, then what is it? It looks to me like you saw your chance and you jumped on it."

Kelly scowled. "I had him first, you know."

"You didn't want him, remember? You were dating Mark and dangling Brian on the end of a string at the same time."

"So? I wasn't engaged or married or anything then. I could do what I wanted."

"You've always done what you wanted, Kelly. You never thought about anyone else but yourself."

I saw it all then: All the times over the years Kelly would flirt with Brian—right in front of me. It wasn't blatant, but a subtle, teasing kind of flirting—a gentle, inviting smile just for him, a hand on his arm as she told him a joke, gazing up at him with adoring eyes, hanging onto every word he spoke. And she was forever complimenting him, telling him how wonderful, how smart, how clever, he was. "That's just Kelly," I'd tell myself, assuming she reacted to all men that way. But I don't remember her ever treating Mark like that. Now I understood why she looked so angry in a candid photo taken at our wedding dinner.

"You're just jealous!" she said to me now.

"Jealous? Of who? You? I don't think so. A shallow person like you isn't worthy of someone's jealousy."

"Shallow? *I'm* shallow?" Her voice went up a few decibels. "Look who's talking. You're the one who worked poor Brian practically to death, wanting this house, giving up your job so you could sit at home all day and watch soap operas while he worked his tail off to give you everything you wanted. And you never appreciated what you had."

"I never watched soap operas!" I matched her volume, decibel for decibel. "I wanted to stay at home and raise my kids—you know that!"

"That was your excuse."

"It wasn't an excuse."

She shrugged. "Whatever."

"I was committed to raising my children, Kelly, but you wouldn't understand that. You don't know what the word commitment means. I felt sorry for Mark after you two got married. You never really loved him, did you? You never loved anyone but yourself. Good thing you never had kids."

A flicker of something—pain?—twisted across her face. I'd gone too far. She yanked on a pair of oven mitts and opened the oven door. As she bent to retrieve the garlic bread, I noticed the glistening under her eyelashes. I picked up the day's newspaper, pulled out the sports section, and scanned the headlines. Kelly put the basket on the table and sat beside me again.

"You don't know anything," she whispered, pulling out the society section. "You think you know me, but you don't."

And so we sat there, neither of us saying a word, pretending to read the newspaper. The next time I looked up, Brian was standing in the doorway, looking around in awe. One look at his hope-filled face, and my heart sank: He thought *I* did all this—for him.

And then it hit me—it had slipped my mind with all the upset of the past few days—today was our thirty-second anniversary.

CHAPTER EIGHT

"What are you doing home so early?" I sputtered.

Kelly hopped down and rushed over to Brian.

"Here, I'll take this," she said, gently pulling his coffee Thermos from his fingers and placing it on the counter. "Supper's ready. I made spaghetti with homemade sauce and meatballs."

Her emphasis on "homemade" wasn't lost on me. I felt like rolling my eyes as if to say, "Who cares?"

"I thought you were working late all week," I said to him.

"My plans changed." His eyes avoided mine. Instead he watched Kelly as she filled serving dishes I never used except on holidays.

Suddenly I felt unsure of myself. Did he know Kelly was going to be here? Maybe they'd both planned this little dinner. And here I thought it was all Kelly's doing. I glanced at Brian. He wore his usual work clothes—a flannel shirt tucked loosely into relaxed fit jeans. Not buff like Thomas, I thought, noting how his stomach sagged over his belt. His haggard face told me he wasn't sleeping much either. I leaned toward him ever so slightly and sniffed. Good. No cologne.

Running his fingers through his hair—he does that when he's nervous or worried—he glanced at me as if to ask, "What's going on here?" Usually I hated that stupid expression, but this time it filled me with relief. I noticed he still wore his wedding ring.

In answer to his silent question, I shrugged, then slipped off the stool and sat in my chair at the table. Taking his cue from me, Brian did the same.

"What do you want to drink?" Kelly asked, plunking the salad bowl on the table.

"Water," Brian and I answered in unison.

"I brought some wine," she purred. "What's a nice Italian dinner without a good wine?"

We don't drink, I wanted to say.

"We don't drink, Kelly," Brian said. "I thought you knew that."

A look of uncertainty flashed across her face. "No," she said, shaking her head. "I didn't know."

Ha, I thought. *Score one for me.*

"This hits the spot, Kelly," I said after Brian said grace. "How on earth did you know I was hungry for spaghetti?"

I wasn't, but I didn't want Brian to suspect her real plans. When he came in, the table had been set for three, not two, as it was earlier when I walked in on Susie Homemaker. Twirling her noodles around her fork, Kelly glanced at Brian, who was intently shredding his to pieces with his fork and knife and scraping his plate in the process. I hated when he did that—the screech hurt my ears. But this time I ignored it and smiled sweetly at Kelly. Her glare could have halted an ice storm at the height of its fury.

"Why, isn't that a coincidence?" she said, putting her hand on Brian's and, thank heavens, stopping him in mid-screech. "I just remembered how much Brian loves Italian food. Do you remember, Brian, the first time you came to my house? I had a pot of spaghetti sauce simmering on the stove."

Forking a meatball in his mouth, Brian nodded. Maybe, if her memory served her right, she'd remember that Brian never liked to talk when he ate. Apparently that little detail slipped her mind because she plunged right on.

"So, Brian, how was your day?"

"A day," he mumbled after swallowing. *He never tells me much either,* I thought with satisfaction.

She got the hint. We finished the rest of the meal in silence. We were sipping coffee and tea and delving into pumpkin pie—which was not as good as mine—when I heard the door downstairs close and footsteps come bounding up the stairs.

"Grammy! Poppa!"

"Lexie, baby doll, come here and give me a big hug and kiss!" I opened my arms for our four-year-old granddaughter and kissed the top of her massive brown curls. Clasping a large, thin, glossy book, she puckered up for another kiss, then scooted over to Brian, who'd pushed his chair away from the table. Climbing up in his lap, she held up the book.

"Poppa, will you play *I Spy* with me?"

I smiled. He never could say no to her.

"Alexis Rae, let your grandfather finish his supper!" Our older daughter Katie, carrying a box wrapped in white tissue paper with a white metallic bow, plopped into a chair and sighed. "I can't keep up with her anymore!"

"I wonder why," Kelly said, smiling. "How many months along are you?"

"Four," Katie said, putting the gift on the table and hanging her jacket on the back of the chair. Katie's godmother, Kelly treated her like the daughter she never had. There had been times during Katie's teen years that I'd resented their special relationship. I knew Katie had confided in Kelly more than she did in me. But once Lexie came along, Katie called me daily with concerns about the baby, and we'd grown closer.

"Happy anniversary!" Katie said, handing me the gift along with a blue envelope.

I scrutinized her pixie face. She could look like the innocent flower, but be the serpent underneath. Her smile was innocent but her eyes challenged me. *Jasmine. Of course.* Now that the stormy teen years were past, my two daughters had become best friends. First the card. I slit open the envelope with my unused butter knife and pulled out the oversized card. Tucked inside was a gift card for Anna's Place, a local restaurant known for its superb food, romantic atmosphere, and high prices, which were willingly paid because the place was so charming.

"It's from all of us—me, Jasmine, and Danny," Katie said, pushing the gift box closer to me. "This year we wanted to do something special."

So Danny knows, too.

"Thank you," I said, tearing off the wrapping paper. Knowing Katie and her fondness for using lots of tape on gift boxes, I checked the sides. I used my butter knife to slit the tape on all four sides then lifted the lid.

"Oh, it's beautiful!" I exclaimed, lifting the ten-by-twelve-inch wood-framed plaque from its bed of tissue paper. A lump formed in my throat as I read the words: "Love is patient. Love is kind...." The words of First Corinthians thirteen printed in shape of a heart. The love chapter of the Bible. The words blurred. I couldn't read them now. Maybe later. I put the plaque on top of the card beside Brian's plate.

"Brian, look what the kids got us for our anniversary," I said, my voice having a hard time getting past the lump in my throat. *Those kids.*

Brian leaned over, glanced at the plaque, and nodded, then returned his attention to Lexie. Kelly pushed her plate of half-eaten pie away.

"Well," she said, standing, "I need to get going. Happy anniversary, you two."

I eyed the table. Cooking I didn't mind. It was the cleaning up that made me the thirty-minute cook. I rose to the challenge.

"Thank you so much, Kelly, for the anniversary dinner. That was sweet of you," I said, gathering the dirty dishes. "Here, I'll help you clean up."

Kelly glanced at Brian, whose nose was in the *I Spy* book, then at Katie, who was ignoring the vibes screaming around her and helping herself to a healthy serving of pie. Kelly shot me a look that could have wilted a silk poinsettia.

"Oh, no," she said, upping the notch of sweetness in her tone. "Sit down and enjoy your family. I'll clean up."

I sat. And poured myself another cup of tea. And cut myself another piece of pie. And enjoyed watching my former best friend clean up the mess she made.

After Kelly's second or third trip to the kitchen, Brian kissed the mass of curls on the top of Lexie's head and gently put her down.

"Why don't you go downstairs and curl up in Poppa's chair?" he said, winking at her. "I'll be down in a few minutes, and we'll finish our game."

Lexie's bottom lip curled out.

"Lex-ie." Warning dripped from Katie's voice. "You heard what Poppa said. Go on downstairs. He'll be right down. And, remember, we're not staying long. Daddy'll be home soon. Go on, now."

Still pouting, Lexie stomped downstairs. Brian rose from his chair and stepped over to Katie.

"Thank you, sweetheart," he said, leaning down and planting a kiss on her filled-with-pumpkin-pie cheek. Straightening up, he turned to Kelly.

"Kelly, thank you for dinner. It was superb."

Superb? He never said that to me.

Picking up the plaque and the card, he headed for the stairs. "Well, it's been a long day, so, if you'll excuse me—"

An emptiness opened up inside me like a huge, yawning gulf. I felt as though I'd lost something precious. I wanted to fill the void with words, but words wouldn't come. So I sat there, poking what was left of my pie with my fork. Dishes clattered in the kitchen. Finally Katie emptied her cup and stood.

"Kelly," she called, "do you need any help?"

Kelly appeared in the doorway, wiping her hands on a dishtowel. "No, I'm done. Thanks anyway."

Done? She makes a mess in my kitchen and my dining room with her romantic dinner, cleans up a few plates, and she's done? But that was Kelly.

"I stacked the dishes on the counter," she told me, tossing the dishtowel on the table in front on me like a gauntlet. "I would have put them in the dishwasher, but I don't know how you load it." She turned to Katie, who was pulling on her coat over her petite, five-foot frame.

"You leaving, Kate? I'll walk you to your car."

Katie leaned over and pecked me on the cheek. "I'll call you tomorrow morning."

When the commotion downstairs ceased and the car engines faded away, silence screamed through the house. The only noises were the popping of the fire in the family room and the soft whirring of the fan at the top of the stairs—homey, comforting sounds at any other time.

I poured myself another cup of tea, fortifying myself for the confrontation ahead.

CHAPTER NINE

"Brian, we need to talk."

He stirred in his recliner. He'd fallen asleep while I cleaned up the kitchen after dinner. Although I wasn't too happy with being stuck with the mess, it gave me time to plan what I was going to say. A lot of good it did though. My insides were churning like an overloaded washing machine. And all the carefully planned words dissolved in the wash of uncertainty.

"Brian, wake up." I tapped his shoulder then stood over him while he slowly awakened. How many times had I done this over the years? Spending half the night in his recliner had become a habit he refused to break—even when I told him how lonely I felt and how cold the bed was without him.

"Brian, wake up." I shook him a little this time. "I need to talk to you."

The Christmas tree blinked in the corner, a cheery presence in a cozy room that embraced a thousand memories. The Christmas decorations—so many the kids made themselves. The family portraits with all of us smiling, looking so happy. Who would get the antique rocker? The old school desk I'd found at a yard sale and restored? How would I ever divorce them from the memories? Divorce. Was that really what I wanted?

Superheated sap in a burning log exploded in a loud pop. Brian blinked and looked up at me, the question in his eyes gradually turning to understanding. I dropped onto the love seat. Kind of ironic.

"You left me." Sad, lifeless blue eyes now met mine. "Without even telling me. You just packed up and hurried off while I was out."

"I didn't leave without telling you."

"A note. A lousy note telling me you were leaving."

"I tried. I tried to tell you Saturday night after the party, but, as usual, you didn't listen."

"I listened."

"Yeah, like you always listen—in one ear and out the other."

He looked up to the ceiling and sighed. "I'm listening now. Talk."

I took a deep breath. "I'm not staying. I'll be here until after the first of the year. Then I'm moving out for good. It'll give us time to tell the kids."

"Tell the kids what? They already know."

Thanks to you, I wanted to say. But I didn't want him to know what Jasmine told me—that he'd cried on the phone.

"They need to know I'm not back to stay," I said. "That their mom and dad are, uh, parting ways."

Twisting the recliner around to the fireplace, Brian reached over and dropped another log on the dwindling fire. Glowing red sparks danced up the chimney, and the flames, with fresh fuel, crackled to life, licking the dry, peeling bark.

Too bad we can't do that—add another log to the dying flames of a marriage that once brightened and heated my life with its passion. But it's too late.

Brian leaned back into his chair, his lips tightened into a firm, thin line.

I told him about the McCormick House.

"Right," he scoffed. "I could just see you in that big old house all winter all by yourself—" He raised his eyebrows. "—or maybe you won't be all by yourself."

"How can you say that? There's never been anyone else. I've been—oh, never mind. It doesn't matter."

He sighed. "I gave you all you ever wanted."

"The only reason I got what I wanted is because you shoved all the decision-making on me. You can't even decide where to eat out."

"Because I wanted you to have what you wanted."

"Yeah, right."

"I did."

"Well, how nice of you. And if the decision was the wrong one, whose fault was it? Not yours. That burden was on my shoulders. I carried the blame—"

"I never blamed you for any wrong decisions!"

"No, you didn't dare! You never could face the hard stuff, could you, Brian? You can't make a decision if your life depended on it. When the kids were sick, I had to decide when to take them to the doctor. Christmas and birthdays, I came up with what to buy for whom. On paydays, I was the one who had to decide which bill wouldn't get paid. Well, Brian, I'm all decisioned out."

"I thought you were happy. I thought you liked being in control."

I gazed into the fire. This wasn't the conversation I had in mind. I was just going to tell him about the house-sitting. That it would give us time away from each other to decide what we each wanted. I hadn't planned for all this—garbage—to come tumbling out.

"Look, Brian—" I reached over and put my hand on his arm. "I didn't come down here to list all that's wrong with our marriage. I just wanted to tell you I wasn't back to stay."

"What made you think I'd care?"

That hurt. "So maybe I did walk in on a planned tryst?" I took my hand off his arm and leaned back. "Well, sorry to ruin your plans for the evening, lover boy. You could at least wait until we're divorced."

"Divorce? Is that what you want?"

"No—I mean—I don't know what I mean. All I know is I've got to get away. I can't take your—your insensitivity anymore. I try—*tried*—so hard to please you, but you always find something wrong with everything I do—every meal I cook. And tonight you had the nerve to tell Kelly dinner was superb. *Superb!* You never told me that even once."

"To tell you the truth, it was nice walking in and feeling as though someone spent the entire day working hard to please me."

"Oh, so you notice it when it's Kelly. I did all those things, too—lit the candles, made your favorite meal, from salad to dessert. Even showered and put on a nice outfit—one that didn't smell like baby spit-up."

"When? When did you do that?"

"On our twentieth anniversary."

He furrowed his brows and frowned, then shook his head.

"See? You don't even remember. And what about Saturday? I spent months getting ready for that party. I started working out three months ago. I lost ten pounds, Brian, and it wasn't easy. I even bought a new dress. And do you know why I did it? Because I wanted to see your eyes light up when you saw me. Like they used to. But you never once even told me I looked nice."

Silence.

I shook my head. "It's not there anymore."

Brian's head jerked around and he glared at me. "What's not there?"

"The sparkle in your eyes when you look at me. And I don't know how to put it back."

He screwed up his face in that what-are-you-getting-at expression that I hated.

"Brian, I want to be *cherished,* not just loved."

I paused, collecting my thoughts.

"Do you remember the night I wrecked the van? You were sleeping in your recliner, as usual. When I told you, you didn't even open your eyes. 'You were going too fast,' you said. You didn't even ask me if I was all right. I needed to hear you say, 'I can replace the van, but I can't replace you.' I know what you thought: 'Something else to fix!' 'What's *this* going to cost?' What if I'd been killed?"

He shrugged.

"I'd like to believe you would've felt as though you'd lost your best friend." I blinked back sudden tears. "But I don't think so. Best friends share everything with each other—their desires, their disappointments, their dreams."

"You know you could always talk to me."

"I tried. But you didn't listen."

"I listened."

"With your ears, but not with your heart."

I could tell by his expression he just wasn't getting it—or didn't want to get it. But all the hurt was tumbling out now, and I couldn't stop it.

"Do you remember when I asked if you wanted to see what I'd done on a music project? 'No,' you said. 'That's *your* thing.' Yet I put on a life jacket, poncho, and that ridiculous fishing hat, sat in a cold, hard rain on a vacation we couldn't afford, just to give you the fishing trip you'd always wanted. Fishing isn't my thing.

"I asked you last Christmas to hang my music award. You never did it. I finally put it away—out of sight—because it reminded me not of success, but of a failing marriage. None of the little jobs I've asked you to do would have cost you any money, only your time."

"But—"

I held up my hand. "Oh, I know you're tired when you get home from work. Yet you have time for ball games, hunting and fishing, and fixing Danny's car. You do everything everyone else asks as soon as they ask." I paused. "I must be very low on your priority list."

I stepped over to his chair and knelt on the floor in front of him. Putting my hands on his, I looked into his eyes.

"I want to feel that I'm the most important person in your life. I want to be romanced."

"I romance you, but you always shut me down."

"That's sex. There's a difference, you know."

I thought he was thinking about what I said. But I was mistaken. He had a record of wrongs too.

"You accuse me of not putting you first. What about you? When did you stop putting me first? When we were first married, you got up at 4:30 every morning to pack my lunch and fix me eggs for breakfast."

"When we were first married, I didn't have to stay up all night with a sick kid."

"And last week I ran out of lunch meat and had to make peanut butter and jelly sandwiches. You know how I hate peanut butter."

I eyed his expanding middle. "You poor starving man."

"You say you want to please me. When was the last time you made mashed potatoes? Or homemade noodles?"

"Well, I've got a career now—one I gave up to raise our family."

"Your career used to be making me happy. Your career used to be us. Whatever happened to that? How many times have I come home and supper isn't even started? So, yeah, it was nice when I walked in tonight. It made *me* feel...loved."

"You know what she was after, don't you? It wasn't an innocent little dinner, Brian."

"I'm not stupid, Lin. You know what? It was nice to be wanted for once."

He sighed. "Somehow, the Linda I knew and loved—the girl I married—got lost in the rush to prove herself with a career. To make herself important. Well, you were the most important thing in my world. The most important thing in the kids' world."

I grabbed his hands. "Maybe—maybe we can start over."

That definitely wasn't what I'd planned to say. But, for the first time in years, I'd poured my heart out to him. Maybe there was hope. Maybe he loved me enough to change. I searched his eyes. For a heartbeat I thought I saw a spark. But then he turned away and stared into the fire.

"I don't think so." He shook his head. "I'm too old to change."

"You're not too old, Brian. You're only fifty-seven. Nobody's too old to change—unless they don't want to."

He sighed. "Then I don't want to. It's just too much effort."

"So what you're saying is that you don't love me enough."

"I'm just too *tired*, Lin. Tired of busting my butt trying to give you things you don't appreciate."

He pushed my hands away and stood. I leaned back on my heels and stared up at him. He looked down at me—Was that pity in his eyes?—and shook his head.

"When I came back Sunday and found you gone, Lin, something died in me. I don't know if I can get it back. I don't know if I even want it back." He stepped away. "I'm going to bed. It's been a long day."

Pausing at the bottom of the stairs, he turned to me. "You can have the guest room. Good night."

How long I knelt on the floor, weeping into his empty chair, I don't know. But one thing I did know. This time there was no coming back.

CHAPTER TEN

"This is the last of it," Danny said, scanning the room for a place to deposit the box he'd lugged in from the carport. Surprisingly, the holidays had flown by, with family get-togethers, packing up the Christmas decorations one last time, and getting ready for the big move. I'd had no clue it would be so overwhelming. What to leave?

I'd spent the first two weeks of the new year organizing and packing while Brian worked twelve-hour days, then came home and holed up in his woodshop until I went to bed. We'd barely spoken to each other since that night he told me it was over between us. I felt like a stranger in my own home.

We told the kids on New Year's Day. The girls, who'd been hoping that I was home to stay, tried to talk me out of it and sulked when I didn't cave in. But Danny said nothing and acted the entire time he was home on semester break as though things were normal.

Now, finally, it was mid-January, and I was moving out of the house where I'd spent nearly half of my life.

"Over here," I said, shoving a carton of books into the corner. "Easy. There's glass in that one."

Danny placed the box on the floor with care. Jonathan and David, the two German Shepherds that would be my house buddies for the next year, plopped down in front of the stone fireplace, tails thumping contentedly on the carpet.

"Do you want me to take anything upstairs?" Danny asked, pulling his cell phone out of his jeans pocket and checking to see if he had any messages. I eyed the clutter strewn about the den. It would take me days to get settled in. I shook my head.

"The upstairs is closed off. I'll be using the room off the tower room as my bedroom."

I stepped over boxes and bags to get to the bedroom doorway and reached around the door jam to switch on the bedroom's ceiling light. Danny peered in the bedroom, decorated in shades of blue—drapes, bedspread, throw pillows, walls, and area rugs.

"You're gonna love it here," he said with a grin.

Pushing aside some clothes on hangers draped over one of the two matching leather recliners, he dropped into the seat, lanky legs swung over the arm of the chair, thumbs busy pecking the phone keys. Outside, the waning sun cast its midwinter rays over the snow-covered lawn.

Suddenly I felt unsure of myself. Was I doing the right thing? Well, too late now. My stomach growled, and I realized that I'd not eaten since breakfast. *That's why I'm feeling so anxious,* I thought, glancing at the mantle clock.

"Hey, Danny, what do you say we grab an early supper? How about Chinese? Or do you have plans?"

Danny looked at his watch then furrowed his eyebrows. Of course he had plans. It was Saturday night. What twenty-two-year-old wouldn't?

He looked up from his phone and grinned. "I'll drive."

A half hour later we were ensconced in a booth, chowing down stir fry and rice and sipping egg drop soup.

"When does practice start?" I asked, blowing on my spoon to cool my steaming soup.

He speared a chunk of broccoli with his fork a little harder than he needed to. "I won't be playing baseball this year."

I put down my spoon and stared at him. I was shocked. Baseball was Danny's first love. "Why not?"

He smiled sadly. "Grades."

"Oh."

I should have known. Danny had been on the borderline of eligibility for two or three semesters now. I didn't know if the classes were as difficult as he said they were or if he just wasn't working as hard as he should have been.

"Have you told your father?" I didn't know who this would be harder on, Danny or Brian, who had big dreams for his only son.

"Not yet. I was going to over break, but then you dropped your bombshell, and I thought maybe it would be better to wait until things cooled down."

I sipped my ice water. "Well, don't put off telling him. That's your problem—you procrastinate too much."

"I won't."

I smiled. He probably would. And I would probably be the one to tell Brian. *Oh, well, I'll cross that bridge when I come to it.*

"Uh-oh," he muttered, his eyes fixed on something behind me.

"Uh-oh what?" I twisted around to see what he was staring at.

He took a breath. "Don't turn around. Dad just walked in with Kelly Windsor."

My heart stopped. My world stopped. With trembling fingers I put my spoon on the table and swiped my lips with my napkin. I felt as though someone was strangling me.

"Be cool. Here they come," Danny whispered. I put my face close to the table, snatched my fork, and chased the rice around my plate. "They're at the buffet."

The waitress came and plunked down our refills. I wanted to ask for the check and hightail it out of there, but Danny wasn't done eating. So I ordered a diet cola and tried not to peek. But peek I did. My heart fluttered when I caught sight of Brian. He was wearing a forest green chamois shirt with jeans. *He's got some nerve. I gave him that shirt last year for Christmas. This is the first time I've seen him wear it.* Kelly wore a maroon sweater with a deeply scooped neckline. *Probably has one of those push-up bras on.* She looked poured into her jeans, as usual. I wondered if she was wearing black lace underneath.

"Didn't take long," I muttered.

"Here they come!" Danny whispered loudly.

"Sh-h!" Putting my elbow on the table, I used my hand to shield my face. I heard Kelly chattering to Brian as they passed within a few feet of our booth. But they were too immersed in each other to notice the other diners, which was both good and bad. Good because I didn't want them to see us. Bad because, well, I wasn't out of the house a day and here they were together, apparently on a date.

"Hey," Danny said. "I thought Dad didn't like Chinese food."

I rolled my eyes and jerked my head toward the side room where Romeo and Juliet dined. "Apparently he does now."

Anger, hurt, and hatred churned inside me. I felt betrayed. *Darn him!* Tears, unbidden, spilled down my cheeks. *Darn him, darn her, darn the whole stinking situation!* I plucked a fresh napkin out of the stainless steel holder on the table and jabbed my eyes. *And darn if I'm going to cower in this booth just because they showed up!*

I blew my nose in the napkin, tossed it down on the table, slid out of the booth, and hurried to the dessert case, slipping on the wet tile floor. *Why don't people wipe their feet?* I grabbed a clean plate from the stack and heaped on several spoonfuls of chocolate pudding, as well as chunks of watermelon and cantaloupe. I decided I wanted more egg drop soup, so I ladled some into a small bowl then headed back to the booth. As I passed the entrance, I heard someone call my name. I turned, saw Thomas—and slipped on the wet floor. The plate and bowl flew out of my hands, clattering on the hard floor. Pudding and soup splattered everywhere. Watermelon and cantaloupe rolled across the floor. And out of the corner of my eye I glimpsed a forest green shirt and a maroon sweater.

CHAPTER ELEVEN

All noise in the restaurant stopped. I felt like a clumsy teenager who'd just dropped her tray in the high school cafeteria, like I was in one of those "want to get away?" commercials. Someone snickered. Kelly. Which gave me the courage to do what I did next.

"I'm so sorry," I said sweetly to the waiter and waitress who had both come running. I pointed to the wet floor. "You know, this is a lawsuit waiting to happen."

"So sorry," the waiter said, waving off the staff that had congregated by the kitchen door. "You are all right? Yes?"

I smiled and pretended to test my movement. "I think so. Thanks." My neck felt a bit like it was out of joint. My nose was for sure.

Another waitress appeared, bearing an armload of towels. As the murmur of conversation resumed, I turned to where I'd glimpsed the green shirt and maroon sweater. Brian, mouth agape, stood about three feet from me, grasping an empty plate, looking absolutely horrified. Kelly, standing to the left of Brian and a step behind him, gave me one of her cat-smiles.

"How did you ever manage to stay on your feet like that?" she purred. "I would have fallen for sure."

I smiled and shrugged.

"Practice," I said simply, grabbing a towel from the waiter mopping up the mess. I bent and swabbed my splattered jeans.

"Brian," I heard Kelly say in that sickeningly syrupy voice of hers, "you've got to try General Tso's chicken. You'll love it."

No, he won't. I almost snickered myself. *It's too spicy for him.* I straightened up in time to see her slip her arm through his and lead him away.

"That was great," a deep voice said right behind me.

"Ooooo!" I spun around. "Oh, Thomas, you startled me." With trying not to make a complete fool of myself and thwarting Kelly's efforts to the opposite end, I'd forgotten about him.

He grinned. "Darn, I wish I had my camera. We could've been on America's Funniest Home Videos."

"It wasn't *that* funny, was it?" Then I got a brilliant idea. "Are you by yourself?" *Please say yes.*

He nodded. "Picking up some takeout and heading back to Wil's. He and Trish are out for the evening, so I'm all alone."

Not for long, I hoped. "Hey, why don't you join us—" I nodded to the booth where Danny sat, fiddling with his cell phone—"my son and me."

Thomas glanced in Danny's direction, arched his neck forward, then turned to me, his gray eyes showing a hint of surprise. "That can't be your son. You're much too young to have a son that old."

I felt myself having an instant hot flash. I put on my most seductive smile. "I take that as a compliment. Will you join us, then?"

He shrugged. "Why not."

Danny's busy thumbs ceased pushing the cell phone buttons when I appeared at the table with Thomas, who slid into the booth beside me. I introduced Thomas as Wil's brother and Danny as my youngest. Danny held out his hand. Thomas shook it.

My brilliant idea was growing. I wondered how I could finagle a ride home from Thomas. *That would really show them.* I glanced at my watch and gasped.

"Danny, what time did you say you had to meet your friend?" *Play along, Danny. Play along. Please.*

Danny's face registered surprise. I shifted my eyes to Thomas, then to the room where Brian and Kelly were.

"Aww, man!" Danny wiped his mouth with his napkin and checked the time on his cell phone. "I totally forgot." He had the presence of mind to look panicked. *Bless you, Danny boy. I owe you.*

"Hey," he said to Thomas, "can you do me a big favor? I've got to meet a friend—actually she's a girl I just met and—well, you know—"

Thomas grinned and nodded. "Been there, done that."

"And Mom needs a ride home. Would you mind?"

Thomas hesitated then turned to me, his pale eyes scanning my face, my neck. "Be glad to."

"Thanks, Dude." Danny slid out of the booth, leaned past Thomas and pecked me on the check. "I'll be in touch."

We watched him hustle out the door.

"Nice kid," Thomas said. The waitress came to take his drink order.

"Tsingtao," he said.

"Put it on my check," I told her. I turned to Thomas. "The least I could do. I really appreciate you helping us out like this."

"No problem." He slid out of the booth and headed for the buffet. As I watched Thomas fill his plate, my mind worked on how to get Brian and Kelly to notice us.

My chance came as they were leaving. Thomas, in Danny's seat across from me, and I were chatting. I couldn't wave to them. It would be too obvious, too uncool. So I reached across the booth and lightly put my hand on Thomas's arm, a gesture I hoped looked cozy and intimate. Thomas's eyebrows arched then he noticed Brian and Kelly. He leaned toward me. I leaned toward him.

"How far do you want to play this?" he whispered with a gleam in his eyes.

He stretched across the table and kissed me. It wasn't a passionate, lover's kiss, but it wasn't a smooch either. I felt myself getting hotter. I opened my eyes, willing myself not to look and see if Brian and Kelly noticed.

"Mission accomplished," Thomas murmured, winking at me. His face was still inches from mine. My heart pounded. My knees turned to jelly. I smiled and rubbed my nose against his. "Thanks," I whispered.

"Your ex?" Thomas asked after they'd left. Wil. Of course. That's how Thomas knew.

"Soon to be. I just moved out today."

"Ouch. Still hurting, then, huh?"

I paused then nodded.

"Who was the blond babe with him?"

I sipped my diet cola. "The blond *babe* is—was—a friend of ours."

"She the reason you left him?"

I sighed. How to explain? I was tired of explaining. I wanted to go home. To bed. Alone. Thomas took my silence for a "yes."

"Hey, babe," he said, running his fingers down my cheek. "You're not too bad yourself."

I grabbed his hand and gave it a little kiss. "Thanks." I turned my head to look out the window—and there was Brian, opening the car door for Kelly, but staring in the restaurant—right at me. For an instant I thought he looked angry, then sad. But it was probably a trick of the street light. I looked away. The next time I checked, he was gone.

I paid for our meals with my credit card then headed out the door with Thomas. I His hand rested on my back as we made our way to his Humvee.

"People call it a that," Thomas explained as he pulled out of the parking lot—and after I'd mistakenly called his "more money than sense" vehicle a Humvee. "But that's the military version. The civilian version, which this baby is—" he tapped the dashboard—"is called a Hummer."

"I see." I settled in my seat. "What all did Wil tell you?"

We approached the mall intersection. Traffic, as usual for a Saturday night, was horrendous. The light turned red. My body jerked back against the seat as Thomas gunned through the intersection.

"Outside of warning me to stay away from you, nothing." We approached another intersection. "Which way?"

"Left." I dug my fingernails into the leather handle on the passenger door and breathed a sigh of relief when the left turn arrow stayed green. "Why did he warn you to stay away from me?"

"He just said that you and your husband were going through a difficult time, and that you'll eventually get things worked out, so stay away and don't complicate things."

I snorted.

"Yeah, that's what I think, too. Especially after seeing him with that babe."

Fifteen silent minutes later, we turned in the driveway to the McCormick House. *Should I ask him in?* While I hungered for romance, after thirty-two years of marriage, I didn't know how to go about this dating thing.

"Around back," I directed him.

He stopped under the portico. *This is it. What next?* I pulled the handle on my door.

"Wait," Thomas grabbed my left hand and pulled it towards him. But he didn't take me in his arms. He just fingered my wedding ring, which was good and stuck on my fat finger.

"Linda." He gazed into my eyes. "I'm not the rapper, no matter what you may have heard and no matter how I act sometimes."

The words of that long-ago song came back to me. I smiled. "You're not? That's good to know. You had me worried there for a bit."

Something like longing flashed through his eyes—but so quick I thought I imagined it. "Linda, I'll be honest with you. I'm tempted. You're not a bad-looking broad."

"Thanks. You don't know how that makes me feel." I leaned against the door. "But don't call me a broad. Please. It's as bad as 'chick.' I hate that term."

He smiled. "You're not a bad-looking *woman*. How's that?"

I smiled back. "Better."

"I make it a policy not to go to bed with an unwilling woman."

"Who...who says I'm...unwilling?" I asked, flustered.

He looked me over from head to foot. I felt as though he could see through my clothes. A chill shot up my spine. Maybe I wasn't as fat as I thought I was. He pulled me to him and kissed me—a hungry kiss that stirred something in me that I thought was long dead. I pulled away from him. The moonlight revealed his expression—and it wasn't anger. It was a strange mixture of sadness and triumph.

"That tells me," he said, turning away and starting the Hummer. "Good night, Linda. Thanks for dinner."

I fumbled with the door handle.

"Good night," I mumbled. Then, more clearly, "Good night, Thomas. Thanks for everything."

Darn it, I thought as I watched him drive off into the night. Then another part of me whispered, *Maybe you should be thankful.*

I shook my head. I must be going crazy for sure, standing outside on a winter night, talking to myself. I unlocked the door and, with a shiver, stepped inside.

CHAPTER TWELVE

The week after I moved in, so did Ol' Man Winter. Snowstorm followed snowstorm, with lake effect squalls adding to the drifts daily. Arctic air howled down out of Canada. I was glad there was nowhere I had to go. Once a week I'd venture out for groceries. Other than that, I spent the days reading to my heart's content, mostly romance novels. And playing piano. And sleeping. And getting over the flu, which I came down with two days after the restaurant incident.

Some days I didn't even get out of my jammies. Television wasn't much of a draw. Most of the programs were inane and plotless. Not a great fan of radio, I turned on The Weather Channel whenever I wanted noise.

Once a day I checked my e-mail. Most messages were spam or promotions from businesses or forwards or something equally impersonal. I did, however, wander into an over-forty chat room, where I met "Matt." I told him I was forty-five, blond, five-foot-two, one-hundred-thirty-five pounds, blue eyes, and was divorced. So I lied a little bit. I didn't tell him where I lived, though he pressed. He posted a picture of himself on blogspot. I checked. Buff. Handsome. Tan. Light brown, longish hair. Looked like a lot younger than the fifty he told me he was. When he suggested we meet somewhere "neutral," I told him no thanks and never went back to that chat room again. Or any chat room. I visited a couple of dating and matchmaking websites—those that I'd heard were reputable, but chickened out there, too. That might be the highway to love these days, but it wasn't for me. I wanted a man in the flesh. And I wanted to meet him the old-fashioned way.

Wil called the week after I moved in to see how I was doing.

"How's your brother these days?" I asked, trying to sound nonchalant.

"Haven't heard from him. As usual, he escaped to someplace warm after the holidays. Who knows where? Florida. California. Aruba."

"He's a real character—that Rudolph costume was a hoot," I said, hoping Wil would volunteer more information. He didn't, and I didn't want to be obvious. But I was disappointed. Why hadn't Thomas told me he was leaving for the winter?

*****

On the evening of January 31st Brian called.

"What in blazes am I to do with all these bills?" he asked.

"Pay them," I said. *Dummy.*

"I don't know where the checkbook is." The whine in his voice grated my nerves.

"On my desk in the folder marked monthly budget," I snapped. "I told you. Remember?"

"No, I don't remember. Hold on." I waited. In the background I heard what sounded like music. Was Kelly there? I heard paper rustling.

"Here it is."

"There should be a spreadsheet with all the bills listed and when they're due. What bills came in?"

I'm sure by now it was a mess, but I didn't feel sorry for him. I was glad that monkey was finally off my back.

"What are you doing?" He sounded more like he was issuing a command than asking.

"I'm getting ready for bed. Why?"

"I'm coming over."

"Now?"

"Yes, now. I can't figure this out, and I need you to show me."

"You can't come now," I stammered.

"Why not? You said you're just getting ready for bed. You *are* alone, aren't you?"

"That's none of your business."

"Well, too bad, because I'm coming."

"Brian, wait—" My voice spoke to empty air. He'd already hung up. Meanwhile I decided to give myself a facial then curl up in the den with my book.

Forty minutes later tires crunched on the snow out back. I peeked out the window. It was Brian, all right.

"Are you crazy—coming out on a night like this?" I said, opening the back door and letting him in, along with a blast of frigid air. "A snowstorm is in progress, in case you hadn't noticed."

He stomped his boots on the throw rug by the door and shoved the budget folder at me. "I want to get these in the mail tomorrow. Some are already late," he said, shrugging his coat off and hanging it up on a coat hook. He bent over, unlaced his boots, and pulled them off. Straightening up, he took the folder out of my hands. "Let's get to it, then." He paused, leaned towards me, and peered at my face. "What on earth is that green stuff all over your face?"

Oops. The facial. I'd forgotten.

"A beauty mask," I said, hurrying to the bathroom. "I'll be right back. Why don't you put some water on for tea?"

We sat at the kitchen table for the next hour while the snow swirled, the wind howled, and the thermometer plunged outside. Inside the temperature was heating up. Brian hadn't known the credit card bill was as high as it was.

"This was to be for emergencies only," he growled.

"Danny's college books aren't an emergency?"

"Wasn't there money in checking? You know I hate credit cards."

I sighed—nice and loud for effect. "One book alone cost one hundred fifty dollars. And he had to have it before the next class. What was I supposed to do?"

"Write a check from our account. That's why I work my tail off, woman."

"I don't have the checkbook. I left it with you—remember?"

"We're still married, and you still have access to the money in our account—for Danny's needs *and* yours."

"But I don't want to access it. I can support myself very well, thank you."

I didn't, of course, tell him about my "mad money" account, the savings account I'd opened in my name only five years ago when I'd started teaching at the college. It wasn't much—I'd been able to squirrel away only fifty bucks or so every payday—but it was enough, with my unemployment checks, to help me get by.

"You can support yourself, all right—by using our credit card. If you left the checkbook, why didn't you leave the credit card, too?"

"Because," I said in my best you-are-such-an-idiot tone, "the checking account will get all screwed up if we both write checks without the other knowing."

He mumbled something I didn't understand and wrote a check for the entire balance. He didn't say anything about Danny and baseball, and I wasn't going to open that can of worms.

"Have I gotten anything from the church?" I asked him while he was getting ready to leave.

He bent over to lace his boots. "Like what?"

"Like the music schedule for February." I was usually scheduled to play the piano once a month, except January, the month I requested no duties. January had always been my personal R&R time. I'd missed church the past two weeks. The Sunday after I moved out I was too exhausted to go. The next Sunday I had the flu.

"Nope." He straightened up. "Haven't seen anything."

I was puzzled. I should have gotten something last week.

"Has anyone called? Left a message?"

"Nope."

I'll just have to call the church then. It probably got lost in the mail with all the Christmas bills.

"Let me know *immediately* when it comes," I said, glancing at the whiteout outside. "And be careful going back."

He got a silly little grin on his face. "Yes, dear."

I watched out the kitchen window as he swept the snow off the windshield and hood of his truck. It wasn't until his taillights were swallowed up in the whiteout that I realized what day it was—we'd met thirty-three years ago tonight.

*****

On February 2nd Punxsutawney Phil didn't see his shadow, which meant spring was just around the corner. He was wrong, of course. But we did have a break in the weather.

So I thought I'd take the day to see about putting in some job applications for next year. I'd have to find my own place when the Thames returned in November, which meant rent and utilities, as well as furniture, pots, pans, dishes, and who knows what else. Panic started to creep in. *Cross that bridge when you come to it,* I scolded myself.

First I stopped in at the unemployment office, officially known as the Department of Labor and Industry, to check on the status of my application for unemployment compensation. My weekly benefits should have begun around mid-January, but there had been some complication I didn't understand, something they told me they had to look into. I'd called every week—I was using my credit card too much for comfort—but the application was still "pending" they said. This time a woman wearing black slacks and a red and white turtleneck sweater with a wooden Punxsy Phil pin on the collar approached me.

"Linda Laverly?"

I nodded.

"Please come with me."

Finally. I grabbed my purse and followed her into her office.

"Help yourself to a shadow cookie and some hot chocolate," she said, indicating the tray of groundhog cookies and a carafe that I assumed contained the hot chocolate on her rather messy-looking desk.

I shook my head. "Watching my weight. How much am I going to get?"

She opened my file, studied it, and bit her lip. "Nothing."

"What?" Maybe I heard her wrong. "Did you say 'nothing'?"

She nodded, her eyes betraying her pity.

"But I thought I was eligible to receive benefits," I stammered. "I was laid off. The college is shutting down."

"Linda, the college never paid in, and you can't get what you didn't pay in."

It was as though someone punched me in the gut. Hard.

"What do you mean I never paid in? I have my check stubs. UEC was deducted from every paycheck."

She sighed. "L & I never received it."

I was stunned. "But...where...what happened to the money?"

She shrugged. "You'll have to ask them."

Speechless, I hurried out, stumbling over her boots near the door.

I stopped at the college in a panic. All I got, though, was the runaround. I tried to talk to every person on the pass-the-buck list, but the wonderful college that had once opened its doors to me had changed its attitude. I felt unwelcome—like an enemy to be dealt with skillfully and tactfully. There was one place on campus, I knew, I'd always be welcome.

"I don't understand, Wil, how can they do this?" I cried after I told him what had happened. Thankfully he had no classes at the time and had no students waiting to see him. In fact, the whole place was a ghost of what it once was.

"I'm sorry, Lin." He sat beside me, handing me a steaming mug. "Have you put in any applications in the local school districts?"

I took a sip and burned my tongue. "Not yet."

"What about private piano lessons? That was always your passion, next to writing music."

"I wanted to wait until spring when I could find a studio in town. I don't want to give lessons at the McCormick House. Too far for students to drive. Besides, I don't feel right asking strangers to a house that isn't mine."

He nodded absently then glanced at the wall clock. "Lin, I'd love to stay and talk to you, but I've got a class in ten minutes."

I placed the mug on the coffee table and pushed myself to my feet. "I understand, Wil."

He wrapped me in a bear hug. A lump filled my throat, and tears filled my eyes.

"Go ahead, Linda Sue. Cry it out. It'll help."

"I'll be fine." I sniffled. "Thanks, Wil, for everything."

He held my coat while I slipped my arms into the sleeves.

"You know," he said softly as I pulled on my gloves. "There *is* one option we didn't discuss."

"What's that?" I jammed my toboggan hat on my head.

"You could always go home. To Brian."

CHAPTER THIRTEEN

On the way to the McCormick House, I stopped at the church to pick up the music schedule. Sissy, the church secretary, seemed flustered when I told her I hadn't received it yet.

"Wait here, please," she told me, getting up from her work station and disappearing down the hall. I dropped into the visitor's chair. Five minutes later I was still waiting. *What is taking so long to get a lousy piece of paper?* I wondered, tapping my boot on the plush carpet and unbuttoning my coat. After another ten minutes—and several phone calls which the machine picked up—her face appeared in the doorway.

"Linda?" I looked up. "Pastor Frank will see you now."

Why would the pastor want to see me? I wondered as I walked down the narrow hall to his office.

"Ah, yes, Linda," he said when he saw me. "Please. Sit down."

I sat.

"I understand you want the music schedule."

Duh. "Yes, please. I haven't gotten it yet, and no one's called me about it. I've called the church twice, but no one seems to know anything. I assume I haven't been scheduled to play; otherwise, I would have heard about it if I hadn't showed."

He fiddled with his tie, avoiding my eyes.

I shifted in my seat.

"You assumed correctly," he said, flipping his desk calendar. Why did he seem so nervous? A knock sounded on the door, and Deacon Dudley stepped into the room, shutting the door quietly behind him and dropping into the chair beside mine.

They exchanged glances.

Pastor Frank cleared his throat. "Uh, Linda, we have some questions to ask you, and we'd appreciate it if you were honest with us."

"Why wouldn't I be?"

"Linda, are you or are you not separated from your husband?"

So that's what this is all about. "Why do you want to know?" I asked.

"Because, Linda, if you are, you can no longer hold any position of responsibility in this church. So, please, answer the question." His stern tone was all business—not a note of sympathy in it. I felt like a child called into the principal's office to get expelled.

"Don't you want to hear my side of the story?" I asked.

"I don't think so, Linda," Pastor Frank said, avoiding my eyes. "A good wife does not leave her husband—unless, of course, he's been unfaithful." He paused. "That's the only biblical grounds for divorce, you know."

"And we know Brian well," Deacon Dudley added. "He's not a man to be unfaithful to his wife."

"What's going on here?" I asked, confusion turning to anger.

Deacon Dudley scratched his bald head. "Just answer the question, Mrs. Laverly—if you still go by that name. Did you or did you not leave Brian?"

"This...this...*inquisition* is ridiculous! I lost my job at the college, and I'm house-sitting for Jordan Thames, the sculptor."

Immediately I sensed I'd just made a bad situation worse.

"Ah, yes, Jordan Thames." Pastor Frank leaned back in his swivel chair and gave me a look like I'd just told him I had AIDS. "We've heard about Jordan Thames and some of the so-called art he produces."

My insides shook with repressed rage.

"And how," I said, clipping my words, "does that have anything to do with the blasted music schedule?"

"Linda, let's not swear," Pastor Frank said in a calm, patronizing voice.

"Swear?" I almost shouted. "You call using the word 'blasted' swearing? That, my dear hypocritical pastor, is not swearing. *This* is swearing."

I used only a couple of swear words, but you'd think I called up an army of demons, the way those two sanctimonious men of God reacted. Deacon Dudley shot up out his chair, his face a blotchy crimson. Pastor Frank, a pink blush spreading across his cheeks, fiddled with his tie some more and stared at the ceiling.

"Mrs. Laverly, I'm sorry, but I'm going to have to ask you to leave," Deacon Dudley said in a stern voice reserved, I was sure, for the worst of sinners.

"You don't look sorry," I shot back. "You haven't even asked for my side of the story. All you wanted to do was to trap me with a question so you could strip me of my music duties. What's the matter? Are you afraid that I, a hopeless sinner, am going to contaminate your holy church building? Well, I've got news for you, buster. There are more sinners in this world than saints. And a church like this does more to drive them away from the love of Christ than to draw them to it.

"You call yourselves Christians. I thought Christians were supposed to show love and mercy and understanding toward one another. I thought Christians were supposed to help a brother or sister who has fallen, not stomp on them harder."

I turned to leave.

"Ah, Mrs. Laverly?" Pastor Frank's voice sounded hesitant.

You wuss. I spun around and glared at him. "What?"

"Please leave your keys."

I rummaged through my purse until I found my church keys then flung them on the desk.

"You know," I said, lowering my voice, "I haven't been to church since the beginning of January. Yet, no one—I repeat—not one of you so-called saints cared enough to call me to find out why. I lost my job, through no fault of my own. Someone who called herself my friend is chasing after my husband and doing all she can to make my life miserable. I just found out the college cheated me out of unemployment benefits. I need a friend more than I've ever needed a friend. And the one place where I thought I'd find love, acceptance, and help has cast me off like a leper."

I stared Pastor Frank in the eye. "Well, I just have one thing to say: Shame on you."

Then I spun around and stomped out of there, trying hard not the slam the door behind me.

On the way home, I stopped at Sheetz and bought a box of Hershey's chocolate bars with almonds, a box of Almond Joys, a giant bag of peanut M&Ms—and the biggest cup of hazelnut coffee I could get. Then I found a booth to try and calm my jangled nerves. I was tearing the wrapper off a Hershey's bar when I saw Kelly's silver luxury car pull up to the gas pumps. She swiped her credit card and fed the nozzle in her tank as I watched, a seed of regret planting itself in my heart. Even if she'd pretended to be my friend so she could stay close to Brian, I missed our occasional gabbing sessions. I didn't have anyone to talk to now.

When she finished pumping gas, she pulled into the empty parking space next to my car. Oh, drat! I didn't miss her that much to want to meet up with her now. Coming through the door, she spied me and headed over.

"I saw your car outside. Do you have a minute?"

She dropped her blue suede gloves on the table, narrowly missing my coffee. I pushed them to the other side of the table and made a show of checking the time on my cell phone.

"I have an appointment in half an hour," I lied. "But I can squeeze in a few minutes if it's important."

"Thanks. Just let me get some coffee to warm up these cold bones. It's freezing out. Be right back."

Why would she want to talk to me? I wondered, watching her pour her coffee. Didn't she know how angry I was? How hurt? How betrayed I felt? But then, I was the one who started this mess. I broke off a block of my chocolate bar and plopped it into my mouth. Placing her coffee cup and a small cup of ice on the table, Kelly slid into the booth across from me, unzipping her blue suede jacket.

"I don't have a lot of time," I reminded her, taking too big a sip of my coffee and burning my tongue—for the second time that day. Kelly pried the lid off her coffee mug and shook in some ice.

"I'll get straight to the point," she began. "I'm planning a baby shower for Katie."

Shame and embarrassment washed over me. Why hadn't I thought of it? After all, I was her mother. When she had Lexie, her best friend had planned and organized the baby shower for her—and her bridal shower. I was too busy launching a teaching career and juggling family responsibilities and trying to convince myself I wasn't a bad parent. At the time Jasmine had some cockamamie scheme to marry her then-boyfriend, who was going to be a big rock star someday. Danny had just started high school and was into the skateboarding scene—and touted the long, tangled hair and baggy cargo pants that barely covered his skinny butt. Brian had just started his business and was hardly ever home.

"She had a shower when she was pregnant with Lexie," I said, stirring my coffee to cool it down faster. "Why would she need another one?"

"Because she's going to have a boy this time. Didn't you know?"

"Yes, I know," I said defensively. "But I never thought of another shower. I was—oh, never mind." I was going to say that I was buying little boy things whenever I had a chance and had planned on giving them to her sometime before the baby came.

"I was wondering if you wanted to help."

"Help?" I was stunned and angry—at her for her audacity, at myself for my negligence and stupidity.

"I figured you have more time now that you're laid off."

What was I to say? That I was too busy? For once, I wasn't. That I didn't want to because she, who was supposed to be my friend, had put the moves on my husband as soon as I moved out? He was still my husband. We hadn't even filed for divorce yet. She had me over the barrel, through the loop, up the creek, in a lurch—however you want to say it, I had no choice. I wanted to do this for Katie, but not with Kelly. The wound was still raw. She'd beaten me to the punch—again. *Darn you, Kelly!* I fumed silently.

Aloud I asked, "Do you have a date picked yet? What would you need me to do?"

"I was thinking of mid-April. We have a couple of months yet. I thought I'd keep it small, so we can have it at the house. And as far as what I need you to do, well, how about helping with the invitations, to start?"

"That sounds fine. Just no crafts, please. You know what a klutz I am when it comes to anything remotely connected with art."

She smiled. But it didn't reach her eyes.

"I'll call you." She picked up her gloves and coffee and slid out of the booth. "Same cell number?"

"Yes, but here's the landline just in case." I scribbled the number to the McCormick House on one of my old business cards and handed it to her. She slipped it into her jacket pocket and turned to leave.

"Wait!" I didn't want to ask, but I had to know. "What about you? If I needed to get hold of you, where—"

"Neither my cell nor my home number has changed," she said, with a trace of a smirk on her face, "so, don't worry, I haven't moved in with Brian—yet."

She pointed to my bag of chocolate.

"Don't eat too much of that," she sneered. "It'll make you fatter."

With that, she turned on her black-booted heel, her slim hips swaying in time with her easy, graceful steps.

When I got to the McCormick House, I built a fire in the fireplace and took a long, hot, bubble bath, slathering myself with lavender body lotion. Then I settled on the love seat in the den, comfy in my flannel jammies— never mind that it wasn't even dark yet—with a pot of hot tea and my chocolate stash on the coffee table in front of me.

I sat there, watching the orange flames stretch up the chimney and the red winter sun sink down behind the pines, until the windows darkened and my tea—and half the chocolate—were gone.

CHAPTER FOURTEEN

I'd noticed the flier for the monthly book club on the community news bulletin board on my way out of Sheetz. Now, three weeks later, after driving forty-five minutes on slippery roads, I settled into my seat and turned my attention to the pleasingly plump, gray-haired lady sitting to my left at the head of the large conference table, where ten other women, not counting myself, sat. Most were my age or older, but there were a couple of younger women there—I guessed in their late twenties or early thirties.

"I'm happy to see so many of you here tonight, especially with freezing rain in the forecast," the head lady said with a warm smile. "I see some new faces, so why don't we go around the table and introduce ourselves? Tell us your name, what you do, where you live, and how long you've been a part of *The Book Marms.* If this is your first time, tell us how you heard of us and why you're here."

She giggled. "Can you tell I'm a retired teacher? That's a lot to remember, huh? Here, I'll start off."

Head Book Marm Betsy—"Bets," as she preferred to be called—was a former high school English teacher from Glenwood who'd launched the monthly book club five years ago when she retired. When she was done, she nodded to the woman on her right, a young mother of three toddlers whose husband encouraged her to join so she could get out of the house for a few hours and do something for herself. *Lucky you,* I thought.

When it was my turn, I said that I was a music teacher who was house-sitting at the McCormick House and that I was a grandmother—and ready to become one again.

"This is my first time," I concluded. "I joined because I love to read and make new friends."

Our book for next month was *The Wedding* by Nicholas Sparks—one of my favorite authors, except that most of his books had sad endings. *I hope this book will be different,* I thought.

"Read it and next month we'll discuss it," Bets said, after a half hour of discussing what we knew about the author and his favorite theme—romance. "Be thinking about what you'd like to read next. Well, that's it. Goodies on the table. Enjoy schmooze-time, ladies. Oh, yes, I almost forgot. There's a clipboard by the coffee pot. Don't forget to write down your contact information. I'll e-mail you in two weeks for your suggestions for our next book."

I was trying to decide whether to give in to the chocolate chip cookies or be a good girl and choose something from the veggie tray when someone tapped me on the arm.

"Mrs. Laverly?" It was the young mother—I couldn't remember her name.

I smiled. "Linda—please. 'Mrs.' is too formal. Besides it makes me sound old."

"Oh, I'm sorry." She giggled, dropping two chocolate chip cookies on her paper plate. "I'm Tina. I saw you last month at the company holiday party."

I frowned, trying to place her.

Uncertainty flashed across her face. "You *are* married to Brian Laverly of Laverly Construction, aren't you?"

"I…uh…yes, as a matter of fact, I am. We're—"

"Oh, he's such a wonderful man!" she gushed. "My husband, Dave—he's a carpenter—works for him. Mr. Laverly took a chance and hired him right out of tech school. Dave's been there five years. Your husband is a terrific boss."

I helped myself to three chocolate chip cookies.

"Isn't it great that he got the bid?" she said.

Oh, so he got the bid. THE bid. The one he said would take care of our retirement. I scanned the hot drink selection and chose decaf coffee. I'd already had my limit of caffeine for the day, and I didn't like tea in Styrofoam or paper cups. Maybe I'd suggest ceramic mugs for the next time or bring them myself. There were only twelve of us.

"Too bad about the community college though," Tina said, following me. I put my cookie-laden plate and coffee on the table. Tina plopped her sweatshirt-and-blue jeans-clad body down in the chair on my right. I was puzzled. I hadn't said anything about working at the community college.

"How did you know—"

"But, from what I hear, what they got for the land and buildings, they could build somewhere."

"But those old buildings are—"

"I know—such a fire hazard. It was time. And a retirement village is just what this area needs. Maybe so many folks won't run off to Florida for the winter."

I was stunned. *This* was the big job he said would take care of our retirement? How could he? He knew closing the school would cost me my job.

"Linda? Are you all right? You look kind of pale."

"Yes...uh...I'm just getting over the flu." I glanced at the wall clock. Brian should still be awake.

"Tina." I forced a smile and pushed myself up from the chair, which suddenly felt hard and unforgiving. "Tt was nice meeting you. But I need to get going. See you next month."

"I heard we're supposed to get an ice storm tonight. Be careful. And tell your husband I said hello."

"I will."

I left my coffee and cookies on the table. Stuffing my book in my purse, I yanked on my coat. I took the stairs—it was faster than waiting for the elevator.

Forty-five agonizing minutes later, I maneuvered up the driveway to the house, where a light shone from the game room window downstairs. The rest of the house was dark. The floodlight, triggered by the motion detector, came on and glared down on the driveway, where Brian's pickup sat all by itself. I slid to a stop beside it, narrowly missing the garage door. A coating of ice glazed the roof of the cab and the bed, but the hood and the windshield were just wet. The LCD numbers on the clock on my dash glowed blue. Eight fifteen.

I shut off the engine. My hands trembled, my knees shook, and my heart jammed itself in my throat. I shoved open the door and nearly fell on my backside. A layer of ice coated the driveway. I turned my face to the sky. Stinging pellets hit my skin.

The front porch light flicked on and the front door opened. Brian watched out the storm door while I slipped up the front steps. The freezing rain was coming down harder now. I'd better have my say quick and head back to the McCormick House before it got any worse.

"I have to talk to you," I puffed when I got to the door. "Let me in."

He stepped aside, and I brushed past him, stopping in the foyer. He pushed the door closed, then turned to me, folding his arms across his chest. I could usually tell from the set of his mouth when he was upset or angry. But not tonight. Tonight his face was a mask. But his eyes looked tired and lifeless. I glanced down to catch my breath and pull my thoughts together. He stood in his stocking feet, his big toe pushing out of a hole in his sock. *If he'd cut his toenails—*

"And to what do I owe a visit from you on a night like this?" His sarcastic tone wasn't lost on me.

I raised my head and blinked in the dim hall light. He wore that ugly brown plaid flannel shirt that I absolutely hated. The sight of that shirt—and his tone of voice—fueled my fury.

"Why didn't you tell me?" I spat out.

"Tell you what?"

"That you put in a bid on the retirement village? You knew it would mean tearing down the college. How could you do this to me?"

"You always take things personally. This has nothing to do with you."

"It has everything to do with me!" I shouted. "Thanks to you, I lost a job I busted my butt to get!"

"Look, Linda, it was bound to happen anyway. The handwriting was on the wall. Somebody was going to get the bid. Why not me? Don't you think I busted my butt all these years?" His voice got louder. "And for what? I land the biggest deal of my life and my loving wife up and leaves me."

"You went behind my back and submitted a bid that, if you got, would mean you'd be the one to tear down the place where I worked."

"I thought you'd enjoy retiring early—I thought we'd buy an RV and take our time touring the country like we always talked about."

"Why didn't you tell me?"

He hung his head. I glanced down, too, and noticed he was wiggling his big toe through the hole in his sock.

"What do you want me to say, Lin? You're always harping about how I can never make a decision on my own. Well, I made one this time, and it blows up in my face."

I didn't know what to say. So we stood there, the anger between us melding into an awkwardness I didn't know how to handle. If he was telling the truth—and I'd never known Brian to lie—he was painfully honest, and the pain was always mine—then he'd done it for me. But it was too late to turn back now.

Words said in anger can't be taken back. And too many words had been said. And no matter what his motivation, I still blamed him for the loss of my job.

"I'd better get going," I said, opening the door. It was raining even harder—everything in sight sparkled with a thickening layer of ice. I'd never make it to the McCormick House in this.

"Stay."

I turned to face him.

"I know how you hate to drive in this stuff."

"It won't change anything."

"I know."

I heard the sound of a car coming up the lane. I peered through the freezing rain.

Kelly.

CHAPTER FIFTEEN

Kelly, who apparently came through the garage, appeared at the top of the basement stairs carrying something wrapped in aluminum foil. Brian avoided looking at me. Kelly didn't. Her glare would have halted the ice storm lickety split.

Brian held out his hand to me. "Give me your keys. I'll put your car in the garage. Then you won't have to worry about scraping in the morning when you leave."

I fished the key ring from my coat pocket and tossed it to Brian. "My purse is on the front seat. Will you bring it up, please? Thanks."

I followed Kelly to the kitchen. It was all I could do to keep the smirk off my face.

"I thought you hated driving when it's icy," I said, slipping onto one of the counter stools and flipping through the stack of mail, which was mostly junk, bills, and a couple of credit card applications for zero percent interest, which I stuffed in my purse.

Ignoring me, she fished through the silverware drawer. I sniffed. A freshly baked pie sat on the counter. A whiff of Chanel No. 5 wafted by as she flitted around my kitchen. I watched her take two dessert plates from the cupboard.

"You miscounted," I said. "We need *three* plates and forks, not two."

She turned, plucked another plate from the cupboard, and placed it on top of the other two. "You're right." She gave me a withering look then pushed the pie towards me. "Help yourself. What's a few more pounds?"

Heck, let her have him. They deserved each other. Just not in my house. I seethed, imagining her using my bathroom, wiping her slim body with my towels, hanging her expensive clothes in my closet, sleeping in my bed, cozying up on my sofa in front of my fireplace. The keys clattered on the counter in front of me.

"It was a tight fit, but I got both cars in," Brian said, dumping my purse beside the keys and dropping on the stool beside me.

"Wait a minute." I turned to him. "*She's* staying, too?"

I could feel Kelly's gloat.

"Yes, of course." Brian sniffed the pie. "What's this?"

Kelly beamed. "I thought some peach pie would be a great bedtime snack on a night like this."

Brian grinned at her. "Thanks, Kelly. Just what I needed."

It's just what he needs, all right. Has she seen his *spare tire?* I yawned loudly, stretching my arms over my head.

"I'm tired," I announced. "I'm going to bed. What are the sleeping arrangements?"

"Kelly can have the guest room," Brian said. "You can sleep in our room. I'll take the downstairs sofa."

The sight that greeted my eyes when I stepped into the bedroom and flicked on the light made me groan in dismay. The comforter lay in a heap on the floor, the sheets twisted on the bed—when was the last time they had been changed? I certainly wasn't going to sleep on those sheets. Brian probably had reverted to showering in the morning, which he preferred. I stepped over a pair of crumpled jeans, balled-up underwear, and dirty socks on my way to the closet, where I kept extra sheets.

I dropped the clean sheets on the blue recliner and rummaged through the closet. Only Brian's clothes and my summer clothes were there. Then I quietly went through both dressers. Only his clothes were in the chest-on-chest. The drawers in my mirrored dresser were mostly empty, except for some lingerie I didn't fit into anymore. Satisfied that I found nothing of Kelly's, I headed for the bathroom. I stepped quietly on the carpet in the hall, listening for any sounds from the kitchen. All was quiet. I tiptoed to the foyer and peeked in the hall mirror, which was angled so that I had a good view of the living room. Brian and Kelly weren't there. I stepped to the top of the stairs. The soft murmur of their voices in the game room rose on the warm air from the fireplace. Was that music, too? Soft, romantic music. I leaned over the banister. The lights were low.

"Linda?" Brian's voice cut into the darkness. "Do you need anything?"

"Yes," I called down as calmly as I could. "I need something to sleep in, so I'm taking a pair of your flannel pants and a sweatshirt."

"You know where they are. Goodnight."

In the bathroom, I turned on the taps, running the water full steam, then flicked on the exhaust fan, which made enough of a racket to drown out the sounds of my search. The only thing hanging on the back of the door was my old green plaid flannel robe—showing years of wear, but more comfortable now than when it was new. I checked the medicine cabinet, vanity drawers, and both closets. I lifted the lid of the white wicker hamper and rooted through the dirty clothes. Nothing. After I showered, I wiped the steam off the mirror and brushed my teeth, using a brand new toothbrush I kept for company. I unwrapped the towel and examined my naked body in the mirror. *I could lose,* I thought. *I could do it.*

Pulling out a pair of Brian's flannel pants from a shelf in the bathroom closet, I stroked the soft gray flannel. The fragrance of fabric softener still clung to them. I rummaged through the hamper until I found Brian's blue chamois shirt, then sat on the commode lid, buried my face in the collar, and inhaled deeply—the cologne, the deodorant, the sweat—imprinting every scent on my memory.

Why am I doing this? I dropped the shirt back in the hamper, mixing up the clothes and arranging them so Brian couldn't tell I'd been snooping. I pulled on Brian's green "World's Best Grandpa" sweatshirt, hung my towel on the shower curtain rod, wiped up the marble vanity top, and sprayed the shower with the daily cleaner. Then I turned off the fan, flicked off the light, and stepped into the hall. The door to the guest room was closed, but Kelly was still up. A light shone under the door. Was she alone?

Back in my bedroom, I picked up Brian's jeans, underwear, and socks from the floor beside the bed and placed them in a pile by the door to take to the bathroom later. Then I started stripping the sheets from the bed.

That's when I found it. Wedged between the top and bottom sheets at the foot of the bed. A black lace thong. And it wasn't mine.

CHAPTER SIXTEEN

I stared at the evidence. Never in a million years would I have ever dreamed Brian would do something like this.

How could he? This was the room where we'd made love and babies and dreamed of what all we'd do when the kids were grown and gone. Sure, I was the one who left, but I hadn't taken up with anyone else. Besides, we were only separated, not divorced. It certainly looked like I had the biblical grounds now. I guess I didn't really know him at all.

I couldn't touch it. I couldn't even touch the sheets. I went to the closet and pulled out an old quilt I kept there for my Sunday afternoon naps. Then I shut off the light, tiptoed across the dark room, and curled up on the recliner, my quilt wrapped around me.

Three hours later I was still awake. I couldn't get the image of Brian and Kelly together out of my mind. I flicked on the lamp. Photographs stared down at me from the pale blue walls. A family portrait of Brian, Jasmine, Kate, her husband Jon, Danny, and me holding a six-month-old Lexie in my lap. Brian, wearing a sapphire blue shirt and tie, me standing behind him, wearing a matching blue dress, my hand on his shoulder. Both taken for our church directory. Two wedding pictures—me sitting in the restaurant at our wedding dinner, long auburn hair cascading over a beige brocade dress, beaming as my laughing bridegroom with shoulder-length, wavy black hair sat by my side in a black suit. Were we really once so happy? Another wedding picture: Brian, trusty Dingo boots peeking out from his suit pants, and me, flanked by the maid of honor and the best man. I winced. Kelly had been my maid of honor. I studied her face in the photo. Was it my imagination—or hindsight, maybe—but did her smile seem pasted on? More family pictures showing the progression from young parents to grandparents.

I glanced at the alarm clock. Three a.m. Maybe I could leave before Brian got up for work. I padded over to the window. It must have warmed up through the night, because rain, not ice, was hitting the windows. Turning back to the recliner, I noticed the plaque Katie had given us for our anniversary. I lifted it off the chest-on-chest, where it had lain for over two months, and blew on the dusty glass. I hadn't read the words the night she gave it to us. Now, dropping into the recliner, I did.

"Love is patient, love is kind. It does not envy, it does not boast, it is not proud. It is not rude, it is not self-seeking, it is not easily angered, it keeps no record of wrongs. Love does not delight in evil but rejoices with the truth. It always protects, always trusts, always hopes, always perseveres."

I stroked the glass over the words—and recalled other words that framed my life with Brian. Criticism instead of a compliment. Silence instead of encouragement. Thoughtless words that tore down instead of building up. In time, I gave up trying to please him. A teardrop splashed on the glass and trickled over the middle of the heart. Maybe if we'd lived them, these words of love, instead just letting them be a useless decoration, things would be different.

*****

Five a.m. was dark, damp, and cool. I couldn't stay in the house another minute. I folded the quilt and put in back on the closet shelf, then tucked the plaque inside my oversized purse. I changed back into my clothes, grabbed my bag, and, ignoring the unmade bed and dirty clothes on the floor, stepped into the hall. The guest room door was closed. I didn't hear any snoring behind it.

The aroma of coffee brewing lured me to the kitchen, where Brian, ready for work, stood at the counter in his stocking feet, spreading mayo on bread. I shook my head sadly. He had the money now to buy lunch every day, but still he packed his bucket.

"Up already?" He slapped a slice of bologna on the bread, then dropped a sliver of cheese on top.

"I couldn't sleep." *Should I mention the thong?* I decided against it. Maybe I should have taken it—for evidence in court. Maybe I should burn it. Too late now. I wasn't going back to that room.

"Coffee's almost ready." He shoved the sandwich in a used bread bag. "I made extra."

"No thanks. I need to get going." I stepped into the hall and lifted my coat off the hook.

"I wouldn't go now, if I were you," he called from the kitchen. "I'd wait until after eight, at least. Give the road salt a chance to work."

I stomped back to the kitchen. "Why do you always have to do that?"

He gave me his clueless look. "Do what?"

"Tell me what to do, when to do it, and how to do it."

"I was just making a suggestion." He poured coffee into his chipped mug—the same one he'd used every day for the past fifteen years

"Your suggestions, Brian, are more like orders. And I resent someone ordering me around."

"They are not!"

"Then why do you pout when your *suggestion* isn't taken?"

"I don't pout."

"You do, too."

"I do not. I'm just—*frustrated* because you won't let me do what I'm supposed to do."

"Which is?"

"To take care of you—"

"I don't need anyone to take care of me."

"I can see that." He opened the bread box and grabbed a package of bagels. I watched as he pulled one apart and popped it into the toaster—a ten-year-old monster that he'd fixed more times than I could remember when I wanted to buy a new one.

"Why do you always have to try to fix things? Why do you always have to come up with an answer?"

"Because that's what I thought I was supposed to do."

I spoke softly now. "It wasn't answers I needed, Brian. Sometimes I needed you just to listen. Sometimes I needed you to put your arms around me and hold me."

The bagel popped up. Using two fingers, he pulled it out, put it on his plate, and smeared butter on it.

"I suppose Danny's first game will be canceled," he said, conveniently changing the subject.

Oh, great. Danny hadn't told him he'd been kicked off the team. I took a deep breath. Now was as good a time as any.

"Danny isn't playing baseball this year."

He stared at me. "What do you mean, Danny isn't playing baseball this year? Of course he is. It's his senior year."

I swallowed. "He wasn't eligible. His grades were too low."

The muscle in his cheek twitched.

"I'm sorry, Brian. He was supposed to tell you."

He slammed his fist on the counter. Coffee jumped out of his mug and splashed on his bagel.

"Danny was supposed to do a lot of things which he never did. Like study. Doesn't the kid ever listen?"

"Brian, he's got so much—hard classes, a part-time job..."

"And a mother who babies him."

"I don't baby him! I just try to soften the blow. You know, you are so hard on that kid."

He glared at me.

"Go ahead." I lowered my voice. It wouldn't do to wake up Sleeping Beauty. "Blame me. You always do."

"If you had been half as hard on him as you say I am, he'd be pitching now—and have a chance for the draft. Now he'll never have the chance to make his dream come true."

"His dream, Brian?" I pulled on my coat. "Or yours?"

His chest heaved with each breath.

I grabbed my purse. "I'm glad I'm out of here. I'm glad Danny's out of here. Because living with you is like living with a hammer over my head. I'm always waiting for it to drop and crush me."

It took me an hour and a half to get to the McCormick House, normally a forty-five-minute drive. I slipped and slid all over the icy road, narrowly missing a couple utility poles, spinning a couple of doughnuts, and nearly ending up in a ditch. By the time I pulled into the carport, my foot was shaking on the gas pedal, my knees felt like they were filled with ice water, and my knuckles hurt from gripping the steering wheel for so long.

When at last my trembling fingers found the right key and I pushed open the backdoor, the dogs bounded up to me, whining urgently. I let them out, then dropped my purse and keys on the table, draped my coat on the back of a chair, and put the kettle on for tea. After I let them in and fed them—adding in an extra dose of coddling, since I'd been gone all night—I started a fire in the fireplace.

I was buttering my toast when I heard my cell phone beep. The voice mail was from Brian, wanting to know if I'd made it back OK. I texted him: "Made it OK. No problems."

Then I took my toast and tea and curled up on the sofa in front of a crackling fire. I took the plaque, which I'd removed from my purse, and placed it on the end table, staring at the words. Somehow last night had been the final nail in the coffin of my marriage. Perhaps Thomas was the answer. He'd shown up like a knight in a shining yellow Hummer. And he was so different from Brian. I smiled, remembering when I'd first seen him in the elevator in those ridiculous Rudolph boxers. Thomas sizzled—Brian fizzled.

An hour and two cups of tea later, I'd made some decisions. I found the phone book and flipped through the yellow pages until I came to "Attorneys." I scanned the listings of those who specialized in divorce. "Shuster and Shuster. No fault uncontested divorce," I read. "Affordable pricing. Payment plans available." I'd start with that one. I checked the time. Another hour before their office opened.

The tension of the sleepless night, the nerve-wracking drive back, and the uncertain future drained away with my resolve. The rain outside was changing back to snow. I placed another log on the fire, pulled the quilt from the back of the love seat, and snuggled down in the cushions.

The time had come to find out just how much mettle I really had.

CHAPTER SEVENTEEN

The wood paneled walls and plush carpeting in law offices of James Alan Shuster spoke of success and money. I fidgeted in the upholstered wing chair while across the huge mahogany desk Elizabeth Morgan-Shuster, James Alan's wife, scrutinized the forms I'd filled out earlier, her mouth puckering in funny motions while she read.

"All your assets are jointly owned?" she asked, peering over her reading glasses.

"Yes. We didn't think to do it any other way."

"I see. What about retirement plans?"

"I rolled over mine into another IRA when I was laid off from my teaching job at GCCA in January. Brian has his own from when he worked for Smithston's Construction. He rolled it over into his own IRA when he went on his own. He's the beneficiary on mine, and I'm the beneficiary on his."

"How much are you each insured for?"

"I'm not sure."

She picked up a gold Mont Blanc pen, scribbled something on a yellow legal pad, and turned her attention to the form again.

"Laverly Construction—your husband's business—it's jointly owned?"

"Yes."

She nodded. "Good."

I was relieved when, a week earlier, I'd called for an appointment and was given the option of a female attorney. A woman would understand and represent me better than a man. The Shusters had quite the setup—accident, divorce, death, malpractice—you name it, James Alan and Elizabeth can sue for you.

"Mrs. Laverly—" Elizabeth Morgan-Shuster laid the forms on her desk, slipped off her reading glasses, and leaned forward so that her elbows rested on top of the papers. Her graying hair was stylishly coiffed, giving her a soft, yet elegant appearance. Today she wore a navy blue silk blouse with a matching blazer. A pearl necklace looped gracefully around her neck, complementing her matching pearl stud earrings. She wore no diamond on her finger, only a simple gold wedding band. Her tone was warm and comforting—grandmotherly, if you will—and, together with her carefully chosen attire, conveyed the image of an intelligent, caring woman who would fight like a tiger to get me what I deserved.

"Call me Linda. Please," I said.

"Yes. Linda. Tell me your reasons for filing for divorce."

"Didn't I check the boxes?" There had been a whole list of reasons on the form, ranging from abuse to mental cruelty to adultery to irreconcilable differences. There was no box for "Love died."

"Yes, you did. Irreconcilable differences. But that could mean anything."

I paused, trying to form the right words. "I guess I just came to the realization that I didn't love him anymore—I didn't think he loved me, either—and I couldn't see beating a dead horse."

"Beating a dead horse"? Oh, come on, Linda, that was stupid! Now she'll think you're a bumbling hillbilly for sure.

"I mean, I didn't want to stay in a loveless, unfulfilling marriage relationship." *There. That sounded more educated.*

"I see you checked the adultery box then scratched it out."

"I thought he...I mean...I found a...I...uh...give me a minute, please." A raging inferno flashed up my neck and my cheeks. I fumbled through my purse looking for a Lifesaver. Sucking on one seemed to calm my nerves. A bottle of water appeared on the desk in front of me.

"Thank you," I murmured, taking a sip. I gave her a fragile smile.

"Let me start again." Then I told her about the holiday party, Kelly, the cozy little dinner, the thong, my suspicions.

"Brian's not a heartless monster," I concluded. "Just totally clueless of my needs. My emotional needs."

Elizabeth nodded. "Do you have any proof of his alleged infidelity?"

"Isn't the thong proof? Should I have confiscated it? I mean, for DNA or something?"

Elizabeth laughed softly. "No, dear, we don't do DNA tests for adultery. How do you know the thong was Kelly's?"

"Whose else would it be? It isn't mine. Besides, I saw her wearing it when she bent over to pick something up the night I interrupted her little romantic dinner. At least I saw the straps."

"Are you sure it's the same thong? Did you check the brand or the size?"

"No, I wouldn't touch the thing, so I can't say for sure it's the same thong or even that it's Kelly's. I guess I just assumed it was."

"Do you have any daughters who could have stayed overnight?"

"Yes, but Katie's pregnant. I'm sure she wouldn't wear anything like that in her condition, and Jasmine and her husband live over fifty miles away."

"If you want evidence that would stand up in court, I could put a PI on it."

"PI?"

"Private eye—investigator." Elizabeth flipped thorough her Rolodex. "Here we are. Mike Clark. Excellent PI whom we use frequently for divorce cases. Ex-cop, very discreet. We could put a tail on Brian, get photos of him and Kelly in a compromising situation, if indeed your allegations of infidelity are true. That's the key to getting an airtight case that would stand up in court—concrete evidence. Then, my dear, you could ask for the moon."

I shook my head. I didn't want the moon. I wanted love. Real love. Romantic, head-over-my-heels, I'm-crazy-about-you-and-can't-live-without-you love. This was getting to sound like *CSI*. "Do we have to put a tail on him?" I asked. "How much will it cost? Wouldn't it be breaking a law or something—invasion of privacy and all that? Can't we just split everything in half?"

Elizabeth smiled and shook her head. "I wish it were that simple. Who's his lawyer, do you know?"

I gave her the name of the attorney Brian used for business, and the name of the one we used to draw up our wills.

"Omigosh," I said.

Elizabeth's eyebrows shot up.

"We'll have to redo our wills, too, won't we? What a mess!"

"Most divorces are, you know—a mess and then some. Be thankful you don't have small children involved."

She scribbled something on a paper and handed it to me. "Give this to my secretary. She'll give you a receipt."

"But I thought I didn't owe you anything unless you got money for me."

Elizabeth laughed. "Oh, no, my dear. That's only in accident and malpractice cases. Not divorce cases. Now here's what I want you to do...."

Before my next appointment, I was to make a list of everything Brian and I owned—and I mean *everything*. It was worse than getting ready for an IRS audit. She advised me to sit down with Brian and the two of us decide how to split the assets. Like that would ever happen. I left Elizabeth Morgan-Shuster's office with a folder full of forms to fill out, two thousand dollars poorer, and second thoughts.

CHAPTER EIGHTEEN

On the way back to the McCormick House, I decided to drive to Pineridge, where Aunt Retta and Uncle Ray lived. It was a good hour drive, but she'd be able to help me sort out this divorce stuff.

My mother's youngest sister and twenty years older than me, Henrietta Merrosky had been my confidante and sounding board when I was growing up. It was to Aunt Retta I fled when my mother and I argued—and that was plenty. A plate of moist walnut brownies with milk chocolate icing, all made from scratch, usually awaited me. Which was probably where I first acquired my affinity for chocolate.

I pulled into the driveway of her one-story stone home. Uncle Ray's beat-up old pickup truck was parked in front of the garage, a separate building that doubled as his woodshop. It was also where Uncle Ray spent much of his time these days.

I tapped twice on the back door then pushed it open and stepped into the kitchen. Aunt Retta was expecting me; I'd called her after I left the lawyer's office but hadn't told her why I was coming. The kettle was whistling as I kicked off my shoes and hung my coat on a wall hook. Aunt Retta stood at the rangetop, pouring boiling water into a flowered teapot. A lavender-colored sweat suit casually hugged her plump curves.

I planted a kiss on her wrinkled cheek.

"Linda honey, good to see you," she said, setting the timer for the tea.

"Mmm—what's cooking?" I asked. The aroma of spices and simmering meat aroused my flagging appetite.

"Crockpot chicken stew," she said, leaning over the table to place the teapot on a trivet next to a plate of iced brownies. I laid the file of legal papers I got from the lawyer on the table.

"How did you know I needed chocolate?" I grinned, lifting a brownie to my mouth and biting into it.

"I didn't." She settled into her chair across the table from me. "I baked these this morning so Ray could have something to pack in his lunch bucket."

"Lunch bucket? I thought he was retired."

"He is."

"Then why—"

"He likes to pack a bucket when he goes to the shop in the mornings. Well, most mornings anyway."

"Why doesn't he come in for lunch?"

"After he retired, he just drove me nuts. 'When's lunch?' 'When's supper?' 'Where are you going?' 'When will you be back?' 'Get me this.' 'Get me that.' And I'd thought retirement would be fun. I kicked him out the day he *cleaned* and rearranged my kitchen."

I giggled. "Oh, Aunt Retta. You didn't."

"Yes, I did—but not before going out to the shop and reorganizing all his tools. Ha ha—he got the message. So now he works on wood projects out in the shop all day—mostly handcrafted furniture, something he'd always wanted to do but never had the time."

The timer went off. Aunt Retta pulled the teabags out of the pot. I poured myself a cup, then dumped in three heaping teaspoons of sugar and added milk.

"I need your advice," I said as Aunt Retta helped herself to a brownie. "I'm divorcing Brian."

"Oh." She placed the brownie on her saucer. "Oh, dear. Why?"

I told her about the holiday party, Kelly, the college closing, Brian bidding for the job, the house-sitting. I didn't tell her about Thomas or the thong.

"Oh, Linda honey, are you sure about all this?"

"I just came from the lawyer's office, Aunt Retta. Look at this." I slid the file across the table.

Her eyebrows shot up. "Lawyer? Already?"

I nodded. "The marriage is over." I took a sip of my tea. "Besides, Brian has been…unfaithful."

Aunt Retta, who'd been drinking her tea, sputtered and coughed. She put down her cup. "Oh, Linda, you're wrong. He'd never do anything like that."

"I found evidence."

"And exactly what is this evidence?"

I told her about the thong.

"Have you asked him about it?"

I shook my head. "I can't. I just can't."

"You should—to get his side of the story."

"Aunt Retta, how would I know he wouldn't be lying?"

"Has Brian ever lied to you?"

"I never thought about it. I trusted him. He didn't seem to be the lying, cheating sort. Always seemed so steady and true blue."

"I can't imagine Brian—that's just not his nature, Linda Sue. Before you go any further with this divorce, talk to him. Tell him what you found. Tell him how you feel."

"I already told him how I felt—the night I came home to Kelly in my kitchen all hussied up. He told me he didn't love me anymore."

"Is that what he said? Or is that what you heard?"

"He told me that when I left, something in him died, and he didn't know if he could get it back. Didn't know if he even wanted to try." Hot tears stung my eyes. A lump lodged in my throat. I shook my head. "It's too late."

"Linda, honey, I'm so sorry. But I think you and Brian need to talk before you go any further with this lawyer. Whom did you see?"

"Elizabeth Morgan-Shuster."

"You didn't sign anything yet, did you?"

"I paid her a retainer fee. Two thousand bucks. She gave me these—" I patted the sheaf of papers. "—to fill out."

She flipped through the forms.

"All financial data." She peered at me over her glasses. "Did you shop around first before you chose Mrs. Morgan-Shuster?"

I squirmed then shook my head.

"Linda Sue!"

"I didn't think. I just reacted."

Aunt Retta sat for a few minutes quietly munching on her brownie. I helped myself to another one.

"Linda, do you remember the time in high school, your boyfriend—what was his name?"

"George."

"Oh, yes, George. Do you remember when you thought he and your best friend were sneaking around behind your back?"

I knew where she was headed, so I didn't answer.

"They were, but they were planning a surprise sweet sixteen birthday party for you."

I took another brownie. I remembered too well. I'd broken up with George and told Karen I'd never speak to her again. A month later I'd heard they were going steady.

Aunt Retta continued. "Don't jump to conclusions, honey. Get the facts first."

A draft of cold air flowed along the floor as the door opened then closed quietly. Gunny, Uncle Ray's Brittany pranced in, stubby tail wagging, pink nose nudging my hand. I rubbed the soft orange and white fur behind her ears.

"Whose car's in the driveway?" Uncle Ray bellowed, yanking off his boots and striding across the kitchen in his stocking feet to give me my kiss. "Linda! Sweetheart, how are you?" He gave me the usual bear hug. Sawdust clung to his plaid flannel shirt and jeans, and wisps of unruly gray hair escaped from under his ever-present navy blue toboggan hat.

"You need to come over and visit the old folks more often," he said, planting a smooch on my forehead and looking around. "Brian come?"

"No." I didn't know how to tell Uncle Ray. He and Brian were buddies. They both loved woodworking and usually Brain spent our visits in the shop. They'd gone on a few hunting and fishing trips together before Brian's business swallowed him up.

"I'm divorcing Brian, Uncle Ray."

"What in tarnation for?" His booming voice thundered off the high ceiling.

"It's a long story. Suffice to say there's no love left."

"Love, shmuve." He shook his head and helped himself to a cup of coffee and several brownies. "Women! Been married to the best of 'em for near fifty years now, and I still don't understand 'em." He inhaled deeply. "Something smells deelishus. When's supper, love?"

"In another hour. Linda, dear, you'll stay?"

I nodded. Uncle Ray stooped down and planted another kiss on my forehead.

"You're just going through a tough time. Even the best of marriages have 'em—we did, didn't we, Hen? It'll just make your marriage stronger. You'll see." He winked at me then kissed the top of Aunt Retta's head. "Well, I'm off to the shop. You gals have a nice visit. And remember—you can call me anything you want, but don't call me late for dinner!"

"Oh, Ray, get out of here," Aunt Retta said, giving him an affectionate swat on the backside as he turned to go.

"Do you think that's all it is, Aunt Retta?" I said after Uncle Ray left. "Just a tough time we'll get through?"

"Oh, honey, I don't know. I hope so." Love and concern poured out of her blue-gray eyes. "But I do understand what you're going through. About twenty years ago I found out Ray was having an affair."

I was stunned. "Uncle Ray? With who?"

She shook her head. "It doesn't matter now."

"What happened?"

She poured herself another cup of tea and took a deep breath. "I hardly know where to begin. It was so long ago. I've put it behind me."

Angst filled her usually placid face. "Aunt Retta, if this is reopening the wound, causing you grief, don't. I don't have to know."

She reached across the table and clasped my hand with cold fingers. "Yes, Linda, I do. If what I went through—what I learned—could help you, I have to."

She pushed herself up from the table, crossed the kitchen, and brought back a box of tissues. Plunking it down in the middle of the table, she pulled one out and dabbed her nose. I waited.

"It was right after Rand left for college. While the boys were home, our schedules were full. Ball games, school activities—you know. So all those extra hours Ray was putting in, working nights and weekends, were filled. Besides,

I was used to it. He was gone so much, I practically raised the boys alone."

I nodded. No matter how busy Brian was, he did his best to take time for the kids. Just not for me.

"Then Rand left and suddenly the house was empty. I knew I couldn't ask Ray to cut back his hours—with Rand's college expenses and Reggie starting his own business. You do what you can to help your kids—you know?

"One Friday night—it was after midnight—the phone rang. Rand totaled his car. I couldn't find Ray. No one answered the company phone. I called the bar where he liked to stop on his way home from work. I called Nick, his drinking buddy. I was ready to call the police, go out looking for him when Millie called. She told me. She and Nick had known about it for months."

"Oh, Aunt Retta, I'm sorry. I didn't know. Who was she? A secretary from the office?"

She shook her head. "She was a waitress—a barmaid."

"How could he stoop so low?"

"It wasn't all his fault, you know."

"He cheats on you, and it's not his fault?"

"I didn't say that. I said he wasn't entirely to blame. You see, a man needs what a man needs, and I wasn't available. I was always too tired, too busy. 'Not now, Ray, later.' But later I'd have another excuse. He finally gave up and went elsewhere."

I squirmed. She was describing Brian and me.

"So what did you do?" I asked.

"I filed for divorce. You know, infidelity is the only legitimate reason the Bible gives for divorce. I had the grounds. I hated him. I hated her. I was filled with hate and anger and self-pity. I wanted to hurt him like he hurt me."

"What happened?"

"Your mother talked me out of it."

"My mother?"

Aunt Retta smiled. "She wasn't only my big sister. She was my best friend. She invited me to a Bible study on love and marriage. I respected her opinion and trusted her enough to go.

"We studied—dissected, really—First Corinthians thirteen. And for the first time in my life, I began to understand what real love was. And I saw where I was to blame—partly, anyway—for Ray's wandering."

I was flabbergasted. "How could you forgive something like that?"

She smiled softly. "You can if you try."

"I couldn't. I could never forget what happened. I could never trust him again."

"I haven't forgotten, Linda. I choose not to remember."

"What's the difference?"

"I choose not to think about it when it comes to mind. Funny, but if that hadn't happened, we wouldn't be as close as we are now. It made us realize what we were letting get away."

"But how could you ever trust him again?"

"It was hard, but that, too, was a choice. We went to a marriage enrichment weekend—and were the oldest couple there! We went to counseling, studied the Bible together, began to pray together. We asked God to be the third partner in our marriage.

"Ray took to heart the words of Paul: 'Men, love your wives as your own bodies, as Christ loved the church and gave His life for her.' He started courting me again, treating me like I was the queen of his life. You can't not respond when a man loves you like that. I started putting Ray first, like the Bible instructs wives to do. And I fell in love with him all over again."

I nodded. "Bells and whistles, Aunt Retta?"

She smiled. "And fireworks and lightning strikes…Linda, have you prayed about this? Have you given God a chance to heal your marriage?"

I didn't want to talk about God. I glanced out the window. It was getting dark. White flakes swirled in the wind. I stood.

"I'd better get going, Aunt Retta. It's beginning to snow, and I have an hour drive back."

She looked disappointed. "I hope I didn't say anything—I know I get to talking. I didn't mean to preach—oh, dear me."

I hugged her. "No, dear Aunt Retta. You've given me a lot to think about. I never knew. I admire you for sticking with it, for working things out. I just don't know if I could do it. I'm just not that strong, that forgiving."

"Neither am I, dear. God gives me the strength I need. He forgave me. I had to forgive Ray. 'Forgive us our trespasses *as we forgive those who trespass against us.*' Forgiveness is not weakness, Linda. Forgiveness is sweet honey. For both the one forgiven and the one who forgives. It released me from a prison of hate and opened the door to more love than I could have ever dreamed possible."

I left with a container of hot chicken stew, a plastic bag of brownies, and a feeling that I was missing something important. But I didn't know what.

CHAPTER NINETEEN

"One hundred ninety two," the trainer at the fitness center announced, writing the despicable number on my chart. I winced. I knew I'd put on some weight—but twelve pounds in three months? *All that sweat and starving for nothing.*

I stepped off the scale and sat on the bench to put my sneakers back on.

"Here." Anna Louise handed me a packet of papers. "We've just started another six-week program to help you ladies jumpstart your weight loss."

"I lost nine pounds the last time," I said, taking the papers and fishing through my purse for a pen. "A lot of good it did me though."

I thought of the twenty-eight-ounce box of chocolate-covered nuts I hid under the bed over the holidays. Just one, maybe two a night helped me sleep better. I thought of the gazillion bowls of homemade chicken soup with generous helpings of noodles I'd practically lived on for the past two months. The rocky road ice cream at bedtime topped with chocolate syrup. The midafternoon candy bar. The cookies I liked to dip in hot, sweet tea. The medium-sized pizza I had every Friday night—and that I didn't have to share with anyone.

"Don't be discouraged, Linda," she said when I confessed my comfort eating. "We all get off track. The important thing is to get back on. And you've made that step."

I flipped through the packet until I came to the questions I was to answer. "Why do you want to lose weight?" *So my husband would tell me I look beautiful. Too late for that. So my husband would realize what he lost. I can't write that. So I can get my stupid wedding ring off my fat finger. That won't do, either.* I settled for "so I can feel good about myself."

The rest of the questions were mostly goal-setting: "What can I do this week to improve my appearance?" *Change my hairstyle. Buy a whole new wardrobe.* "What can I do this week that will increase my energy?" *Fly to Florida and not come back until June.* "What can I do this week to boost my self-confidence?" *Hook a man.*

"Anna Louise, where do you want me to put this?" I asked when I finished.

"In your bag. That's for you. By the way, we're having a certified image consultant come in two weeks. If you want an appointment with her, you'd better sign up soon. The slots are filling up fast."

"An image consultant? What does she do?"

"She helps women improve their image—advises on what colors and style of clothes they should wear."

"That sounds like something I could use. What does she do during the color session?"

"She'll take a look at your coloring—skin, hair, eyes—and suggest what colors you should wear in clothes and in makeup."

"What about the style session?"

"She'll advise you what style of clothing would look best on you with your body build and shape and personality. Each session is a half hour long. I had an hour-long session with her at the last trainers' seminar I went to. She was terrific. I took her advice, and now I get lots of compliments on how I look."

Anna Louise, like me, had struggled with weight, losing pounds and putting them back on. Yet she always looked great, never overweight. Maybe it *was* the style of clothes.

"How much will a half-hour session cost?"

"She's giving us a special price—seventy-five dollars. She usually charges a hundred."

"For a half hour? Maybe I should become an image consultant."

"You can sign up for a double session for both color and style."

"Will it cost any less that way?"

Anna Louise shook her curly blond head. "She's giving us a price break on the half-hour sessions."

"When do I pay?"

"Half when you sign up, the balance when you come in for your consultation."

I rooted through my purse for my checkbook. I'd opened my own account the previous month. I checked the balance. I had enough to pay my credit card payment for the month and buy some groceries. The dues for my membership at the fitness center was automatically deducted monthly and would be coming out next week. My "mad money" account was getting low. I'd been drawing from it ever since Brian had a fit about the credit card bill at the end of January.

"Will you take a credit card?" I asked.

She shook her head. "JayCee will, but we're only taking checks or cash for the deposit."

I didn't have enough cash, but if I charged my groceries, I could write a check for the deposit.

"I'll sign up for an hour-long session. Who do I make the check out to?"

*****

I thought I would die before my consulting session. Thirty-minute workouts three times a week, a mile on Glenda's treadmill on the days I didn't work out, and stretches every day. I added a few leg lifts and butt-firming exercises to the routine. I faithfully followed the eating plan outlined in my packet: no more than 1,350 calories a day, mostly low-fat protein, fruits, and vegetables. The first week was pretty rough without pasta, chocolate, and pizza. But soon the cravings disappeared. I wished the weight would just disappear, too—the numbers on the scale decreased agonizingly slow.

But I did manage to lose four pounds before my appointment with JayCee on St. Patrick's Day. I wore emerald green. And found out green is my power color.

"Your power color," she explained, "is the color that gives you a strong sense of confidence and boldness when you wear it." At the end of the hour, I came away with a little book of color swatches to take shopping with me, note cards with suggestions for makeup and clothing styles, three fifteen-dollar scarves, and JayCee's book, which cost another twenty-five dollars.

The next day I cleaned out my closet, pitching anything that wasn't right for me or was old, tired, and shapeless. I didn't have too much left, but in six weeks, I planned to be ten pounds lighter and celebrate with a clothes shopping spree. I called Janice Evers, a makeup and hair consultant I knew, and made an appointment for a complete makeover. It would probably wipe out my mad money account, but it would be worth it. When Thomas came back from Florida—or whatever warm place he was wintering in—I'd be a new woman. And maybe a free one.

CHAPTER TWENTY

Once a week after my workout, I stopped at the house to pick up my mail. Which was what I was doing on April Fools' Day when Brian walked in. Which was unusual because it was early afternoon. I timed my visits for when I knew he'd be at work.

"Home early or just stopping by for lunch?" I asked, leafing through the stack. I noticed they'd already been opened.

"Neither. I wanted to talk to you." He pulled out a chair. "Sit."

"I don't have much time, Brian."

"Sit down, Linda."

"Don't tell me what to do."

"Just once, woman, would you do what I ask?" *Was that exasperation or anger?*

I sat. "Make it fast."

He leafed through the pile, plucked out some envelopes, and tossed them across the table. "What in heaven's name is all this?"

I picked them up. "My credit card bills. What are you doing opening them, anyway?"

"No, *our* credit card bills." With each word, he cranked up the volume. "My name is on them, and they were sent to this address. I have a right to open something with my name on and that was sent to my home address. How did you manage to get the balances so high?"

"What I do and how I spend my money is none of your business."

"It is if my name is on the bill."

"I'm making the payments, so chill, okay?"

"How much of a payment are you making? The minimum amount?" He snatched one of the envelopes and ripped out the statement. "Have you bothered to check the finance charges on this?" He shoved the paper in front of my face. "Look at the APR! Twenty-two percent! All you're paying is the interest, nothing on the principal. At that rate, you'll never get it paid."

I pushed his hand away. "They don't care, as long as I'm making the minimum payment."

He plucked another envelope from the pile. "What about this one?" Tossing the first statement on the table, he reached in his shirt pocket and pulled out his reading glasses. "Look at these charges!" He jammed on his glasses and maneuvered the paper under his nose. "Thirty dollars for gym membership." He peered at me over his half frames. "Is that every month?" I nodded. He snorted. "Two hundred dollars to JayCee Consulting. Who in blazes is JayCee Consulting? Don't answer. Fifty dollars to the Greatest Mysteries of All Time—whatever that is."

"A book club."

"Another book club? By the way, I returned the last book you got."

"You didn't."

"I did. Marked 'refused' on it with a thick black marker and sent it back. I also canceled your membership."

"You have no business—no right!" I sputtered.

"I do when I'm the one paying for it."

"I paid for all my books with my own money."

"When you were working. You're not working now."

"Thanks to you."

"Don't start that again."

"Start what? I—"

He snatched his glasses off and thrust the statement under my nose.

"Three hundred dollars to Janice Evers. For what?"

"None of your business."

He shoved his glasses back on and snatched the statement off the table. "And—I added this up—you must have had one doozy of a shopping spree—seven hundred dollars for clothes! Two hundred for shoes!" His face grew redder the louder he got.

"Don't yell at me."

"I'll yell if I want to! Blast you, woman! Have you no control over your spending? Whatever happened to you? You used to be so—so—" he shook an envelope at me. "You used to be so good with money, so sensible."

"Cheap, Brian. We were cheap. You made me that way."

"*I* made you that way? How did I make you that way?"

"You are a cheapskate. A miserly scrooge! You never let me get anything new. Always had to fix up the old. Well, I'm sick of living that way. After all these years, I think I deserve new things."

"I'm economical. I've saved this family plenty over the years."

"And robbed us of a lot of fun, too. Can't you ever be spontaneous? Do you have to plan everything down to the last penny? To the last mile? To the last second? To the last drop? To the—"

"Oh, shut up."

"What did you tell me?"

"Something I probably should have told you years ago." He ran his fingers through his hair. Was it getting thinner on top? "What, by the way, is this charge to the Westmont Township Police Department?"

"That was for Danny's speeding ticket."

"Did Danny pay you back?"

I gave him my best you-ought-to-know-better look.

"I didn't think so. Well, from now on, he can pay for his own tickets."

I never—and I mean never—had seen Brian this angry—this verbal—about anything. I kind of liked him this way. More sizzle.

"You can be the one to tell him," I said. "He doesn't have any money, you know, being in college and all. You want him to end up in jail?"

"Maybe some time in the clink will slow him down. Get him to think before he acts."

He grabbed another envelope and pointed it at me. "You missed a couple of payments on this one. Do you know what happens when you miss payments? I'll tell you what happens. They call you. They harass you. I don't like getting calls from credit card companies, especially when I didn't make the charges."

"I must have forgotten that one," I mumbled, reaching for it, but he pulled it back out of my reach.

"I have—we had—a good credit rating, Linda. We worked hard and made a lot of sacrifices over the years. Don't screw it up now."

I grabbed the mail off the table and stood. "Are you done? I have to go." I tried to pluck the envelope out of his hand.

"Here's what I'm going to do." He snatched the mail out of my hands. "I'm going to get money out of savings and pay these infernal things off. Then I'm going to cancel every one."

"You can't do that!"

"I can and I will."

"But I need the credit cards, Brian. I'm not getting unemployment. The only money I have coming in is for house-sitting."

"Learn to budget. I listen to Manage Your Money every day—"

I held up my hand. "Oh, spare me, please. Who's the one who took care of the family finances all our married life? You never—not once—wrote a check for anything. It wasn't easy when the kids were little. I had to rob Peter to pay Paul. I never complained. I made like everything was fine. I didn't want you to go into the funk you go into when the money's tight."

"Don't think I didn't know. I did. And I appreciated it, Lin. You've always been so reliable. That's why this—" he waved the bills in the air—"came as a shock."

"Well, Brian, I'm tired of being good ol' dependable Linda. I'm tired of giving up what I really want. I'm not getting any younger, and I want to enjoy life before I die."

I zipped up my jacket. Should I tell him about the lawyer? I'd paid her retainer fee with one of those credit card checks that hadn't shown up on the bill yet. I turned to go.

"Lin?" I felt his hand on my arm. "If you need money...."

I searched his face then shook my head. "Thanks, but no, Brian. I have to do this myself. I'll figure something out."

He looked like he was ready to take me in his arms. I felt as though that was where I wanted to be. This had been the first meaningful conversation we'd had in years. But it had come too late. Patting his cheek, I turned and left.

CHAPTER TWENTY-ONE

"Linda Sue! How are you?"

Wil grinned and opened his big arms for a hug. I'd stopped at the college to confirm some references and verify that I'd attend graduation, which would be held May 7th, three weeks away. While I was there, I decided to pay my former colleague a visit.

"I'm good. I miss teaching, though." I stepped into his open arms. "And, of course, I miss you. How are things?"

He shrugged. "Coming along."

Putting his hands on my shoulders, he held me at arms' length, looking me over from head to foot. He let out a low whistle. "You're looking great. Love that new hairdo. It brings out your beautiful eyes."

My cheeks grew warm. "Aw, thanks, Wil."

I felt almost skinny in my new jeans—down a size and no longer the "relaxed" fit that expanded when you zipped them up. And my new emerald green sweater made me feel like a new woman.

"I've got a new motto," I said, dropping my purse on top of his cluttered desk and plopping into one of the two student chairs.

"What's that?"

"When I look good, I feel good, and when I feel good, I do good." I smiled up at him. "And you, dear friend, always make me feel good about myself."

He gave my shoulder an affectionate squeeze then stepped behind his desk and began organizing papers scattered over the top.

"Got your piano lessons set up yet?" he asked.

I shook my head. "I'm checking some places today to see about setting up a studio."

"Good. Getting any subbing in?"

Again I shook my head. "I submitted my application to several area districts, but music's pretty hard to break into. There are more teachers than available positions. What about you? You'll be clearing out, too, soon."

"I'm ready. Retirement looks better every day." He stopped shuffling papers and looked at me. "You've heard about Goldie?"

"No." I'd heard that Sam had gotten another job, but the new insurance company had refused to pay for Goldie's cancer treatments because it was a pre-existing condition.

"She's in hospice."

"How...how much time?"

He shook his head sadly. "Not much."

Poor Sam. Goldie was the sunshine of his life. I made a mental note to visit her. Maybe take a casserole to the house for the family.

"How's Brian?" Wil returned to his paper-organizing. "Have you two patched things up?"

I pulled at a loose thread on the inseam of my jeans. "That's not going to happen."

He sighed, stacking a pile of papers off to the side then looked up at me. "You two have been married too long not to try to work things out."

I yanked at the thread, but it slipped through my fingers. "I found out he'd been unfaithful."

Wil's eyebrows shot up. "That doesn't sound like Brian."

Here we go again. Why does everybody take his side? Maybe I should hang the dang thong around my neck with a sign: "Found in Brian's bed—it isn't mine."

"Can we talk about something else?" I asked. "Do you have a pair of scissors?"

He lifted a pair of yellow-handled scissors from a Steelers mug that served as a pen holder and held them out. I snipped the annoying thread and blew it into the trash can.

"Thanks." I placed the scissors sharp-side down in the mug.

"Any time you need to talk, Lin, you know where I am."

Out in the hall a bell rang.

"Hey," he said, "why don't you come over for dinner this weekend?"

"Saturday I'm meeting Jasmine and Kelly at the house to get ready for Katie's baby shower Sunday. But other than that, I'm open."

"What about Friday? No, that won't do. Trish and I have tickets for the Pirates game. Would Saturday evening work for you?'

"I can make it work."

"Good. Let me call Trish and double check."

While Wil phoned his wife, I stepped over to the window and watched the heavy construction vehicles maneuvering beyond the orange netting that marked no trespassing zones. In two months, there wouldn't be anything left of Glenwood College of the Arts.

"Love you, too." He disconnected. "Lin? Saturday evening. Six o'clock."

I turned around and tilted my head toward the window. "Does that bother you?"

"Not any more. I've accepted and adapted. The key to survival, my dear. You know they're keeping the old trees, don't you? They reworked the design for the landscaping. Brian came up with some new drawings."

I turned back to the window.

"Anybody home?" I turned to the door. In hopped the Easter bunny. It could only be—

"Thomas!" Wil roared. "You old son of a gun! Back from the Sunshine State early, are you?"

Thomas pulled off the bunny head and grinned sheepishly. "How'd you know it was me?"

My heart beat an extra beat. He was handsomer than I remembered. The southern sun radiated from his tan face, and his hair, which was longer than the last time I saw him—in January—was beach-blond and pulled back in a ponytail.

I was about to say, "Hi, Thomas" when he said, "Hey, Wil, who's the dish?"

I didn't know whether to be embarrassed or flattered. He either didn't remember me—how could he forget the kiss in the restaurant or driving me home the night I moved to the McCormick House? Or he didn't recognize me. I decided it was the latter. I was, after all, nearly twenty pounds lighter than when he saw me last. And no longer a W. And, of course, the new hairdo and clothes.

"Don't you remember Linda Laverly?" Wil said. "You met her in December when you showed up here in your Rudolph boxers."

Thomas stared at me. After a heart-stopping interval—it was probably only five seconds, but it seemed like an eternity—recognition dawned in those cool gray eyes.

"Lulu! Now I remember! Your office is next door, right?"

"Linda. *Was* next door. I was laid off in January." *How could he not remember?*

He turned to Wil. "Hey, Bro, can you put me up tonight?"

"Of course. I'll call Trish and let her know you're coming. Will you be around for supper?"

"Nah, I've got plans. I'll come by later on this evening."

While Wil called home once again, Thomas slipped out of the bunny suit. My face grew hot, remembering the last time.

Wil reached out and stopped him. "You *do* have something on under that, don't you? I mean more than boxer shorts. There's a lady present."

Thomas winked at me and let the costume drop to the floor. Yes, he had something on—tight blue jeans and a Florida Marlins T-shirt about two sizes too small. Bending over, he
scooped his costume off the floor and rolled it up.

"Hey, Lana." He tossed the rolled-up costume on the floor by the coat tree. "Do you like Chinese food?"

Was he kidding? Was January just a blip in his mind? I looked at the time. I had a job interview at the local newspaper in fifteen minutes.

"Wil, I've got to run. See you Saturday," I said, giving him a peck on the cheek and grabbing my purse.

"Hey, what about me?" Thomas said, stretching his neck and holding out his cheek. I ignored it.

"Woman's got nerve," I heard him say as the door shut behind me.

Then I popped my head back in the door. "By the way, the name's *Linda*."

*****

Thirty minutes later I was sitting in the newspaper editor's office, if you want to call a twelve-by-twelve crammed cubbyhole partitioned off from the rest of the newsroom an office. There was no door, and the partitions stopped two feet short of the ceiling. Voices drifted in from the newsroom, as did the beep of the fax. Occasionally there was a burst from the scanner. Someone had a radio tuned to a baseball game.

I sat in the hard plastic chair in front of his cluttered desk as he read over my application. After a few minutes, he looked up and gave me a weary smile.

"I like that you're a...*mature* person," he said, rubbing the back of his neck. "I've had a heck of a time with some of these young ones who don't show up when they're supposed to. Just because we're a small community newspaper, they seem to think we're unimportant."

I nodded. Rick flipped over the application and scribbled something on the back page.

"It's been awhile since you worked at your college newspaper, so we'll start you out as a stringer," he said, dropping my application on top of the mess. "You'll cover government meetings—school board, borough, township, county commissioners—and help with the family page. You could come in and write your stories or write them at home on your own computer and e-mail them in."

I'd be responsible for one school board meeting a month. Other meetings I'd cover as needed, whenever the regular stringer wasn't available. And I'd come in two hours a day to help with the family page.

While I was there, I took out an ad for piano lessons.

"Oh, you give piano lessons?" the lady asked when she read over my ad.

"My daughter wants to start."

"I'm still looking for a place to rent for the lessons," I said. "Would you have any suggestions?"

"Why don't you try the community center? They have lots of rooms—it's the old junior high building, remember. There's a grand piano in the auditorium and I think a piano in each of the two music rooms."

"Do you happen to know how much they'd charge me if I were to rent one of the rooms?"

She checked her wristwatch. "I'm good friends with the director, Denise Bronsen. Why don't we give her a call?"

Thirty minutes later, I was fingering the ivory on one of the community center pianos.

"We have them tuned regularly, but if you think they might be out, let us know," Denise told me.

"It sounds good," I said, pulling the cover over the keyboard of the baby grand. "You're lucky to have such fine pianos. How much did you say the rent would be?"

"Ten percent of what you charge."

Mentally I did the calculations. I wouldn't be locked in to a fixed rent, and I wouldn't be responsible for utilities. The community center, in the heart of the downtown, was easily accessible. Another big plus is that they would advertise at no cost to me. It was a no-brainer.

On the way home, I picked up a single-serving diet pizza from the grocery store and a two-liter bottle of diet root beer. Finally, something to celebrate. I had a job and was going to be giving piano lessons again. I'd rented a post office box and mailed out three applications for credit cards in my name only at a zero-percent introductory rate for a whole year. I was on my way to being a self-sufficient, independent woman. *Take that, Brian, ol' boy! I'll show you!*

And Thomas was back.

One hand on the wheel, I used the other to flip through the CDs until I found the one I wanted, slipped it in the player, and forwarded to the song that was on my lips, "My Boyfriend's Back." I rolled down the window and belted out my own lyrics: "Hey, Brian, hey, the hunk is back."

CHAPTER TWENTY-TWO

"Uh-oh." I flicked on the blinker and pulled onto the berm. The flashing blue lights were a pretty good indication that the car behind me wasn't just a tailgater. I shut off the engine and pushed on the four-ways, then reached into the glove compartment for the registration and insurance cards. Why did he stop me? Surely it wasn't against the law to drive and sing at the same time, was it?

"What's wrong, officer?" I smiled politely at the stern-looking young man who approached my car. He looked too youthful to be a state policeman. But his crisp uniform, Smokey-the-Bear hat, holstered handgun, and badge told me, indeed, he was.

"May I see your drivers' license, registration, and proof of insurance, please?" Not even a hint of a smile. I handed them to him.

"Do you know you ran a red light back there, Ma'am?"

I was floored. "Ran a—*where*?"

"Right before the entrance ramp."

I shook my head. "I don't remember any red light."

"There was a traffic signal about a hundred feet before the ramp."

I was puzzled. "There was a traffic signal there?"

He ignored me as he studied my driver's license.

"Do you know this license is expired, Ma'am?"

"What? Are you sure, Officer—" I peered at his name badge. "—Dorque. Your name is *Dorque*?"

"Yes, Ma'am. This license expired at the end of November."

"Expired? How could it be expired? Let me look at that."

He held it so I could read the expiration date. Yep. It was expired, all right. I swore under my breath.

"I don't understand. I never received anything from the Department of Transportation."

"Wait here, please." While Officer Dorque stepped back to his car, I wracked my brain. I was sure I hadn't received a renewal notice. After what seemed like an interminably long time, he returned and began to scribble on his tablet.

"Wait a minute!" I said. "You can't write me up. It's not my fault if I didn't get a renewal notice. I mean, come on, how do you expect people to remember? These licenses are good for four years, for crying out loud! I can't even remember something for four days—four *minutes*—let alone four years."

I wanted to cry. I'd sobbed my way out of a speeding ticket thirty-five years ago. But I didn't think Officer Dorque would offer the same sympathy to a blubbering grandmother that he might for a slim young thing. Maybe I could reason with him.

"Besides," I rushed on, "I really don't remember seeing any red light. Are you sure there was a red light back there?"

Officer Dorque stopped writing. "You don't remember a traffic signal at the intersection by the shopping plaza?"

I shook my head. *Maybe I can beat this thing.*

"Then I'm going to have to ask you to step out of your vehicle, please."

"Step out—what for? I didn't do anything—"

"Just step out of your vehicle, please."

"Do I need a lawyer?"

"Just step out of your vehicle, please." His hand dropped to his gun. I got out.

He pointed to the berm in front of my car. "Put one foot in front of the other, toe to heel, and take ten steps."

"A *sobriety* test? You're giving me a *sobriety* test? I don't believe this!" Cars were slowing down as they passed. "I don't even drink, for heaven's sake. And drugs—I take Advil for headaches—and Synthroid. I take Synthroid for an underactive thyroid. That's all."

Officer Dorque's stoic face told me I was wasting my time.

"This is ridiculous," I muttered, gingerly placing one foot in front of the other. "There!" I said when I was done. "Are you satisfied? May I get back in my car now?"

After receiving the good officer's permission, I slid back behind the wheel while he wrote out my ticket—or tickets, I should say. I remembered somebody at the college got a ticket last semester for running a stop sign. When the cop checked his cards, he found that his vehicle registration had expired. He ended having to pay, with court costs and other legal fees, almost five hundred dollars in fines. Then his insurance went up. I groaned inwardly. I didn't have five hundred dollars. I didn't have a hundred. Heck, I didn't even have ten.

He handed me my tickets and cards. "You can renew your license tomorrow at the drivers' license center. They'll issue a new one on the spot."

I took them meekly. "How much will that cost?"

"Thirty-one dollars."

"Do they take credit cards, by any chance?"

"I believe they do."

"What about my fine? When do I have to pay it?"

"You'll receive a citation in the mail from the district magistrate in about seven to ten business days. You'll have thirty days to pay."

Thirty days. By then I'd have a new credit card. I hoped. I wasn't sure if the newspaper held the first paycheck or not.

Well, I thought as I drove away, there goes my good day.

The next morning I pulled into the parking lot outside the fitness center and shut off the engine. I was legal now—as long as the state was true to form and didn't cash the check right away. If they did, they'd have me for bad checks. And wouldn't Brian be gloating. But I'd go to jail before I went to him for money.

I signed in then began my workout. I didn't recognize the two younger women gabbing away on the machines. *Oh, brother, I should have brought in my iPod.*

"D'ya know what I did after I threw 'im out?" the short, chubby blonde one told the tall, athletic brunette who exercised like she was a cheerleader. "Took every one of our wedding pictures and cut 'im out!"

Rah-rah shook her head in sympathy. "I know how you feel. When my ex left me for someone he met online, I went out and bought a whole bunch of new stuff and put it on his credit card. Clothes, furniture. Thousands of dollars of stuff. Sure fixed him!"

Another woman—from her gray hair and weathered face, I guessed she was about ten years older than me—stepped onto the machine next to me. I glanced at her left hand. Her diamond engagement ring and matching wedding band glinted under the fluorescent overhead light.

Blondie exhaled through her mouth. "Mine was so cheap, but only with me. He took his mistress on a cruise. Told me he was on a business trip. But I found out. The lousy cheat."

Rah-rah moved over to the next machine. "Well, my ex could probably win the Scrooge Award. He actually washed the lava rocks from gas grill!"

Blondie hooted and wiped her face with the white towel hanging around her neck. "Men!" she sneered. "Are there any good ones?"

"I had one." The lady next to me spoke gently but firmly.

"Had?" I pointed to her rings.

She smiled softly and gazed down at her left hand. "Bill died in December. We were married forty years."

"I'm sorry," I mumbled. Blondie and Rah-rah muttered their condolences.

Gray Hair straightened her back, took a deep breath, and eyed Blondie and Rah-rah. "Forty wonderful years." She dropped her eyes, her face a mask of grief. "What I wouldn't give...."

Her last words shut up the disgruntled ex-wives. For the next twenty minutes the topic of conversation ranged from the weather—finally warming up—to the outrageous gas prices—four bucks a gallon—to the best place to buy walking shoes. I finished my workout and was doing my stretches when Gray Hair sat down on the floor next to me.

"I'm sorry about your husband," I said, reaching for my toes. "You must have had a good marriage."

Her eyes glistened. "It was better than any fairy tale."

"Was Bill's...was it sudden?"

"His death? Yes and no. He had cancer. Started in the prostate. But Bill ignored the early signs. Thought it he was just getting older. By the time it was discovered, it was too late."

"I'm sorry."

She nodded toward my wedding band. "How long have you been married?"

"I was married for thirty-two years."

"Was?"

"I'm in the process of getting a divorce."

"Oh, I'm sorry. I thought...."

I tugged at my ring. "Won't come off. Maybe in another ten pounds." I giggled, feeling self-conscious.

"Maybe," she said, pushing herself up from the floor and winking at me, "it's a sign."

CHAPTER TWENTY-THREE

The first thing I noticed when I turned into the driveway were the daffodils. They'd been buried under several inches of heavy, wet snow following an early spring snowstorm the first week in April and had lain wilted on the ground after the snow melted. But here they were, two weeks later, bobbing their yellow heads in the morning breeze.

I was glad Kelly had recruited Jasmine to help get the house ready for the shower. I still wasn't sure I didn't want to kill her. Remembering that black lace thong in my bed still made me feel like throwing up. Every time I came to the house to pick up my mail, I kept seeing the thing in my bed. And today we'd be cleaning the entire house. I couldn't assign the bedroom to Jasmine. I didn't know what else she'd find. I sighed. I'd just have to put on my big girl panties and do it myself.

I parked beside Jasmine's car, relieved, for once, she wasn't running late. True to form, though, Kelly was. Good. Jasmine and I could start without her. I'm sure that's what Kelly had planned anyway.

After checking the garage to make sure Brian wasn't home, I followed the stone walkway to the back deck where my woven kitchen throw rugs hung over the wooden railing, fluttering in the soft breeze. The aroma of coffee brewing welcomed me as soon as I opened the patio door and stepped into the kitchen, which, to my surprise, was clean. No dirty dishes in the sink. No greasy pans on the stove. Uncluttered counters. I caught a whiff of pine cleaner as I stepped across the gleaming white linoleum floor. Jasmine must have gotten here hours ago. The breakfast nook was set for a cozy tea-for-two, with a coffee cake sliced and ready to be served.

"Jasmine?" I called. A second later she barreled around the corner, lugging a bucket and mop.

"Oh, hi, Mom." A sheepish grin spread across her cheeks. Her curly black hair was pulled back in a ponytail, nearly hidden under a red paisley print bandana. An oversized white

T-shirt hung loosely over gray sweatpants, masking her tall, athletic frame.

"Let me empty this outside," she said, slipping past me in bare feet. "Get yourself a cup of coffee."

On the table a bunch of daffodils fanned out from a white, milk-glass vase. I hoped this wasn't one of her get-Mom-and-Dad-back-together schemes. If so, she was about to be sorely disappointed.

"I'm glad we got good weather for our cleaning day," she said when she returned. The bucket was upside-down on the deck; the mop lay across the corner of the railing. She went to the coffeemaker and filled two cups, handing one to me.

"Aunt Kelly won't be here for another hour or so. She's finishing the cake and picking up the decorations. I told you to come earlier so we could have some time together without *her* around."

Jasmine never did like Kelly. She tolerated her only because she'd been my best friend and was Katie's godmother.

I helped myself to a slice of coffee cake. "How long have you been here?"

"I came last night. I knew the place hasn't had much more than a lick and a promise, if even that, since you moved out."

I forked a piece of cake into my mouth. "Mmm, this is good. Make it yourself?" She nodded. "Very early this morning. I gave Dad a piece before he left."

"Where'd he go?"

"Mom, look at the calendar. What day is it?"

"Oh, right. The first day of trout."

We sat in silence for a few moments, nibbling on coffee cake and sipping our coffee. The morning sun reached into the kitchen, glinting off the white cabinets.

"I wish you'd change your mind about the divorce, Mom."

Jasmine's soft voice belied the harshness of the word. I'd tried to get Brian to sit down with me and go over our assets and decide between the two of us who would get what, like Elizabeth Morgan-Shuster had suggested. "Some other time," he'd told me. And after the big blowup over the credit card bills, I figured it would be best to wait.

"He doesn't want it, you know," she said softly.

"Well, it's too late."

"Mom, he still loves you."

The coffee cake suddenly tasted like sawdust. I pushed my plate away. "Jasmine, I don't want to discuss it." I gulped the last of my coffee and slid out of the booth. "Let's get this place cleaned. I have plans for tonight."

"A date?"

I wish. "Wil and Trish asked me to dinner."

"Will his brother be there?"

I stared at her. How did she know?

"Yes, Mother, I know all about Thomas. Danny told me. We kids stick together, you know."

"Jasmine, please. This is none of your business. Or Danny's. Or Kate's. This is between me and your dad."

"How could it be none of our business when our parents are splitting up? You always told us if we stepped out into the street and you saw a Mack truck barreling toward us, you'd stop us. Well, Mom, you're in the street, and there's a big Mack ready to hit you."

"This is different."

"How is it different?"

I sighed. And here I thought she never heard anything I said.

"You're all grown up now, Jasmine. You're married and have a home and a life of your own. I raised you kids. Now give me the freedom to have my own life too."

I scraped the rest of the coffee cake into the food disposal and rinsed my plate and cup. Jasmine placed her cup and plate in the sink, then grabbed the dishcloth and wiped the table top.

"Mom, you're making a big mistake," she said, shaking the dishcloth over the sink.

"Jasmine, you don't know the whole story. You don't even know the half of it."

"Tell me."

"I'd rather not."

"Come on, Mom, tell me why you and Dad are splitting up. The *real* reason, not some cockamamie story about being different people and drifting apart. For heaven's sake, you were married for what, thirty years?"

"Thirty-two."

"Thirty-two years. And I don't remember you guys fighting—ever. Then suddenly you up and leave? Something happened, Mom. What was it?"

I was tempted. But then this was Daddy's girl. She thought he could do no wrong. I was always the bad guy. But I didn't want to taint the hero image. Brian might have been a neglectful husband, but he was a darn good father. I couldn't—wouldn't—take that away from him. And I refused to play the take-my-side game and try to turn my children—our children—against him. So I just said, "I don't love him anymore."

Jasmine shook her head. "I don't believe that."

"Sometimes love dies. You don't want it to, but sometimes, no matter how hard you try to keep it alive, it dies."

"I refuse to believe that. Love is eternal."

I snorted. "That's a bunch of bunk."

"Mother! How could you say that?"

"I can say that because I know. Love dies. It dies, Jasmine. You spend your life raising your kids and paying the bills and trying to get ahead, and when the last kid finally leaves, you look across the table and suddenly realize you don't even know him anymore. That you feel nothing for him. And you wonder where the love went. You thought it would last forever. But here you are, thirty-two years after pledging 'til death do you part, and you don't even like him. You hate the way he sneezes. You hate the way he laughs. You can't stand his stupid jokes. You feel trapped in a boring, dead-end marriage, empty inside.

"Don't judge me, Jasmine. You'll get here soon enough. Be glad instead we both have another chance for happiness."

"You call Kelly a chance for happiness for Dad? Boy, are you blind or what?"

"Jasmine, I don't want to argue with you. Let's just drop it."

"Mom, Dad doesn't love Kelly. He loves you."

"Jasmine, I said drop it. Please."

She shrugged. "Whatever. But don't say I didn't warn you. You're making a big mistake."

"Jasmine, I gave you the freedom to make your own mistakes. It wasn't easy, but I did. Now, please do the same for me. Besides, if it is a mistake, it's mine. It won't hurt you or Katie or Danny."

"That's where you're wrong, Mom. It already has."

*****

I volunteered to clean the master bedroom. With the exception of more dust, it looked exactly as I left it the morning of the ice storm. I was pulling the sheets off the bed when the thong dropped to the floor. I hurried to pick it up. It wouldn't do for Jasmine to see it.

"So that's where it is!"

I spun around. Jasmine stood in the doorway.

"Where *what* is?" I asked innocently, trying to nudge the thing under the bed with my foot. The stupid straps got tangled in my toes. I felt my face redden.

Jasmine strode into the room and pulled the thong from under my foot. "This." She waved it in my face. "I've been looking all over for it. Do you know how much this skimpy thing cost me? You can close your mouth now, Mother."

"That's—" I exhaled sharply "—*yours?*"

"Yes, it's mine. Whose did you think it was?"

"You're not just telling me it's yours to cover up for—"

"To cover up for what? Mom, you surely don't think—"

I nodded weakly. "I thought Dad and Kelly...."

I sank to the mattress, feeling as though I'd been kicked in the gut.

Jasmine thrust her hands on her slim hips. "Mother! Did you really think—how could you? Don't you know Dad at all? He'd never do anything like that! Besides—" she thrust the thing in my face again. "It's too big to be Kelly's. See the tag?"

A coldness worse than a polar vortex engulfed me. "I found it the night of the ice storm," I whispered, more to myself than to her. "I thought it was Kelly's. That's why I went to the lawyer."

Jasmine dropped down on the bed beside me. "Mom, I'm surprised at you. Dad doesn't love Kelly. He loves you. But he's afraid to say anything. Mom, he hasn't slept in this room since you moved out."

I turned to her. "But how did your thong end up in my bed?" It was her turn to blush. "Josh and I came over one Saturday to spend some time with Dad. He was lonely and missing you so much. Aunt Kelly was always wanting to come over, but, believe it or not, he told her no lots of times. Long story short, the weather got bad and we ended up staying the night. Dad told us to sleep in your big king-sized bed, and, well, the thong just got too itchy and I kicked it off. In the morning, I couldn't find it and didn't have time to look."

Tires crunched on the gravel in the driveway. Jasmine got up and stepped over to the front window.

"It's Aunt Kelly. I'll go help her carry stuff in." She gave me a sad smile and wrapped it in a hug. "Stay in here until you get your bearings."

After she left, I stared at the door she'd closed behind her. *Get my bearings?* My insides felt like ice. *Now I know what it would be like to bleed to death inside.* I covered my face with trembling hands.

Oh, dear God, what have I done?

CHAPTER TWENTY-FOUR

Thankfully, I didn't have to face Kelly. She dropped off her contributions and left, leaving Jasmine and me with the cleaning and decorating. Jasmine griped, but I was glad. The less I saw of her, the better. So the thong wasn't hers. But she still could have waited until after the divorce before making her move on Brian. And Brian still could have told me I looked nice.

We finished up early enough for me to take an extra long soak the old-fashioned cast-iron tub back at the McCormick House, pouring in a healthy measure of lavender bubble bath. Lavender is supposed to be calming for the nerves. Wil and Trish were casual hosts, so I pulled on jeans and chose a sea green blouse and soft white sweater.

Thomas's Hummer wasn't in the Benedicts' driveway when I pulled in. Ignoring the twinge of disappointment, I brushed the shiny spots on my forehead and nose with face powder and freshened my lip gloss. Maybe little brother would pop in.

An hour later Wil, Trish, and I were enjoying coffee and dessert in the family room when the patio door slid open and in stepped Thomas—tonight the man in black: black leather jacket, matching chaps, black stirrup boots, and black headband. His long blond hair was pulled back in a ponytail. Those cool gray eyes scanned the room then stopped at me. My heart did a skippity-do.

"Any cheesecake left?" he asked, eying the piece dangling at the end of my fork.

"In the kitchen." Trish stood. "I'll get some for you. Coffee?"

"Unless you have something stronger." Thomas unzipped his jacket and dropped into the chair across from me. I tried not to stare. *The man must work out every day.* I dropped my eyes to my place and took another bite of cheesecake.

"Everything's settled," he told Wil. "I'll be moving in the end of next week."

"Good," Wil said then turned to me. "Thomas got himself a condo in Pittsburgh."

"Oh?" I flashed Thomas a coy smile. "And here I thought you were a country boy."

He roared with laughter. "Not on your life! I'm a city man to the core."

"Not me," I said. "Give me sunsets and birds and trees, not horns and sirens and concrete, not to mention muggings."

"Bet you've never seen the city skyline at night," he said.

Actually I have, I wanted to say. *And it will never come close to a country sunset.* "Was that a Harley I heard just before you came in?" I said instead.

Thomas's face lit up. "You bet. Ultra Classic Electraglide. Six speed, Twin Cam 96 engine. Fire red and black."

"His baby." Trish placed a tray with cheesecake and coffee on the coffee table. "Brand new."

"Maybe we should get one, Trish," Wil said, "and tour the country."

Trish grinned. "You know, I could do that. But I think I'd prefer an RV."

"We had a Harley once," I said. "A '73 Sportster. A thousand cc. Blue." I smiled, remembering the rides Brian took me on when we first met, the soft feel and smell of his brown suede fringed jacket as I wrapped my arms around his slim waist and rested my cheek on his back. "We sold it when Danny was little."

"That's why I never had kids," Thomas said, forking a piece of cheesecake into his mouth. "And never will."

In my mind I saw Brian standing in our driveway, watching the truck with his Harley strapped on the back until it was out of sight and the dust settled.

"More coffee, Lin?" Trish asked.

"No, thanks. I was just thinking...it's been a long time since I've been a motorcycle mama!" I laughed to cover up the nostalgia that washed over me. I shot a discreet glance at Thomas. Maybe he'd offer to take me for a ride.

He didn't. After further chit-chat about motorcycles versus RVs, Thomas glanced at his watch.

"Well, folks, this Hell's Angel is gonna hit the road," he said, standing up. "I want to feel the bugs in my teeth before it gets too dark."

"Have you ever seen the sun set on Crazy Woman Cliff?" I asked. "It'll beat a city sunset any day."

Thomas glanced at me, looking a bit uncertain. Then he grinned. "You think so, huh? Let's just see about that. Come on."

*****

I froze. I hadn't dressed to ride, and even though the day had been warm, evenings this time of the year were cool and damp, a fact my bones so cruelly reminded me of a few minutes into the ride. I should have accepted Trish's offer of her winter coat, but I wanted to show off my new leather jacket. I snuggled close to Thomas more for warmth than budding romance. I didn't feel safe riding without a helmet, but I didn't want Thomas to think I was a prude. So I'd wrapped a bandana around my head, shoved my wallet and cell phone into my pocket, and hopped on. I was glad when we finally stopped at the scenic overlook. By then my butt was buzzing from the vibrations and I was shivering.

Thomas dropped down on the grass and leaned back on his elbows. "There's your sunset. Enjoy."

I casually settled beside him. The clouds glowed red-orange, reflecting the last rays of the setting sun, which had already slipped below the tree-silhouetted hilltop across the valley.

"See? What'd I tell you?" I said, hugging myself to try to get warm.

He unzipped his jacket. *Maybe he'll give it to me.* "Nice," he mumbled, reaching inside his jacket and pulling out a pack of cigarettes, which he held out to me.

I shook my head. "Cigarette smoke makes me sick."

He laughed. "Then I'll blow the other way."

He fumbled in his jeans pocket and pulled out a gold lighter. The blue flame flared and the end of the cigarette glowed briefly. He flicked the lighter shut and slipped it back in his pocket, inhaling deeply.

"Why do they call this Crazy Woman Cliff?" he asked, turning his head and blowing the smoke away from me. The breeze carried it back. I fanned my hand in front of my face.

"According to an old Indian legend, the young wife of a warrior jumped off the cliff after finding out her husband had been unfaithful to her."

Thomas snickered. "She'd be crazy, all right."

"But the sad thing is that what she was told wasn't true. A jealous friend made it all up because she wanted the warrior herself. But she never got him because after he found out about his wife, he threw himself over the cliff, too."

"Stupid," Thomas muttered.

I shrugged. "You asked."

Watching the mist rise in the valley below us, I wondered if he really didn't get it or was just acting macho. He made no move to take my hand or move closer to me. Or was that my role? I didn't know. You can get out of practice in three decades. I shifted my weight, discreetly edging closer to him.

"Why are you still wearing your wedding ring?" he asked, breaking the silence. I tugged at the ring. "It's stuck. A few more pounds, though." I giggled nervously and turned my attention back to the fading sky.

"You can get it cut off, you know."

I glanced down at the shiny gold band. When Brian first slipped it on my finger, it had been etched, not shiny. Time and duty had worn down the etchings.

I'd never do that.

"That's an idea," I said, trying to sound like I was seriously considering it.

"Then do it. Don't think about it, just do it. How do you think I got to be a millionaire? I didn't wait around for things to happen. I *made* them happen."

"You're a millionaire?" I pointed my thumb toward the Harley. "I figured you had some extra cash to throw around, but a million?" Then I pictured him in his Rudolph boxers and Easter bunny getup. "You're not pulling my leg, are you?"

He turned to me. "Do I look like I'm joking?"

I scanned his face in the fading light. "No. How'd you make your million?"

"I was good at what I did. And what I did was invest other people's money for them. And then invested some of my own."

"And made enough to retire early, Wil told me. How old are you anyway, if you don't mind my asking."

"Not at all. I'm fifty-five. And been retired for fifteen years."

"I'm impressed. How long were you an investor?"

"Twenty years."

Mentally I did the math. "So you got started when you were still in college?"

Clasping his hands behind his head, Thomas lay back and closed his eyes. The clouds had lost their glow and were now an ordinary, dirty gray. "I didn't go to college." He paused. "I went to Canada."

"Canada? Why?"

"Because in those days being a single working man in America was dangerous."

Something in my heart fell. "Vietnam."

"I flunked out of college. You know what that meant." He sighed. "Too many guys I knew never came back. And the ones who did were never the same."

"My hus—Brian never finished college, either. After his best friend, Buddy, went MIA, he dropped out and joined the Marines. But he never went to Nam. The closest he got was Hawaii, where he did maintenance work on F-4s."

"Good for him," Thomas muttered.

I ignored his snide remark. "He put up two flagpoles in our front yard, one for the Stars and Stripes and the other for the black and white MIA flag. He even put in a floodlight so the flags could fly at night."

And I've always been proud of him, I wanted to say. My cell phone vibrated. I pulled it out of my pocket and glanced at the caller ID. Jasmine.

"Excuse me," I said to Thomas, answering the phone.

"Mom? Where are you?" Jasmine's voice sounded frantic. "I've been trying to get you for the past hour."

"What's wrong?"

"I'm at the hospital. It's Kate. She's got toxemia. They want to do a C-section and take the baby."

Oh no. The baby wasn't due for another six weeks.

"Dad's here," she continued breathlessly. "Jon's flying back from the West Coast as soon as he can get a flight."

"I'm on my way." I disconnected and pushed myself up from the ground, stiff joints protesting painfully.

"I have a family emergency." I told Thomas about Kate. "I have to get my car and hurry to the hospital."

"Which hospital?"

I told him. He stood up, brushing himself off. "We'll waste time going back. I'll take you."

As we roared off into the night, I breathed a silent prayer. *Lord, let her be all right. Let the baby be all right. Please.*

CHAPTER TWENTY-FIVE

The first thing I saw when we rushed into the waiting room was Kelly sitting next to Brian, her arm loosely entwined through his. With her free hand, she gently stroked his forearm. Jasmine, still wearing her cleaning clothes, sat on his other side, flipping through a magazine. Brian leaned forward, elbows on his knees, hands clasped in front of him. The sleeves of his light blue Oxford shirt were rolled up to his elbows. All three looked up when Thomas and I approached.

"How's Katie?" I asked.

Jasmine stood and hugged me. "Oh, Mom, I wish there was something I could do besides sit here."

I smoothed her hair back out of her face. "Have you talked to the doctor yet?"

"No, but the nurse on duty is keeping us informed. This waiting is torture."

"I know, honey, I know." I glanced around the waiting room. We were the only ones there. I asked about Jon.

"He's booked for the red-eye out of LAX and should arrive in Pittsburgh around six. Danny's picking him up at the airport." She stepped back, giving me a puzzled look. "Your jacket feels like ice."

"We rode here on Thomas's new Harley," I explained.

They gaped at Thomas. I realized introductions were in order. "Thomas, this is my daughter, Jasmine, her father Brian, and, uh, a family friend, Kelly. Kelly is Kate's godmother. Thomas is Wil Benedict's brother."

Brian nodded, Kelly smiled demurely, and Jasmine ignored him. I could have explained that I was having dinner with Wil and Trish when Thomas happened by on his new bike. But if they—meaning Brian and Kelly—wanted to think I was on a date with him, that was fine with me. I glanced at Kelly. She was studying Thomas, her hand on Brian's arm—protectively, possessively, or both, I couldn't tell.

The automatic double doors swung open with a slow swoosh, and a middle-aged woman in green scrubs approached us, her rubber soles squeaking with each quick step on the waxed terrazzo floor. She scanned the group then settled her gaze on Brian and Kelly.

"Mr. and Mrs. Laverly?" She held out her hand. "I'm Dr. Lamb, Kate's ob-gyn."

I stepped in front of Kelly and grasped Dr. Lamb's extended hand. "*I'm* Mrs. Laverly." Behind me, Brian stood.

Dr. Lamb glanced uncertainly at our little group huddled around her. Assuming she was concerned about privacy laws, I made the introductions.

"I'm Kate's mom, Linda. Her husband, Jon, is flying in from California and should be here in the morning." I put my hand on Brian's shoulder. "This is Kate's father, and this—" I pointed to Jasmine—"is her sister Jasmine." Dr. Lamb glanced quizzically at Kelly and Thomas. "Kelly and Thomas are family friends," I added.

"Kate gave permission for information to be released to family only," Dr. Lamb said firmly.

Inside I smirked. Then shame flooded me. What kind of a person was I becoming?

"Come on, Kelly," Thomas said. "Let's go get a cup of coffee."

Kelly hesitated then grabbed her purse. After they left, Dr. Lamb spoke frankly.

"At this point, we know the baby is stressed. The toxemia is not responding to medication as quickly as we'd hoped. Kate's blood pressure is still dangerously high, and her symptoms—abdominal pain, blurred vision, edema—are getting worse. She's having trouble breathing and has complained of nausea. At this point, we're concerned about seizures."

"What about the baby?" I asked.

"We're monitoring the level of fetal distress very carefully. If we take the baby by C-section, we can administer much stronger drugs to fight the toxemia."

Brian spoke up. "Isn't this kind of early? He isn't due until the end of May."

"Yes, he will be premature," she said, "but we've injected Kate with an antenatal corticosteroid to speed up his lung development before delivery. In addition, we have a medical helicopter on alert in case we need to transport him to Magee-Womens Hospital in Pittsburgh, which has one of the most up-to-date NICUs in the state. With a little technical support for two or three weeks, barring any birth defects or complications, he should be fine."

"What's a nickyoo?" Brian asked.

"Neonatal intensive care unit."

"What about Kate?" Brian asked.

"She's being prepped for surgery now. As I said, once the baby is born, we can administer more potent medication. How her body will respond, I don't know. Every case is different. If she responds as we hope, she should be out of danger within twenty-four hours. Of course, bed rest once she gets home."

She glanced at the wall clock. "Do you have any more questions? If not, I've got to get back to the OR. You can go in now for a few minutes. She's asked to see you."

As we followed Dr. Lamb, I noticed a middle-aged black couple in blue jeans standing by the door. The man nodded to us as we passed them. The woman smiled encouragingly.

Katie was lying on a gurney next to the wall in the hallway. The amount of swelling from the toxemia took me by surprise. Her coloring was grayish-yellow. She smiled at us, lips trembling slightly. She was trying to be brave, but I knew she was afraid. Not for herself, but for her baby.

Brian and I stepped up to the side rail. Gently he enclosed her hand in both of his, careful of the IV needle. Jasmine stood on the other side of Brian, her hand on Katie's pregnant abdomen. Her eyes were closed, and her lips moved soundlessly.

"It'll be all right, honey," I said, caressing Katie's bloated cheek.

"The baby…it's a boy, you know. B. J., for Brian Jon." Her fear-filled eyes gazed into mine. "If anything happens, Mom, take care of Lexie and B. J."

I wanted to say, "Nothing is going to happen to you," but I'd been where she was now when Danny was born. Not with toxemia. Danny was breech. Feet first. The danger of the cord snapping drove me almost insane with panic. You don't deny the danger. You don't deny the fear.

"We'll be here, sweetheart," I said.

"Pray," she said. "I know God is in control, but I'm afraid. Not of dying, but of what's going to happen to Jon and Lexie and B. J. if I die."

"You're not going to die," Brian said. His voice sounded strangled. "You and B. J. are going to be just fine. We'll be here when you wake up. Don't you worry about anything."

Jasmine cried softly, tears coursing down her cheeks and splashing on the starched white sheet.

"I love you, sis," she whispered.

"I love you, too—" Kate glanced at each of us briefly. "And Mom? Dad?" She grasped my hand and placed it in Brian's. "Love never dies. Don't ever forget that."

And then they wheeled my baby, my firstborn, off to an operating room, where they were going to try to save her life and the life of our second grandchild, little Brian Jon.

Oh, God, please, I prayed as I stood in the sterile hallway, feeling helpless and adrift. As I turned to leave, I realized I was still grasping Brian's hand—and he was squeezing right back. I glanced up at his face. He was crying.

CHAPTER TWENTY-SIX

The couple was still in the waiting room when we returned. They stood when we entered and approached us. The man was tall—at least six-feet-five inches—and built like a linebacker. The woman wasn't much shorter than him, with a sculpted build and a regal beauty that set her apart. Her brown eyes exuded warmth and compassion, as did his.

"Mr. and Mrs. Laverly?" He extended his hand. "My name's Wes Hunt. This is my wife, Aaliya. I'm Kate and Jon's pastor. We came as soon as Jasmine called."

So this was the couple of whom Katie and Jon spoke so highly. "They encourage me so much," she'd told me. Jasmine and Josh drove forty-five minutes every Sunday to attend the church and had also joined a small Bible study group led by this couple.

"Thank you for coming, especially on a Saturday night," I said. "Jon and Kate have spoken of you often. All good, of course."

Brian nodded in agreement then turned to me. "I don't think Katie will mind if we brought them up to date, do you?"

I shook my head. "I'm sure she wouldn't. Go ahead."

"Why don't you tell them? You're so much better at explaining things than I am."

"You were here first," I insisted, "at least an hour before I got here."

"Oh, for Pete's sake," Jasmine interrupted. "I'll tell them."

Embarrassed, I headed for the setting in the corner of the room close to the TV. Brian, with a sheepish look on his face, eased himself onto the sofa next to me. "Guess she told us, huh? Sorry."

"We deserved it."

"But you're so much better than I am with this sort of thing, Lin. I get things mixed up, you know that."

"Brian, I am no longer your brain. Haven't you learned anything in the four months since I left? Sh-h—here they come."

"Mom, Dad, I've asked Pastor Wes to lead us in a prayer," Jasmine said, eyeing us meaningfully. "Let's join hands and make a prayer circle."

We clasped our hands, Jasmine on my left, and Brian on my right. This was the second time tonight my hand rested in his. *Our hands fit together so well. It feels like coming home.* I was still mad at the church and God, so I bowed my head and started to tune out. The sound of the pastor's voice, however, drew me in. I liked the way he prayed. He didn't sound pompous or use a prayer voice like some preachers I knew. He just talked to God the same way he'd spoken with us. Down-to-earth. Maybe when this was all over, I'd try that church. I'd get to see my grandchildren in the children's programs, and maybe they'd let me get involved in the music. Brian squeezed my hand. I opened my eyes and lifted my head. I'd missed the "Amen." Maybe they'd think I was spiritual or something, praying longer than anyone else.

Thomas and Kelly appeared in the doorway, each holding two large Styrofoam cups.

"Here, Brian," Kelly said in that syrupy tone of hers, handing one to him. "Just the way you like it. Decaf. Black. I put a couple of ice cubes in to cool it down quicker."

When did he start drinking decaf?

Thomas thrust a cup in my hand. "Here's a hot chocolate. I figure all women like chocolate."

I smiled. "Thanks."

"Oh, and I had them put some whipped cream on top." He looked proud of himself.

"Oh, extra good!" I gushed—for Brian's benefit—and gingerly took a sip. Just as I liked it. "This is excellent. Thank you, Thomas. You are so thoughtful."

We did the introduction thing again, tagging Kelly and Thomas as "family friends," and then settled in for the wait. Kelly sat close to Brian. Jasmine plopped down on the other side of her dad. Thomas chose an overstuffed chair, the pastor and his wife settled on the love seat, and I got what was left in the setting: a chair opposite Thomas. I glanced at the wall clock. Ten-thirty. It had been about a half an hour since they wheeled her away.

"How long will this take?" Kelly asked.

"Actually, not long," Brian said. "Once Katie goes under, they'll take the baby immediately. They don't want any anesthesia crossing into the baby's system."

Thomas grabbed the remote and pushed some buttons. The huge TV screen mounted on the wall came to life. He surfed through the channels until he found a baseball game. The Pirates were playing the Giants on the West Coast, so the game had just gotten underway.

He grinned at the group. "Hope you all don't mind."

Pastor Wes laughed. "Not at all. We've got three boys, and they're all into sports, so we watch a lot of ballgames at home."

I couldn't focus on the game. My mind was on what was going on beyond those doors marked "No Admittance." Brian stared at the screen, but I could tell he wasn't really watching either. Kelly caressed his arm. I wanted to snap, "Stop that!" Jasmine leaned against Brian, her head on his shoulder, her eyes closed.

I shrugged out of my jacket and draped it across my chest, slipped off my shoes ,and folded my legs beneath me. The combined effects of the motorcycle ride, hot chocolate, the warmth of the room, the soft murmur of the men's voices as they talked baseball, not to mention the emotional roller coaster I'd been riding, made me drowsy. I laid my head back and closed my eyes. What was taking so long?

It was nearly an hour before Dr. Lamb strode in and gave us the news. B.J, as far as they could tell, appeared healthy and robust, for a preemie. He would have been a big baby had he gone full term, she said.

"His lungs aren't quite fully developed, which is normal for a baby born six weeks early, so he's in the NICU here."

"You won't have to transport him to Pittsburgh?" I asked.

"At this point, no. Other than needing breathing support, which we can take care of here, he's doing just fine."

"Thank God," Brian said. "What about Katie?"

"She's in recovery. We'll let you know when she's moved to her room."

"Can't we see her now?" Brian asked.

The doctor hesitated.

"I was allowed in after my wife had a C-section," Brian hurried on. "With her husband not here yet, couldn't you let someone from the family in?"

"Fine," Dr. Lamb said, with a nod. "But just Dad and Mom, and no longer than two minutes." She headed for the door.

"Thank you, doctor," Brian said, striding after her.

Crisis brings out the man, I thought, hurrying after him in my stocking feet.

Our two minutes with Katie seemed like two seconds. We murmured encouragement in her ears—Brian on one side, I on the other—kissed her cheek, which was still bloated, then followed Dr. Lamb to the NICU, where Jasmine waited. We donned gowns and stood at the sink washing our hands and arms with antibacterial soap, lathering for one full minute.

Little B. J.—all four pounds of him—looked lost in the maze of wires and tubes. Machines blipping, humming, clicking reminded me of his fight for life. *Welcome to the world, little B. J.* A soft blue knit cap covered his head. I wanted to touch him, but he was so tiny. He didn't look much bigger than Brian's hand. I wanted to cuddle him on my shoulder and sing the silly lullabies I sang to Lexie. In time, I told myself, in time.

Back in the waiting room, we gave our report to the pastor and his wife. Then Brian went to the men's room, and Jasmine retreated to a quiet corner to call Josh, Danny, and Jon. Thomas had disappeared.

"Where's Thomas?" I asked.

Aaliya spoke. "He left right after you and your husband went with the doctor."

"Did he say where he was going?"

She shook her head. Behind me, I heard Kelly snicker. The pastor and his wife returned to the love seat, and I curled up in my chair. A few minutes later, Brian and Thomas walked in.

"Went to check the Harley," Thomas said, stepping past me to his chair. *And have a smoke*, I thought, sniffing.

It was now after midnight, Katie was out of recovery, and the baby was holding his own. Pastor Wes and Aaliya left, with instructions to call them should the situation change. Before she left, Aaliya gave me a hug and whispered in my ear, "Don't let her get to you. Hurting people hurt people. Remember that."

Jasmine announced she, too, was leaving.

"You're not driving all the way to Pittsburgh tonight," Brian told her. "Go home. Sleep in the guest room."

"That's what I intended to do," she said, shooting a knowing look at Kelly.

"I'm staying," I announced. "Thomas, tell Wil I'll get my car tomorrow sometime."

"I'm staying, too," Brian said. "Kelly, I'll take you home then come back."

There is a God in heaven.

Thomas stood. "I'll take Kelly home. This way you can stay with your family, Brian. That is, if Kelly doesn't mind riding on the back of my hog."

"Mind?" she said, triumph oozing out of every pore of her lithe and mean body. "I'd love it!"

When everyone had gone, Brian and I headed for Katie's room, where I settled in the sleeper chair, and he pushed two hard-backed chairs together and sprawled out. An hour later I was still awake. I checked on Katie then settled back down. The room felt cool, so I huddled under my jacket. A few minutes later, I heard a familiar sound. I smiled. I'd always complained to Brian that his snoring kept me awake. But tonight, in a world of uncertainty and fear, it gave me a sense of comfort and stability. The next thing I knew, it was morning and the day shift was bustling about. And someone had covered me with a blanket.

CHAPTER TWENTY-SEVEN

Danny and Jon showed up around eight. Usually trim, tidy, and self-controlled, Jon looked haggard—suit rumpled, tie loose, weariness and worry in every line of his face and body. Katie had passed the crisis point during the night and was sleeping peacefully. Gently, tenderly, Jon lifted her swollen hand to his lips. She stirred and blinked. A smile lit up her pale, puffy face.

"Sweetheart," she mouthed. Her eyes shone as he bent over the bedrail. I could feel their love. A hand squeezed my elbow.

"Let's go," Brian whispered in my ear. I didn't want to leave. I wanted to reach out and capture some of that tender love and inject it in my heart, in Brian's heart.

Danny followed us to the waiting room. Outside, a steady rain. The tension of the night had dissipated, leaving me weak and weepy. I gently pulled my elbow out of Brian's grasp and slid onto the sofa. Danny folded his lanky frame into a chair opposite me. Brian eased in beside me.

He looked at Danny. "Long night, huh?"

Danny's lips stretched into that lopsided, lazy grin of his. "What are families for?"

"To ruin your plans?" I quipped.

"I had no plans, really. Just hang out with some guys and play poker."

"Don't you have finals coming up?" Brian asked.

Danny rubbed the stubble on his chin. "Not for another week."

Brian drew his lips in a firm, taut line. "You could get a head start—academic probation is nothing to mess with."

"I know, Dad, I know." Danny glanced at his cell phone. "I'm starving. What are we gonna do for breakfast?"

"Hi, guys." Jasmine, wearing a yellow sweatshirt and jeans, curly hair still damp from the shower, plopped into the chair opposite Danny. "How're Katie and B. J.?"

I brought her up to date.

"I take it from Danny's presence that Jon made it?" she said.

I nodded. "He's with Kate now."

"Good. He was so worried about the toxemia, he didn't want to go. But Kate talked him into it."

"Wait a minute." I took a breath. "Are you saying Jon knew about the toxemia before his trip?"

"Oops."

"They *knew*?"

Jasmine looked up at the ceiling and sighed. "Yes, Mom, they knew, but it wasn't that bad. Her blood pressure had risen a bit, and her hands and feet were only starting to swell a little. They were keeping an eye on it."

"*You* knew?"

She nodded.

I looked at Brian. "Did you know?"

He shook his head. I shot a questioning glance at Danny. He shrugged.

"Why didn't she tell me? Tell us?"

Jasmine shifted in her seat and glanced away before meeting my eyes. "Because she felt you had enough to deal with."

"I'm still her mother."

"That you are, but you've been, well, let's put it this way, you haven't been yourself lately."

"Just Jon, Kate, me, and Josh." She paused. "And Pastor Wes and Aaliya, and, oh, yes, the prayer chain."

My face grew warm. Anger tinged with shame flooded me. Anger because I should have been told—before the pastor, before the pastor's wife, before the prayer people. Shame because I'd been so wrapped up in my own world I'd been unavailable to my daughter when she needed me.

*****

"I could throttle that Jon," I said on the way to the restaurant. Danny and Jasmine followed in Jasmine's car. "How could he fly out to LA when he knew Katie was in danger?"

Brian shook his head. "She wasn't in danger when he left. No one knew she'd get bad so fast."

"But to put business before his wife, his family!"

"A man can't stop everything because of something that may or may not happen, Linda. Jon's got a lot of responsibility. He's a hard worker. A good provider. Why do you think he's risen in the company so fast?" He turned his attention back to the puddled pavement ahead. "A man's got to do what he can."

I stared out the side window and shook my head.

Breakfast was more pleasant than I'd thought it would be. I thought for sure Brian would use this opportunity to lecture Danny, but to my surprise and relief, he said not a word about grades, school, work, or baseball. Instead, he chatted with Jasmine about Josh's fishing trip and boasted about his growing culinary skills.

"I've got lots of menu choices," he said, cutting through the mass of breakfast jumble before him, silverware screeching against the plate. "Take-out, drive-through, delivery, or one of the three Cs—canned, cardboard, or crockpot."

"Crockpot?" I joked, slathering butter on my wheat toast. "You mean you actually know what a crockpot is, let alone how to use it?"

He grinned. "Sure do. Best way to do a pot roast. The meat falls apart, and the veggies are tastier than if they'd been cooked by themselves."

I nearly choked on my toast. "Did I hear you right? Did you say 'pot roast'?"

"You heard me right, woman. It's so easy to throw everything in the crockpot in the morning, turn it on low, and let it go for the day. When I walk in the door at night, the smell of a nice, hot meal greets me. I can almost pretend...." Brian lifted his coffee cup. "Never mind."

"What you mean," Jasmine said, giving me a knowing look, "is that walking into a cold, dark, silent, empty house really sucks, right, Dad?"

*****

Back at the hospital, we were allowed to hold our newest grandchild—but not before doing the scrub-and-gown routine again. I went first, cuddling little B. J. as best as I could with all the wires and tubes attached to him. I cooed in his ear, planted butterfly kisses on his skinny cheek, and softly crooned a lullaby while Brian leaned over my shoulder behind the rocking chair. Once I glanced up and thought his eyes glistened. When my time was up, I reluctantly and carefully handed the baby to Brian. As I placed B. J. in Brian's big, work-worn, calloused hands, I noticed they were trembling.

"Are you all right?" I whispered.

He nodded and lowered himself into the rocking chair. He held B. J. close to his chest, bending his neck so that his face barely touched the baby's face. A tear meandered down his cheek, losing itself in the stubble that had sprouted overnight. *I'll bet he'd look good in a beard,* I thought. As I watched him hold his tiny four-pound grandson as though he'd break, my throat tightened and my vision blurred. What was it about watching this man, whom I'd practically accused of having no feelings, hold our first grandson that made my heart feel like it was about to burst?

I didn't know, but I did know that this was something that I could never and would never share with any other man.

CHAPTER TWENTY-EIGHT

The Saturday evening before Mother's Day, Jasmine called.

"Mom?" She sounded excited—but a controlled excitement I knew well.

"What are you doing tomorrow?"

I had planned on a quiet day. Sleep in, have a leisurely brunch over the Sunday paper, maybe take the dogs for a walk in the woods, eat supper out. Alone. Danny was at college, getting ready for summer classes. He'd sent flowers, which I'd probably have to pay for. Jon had taken Katie and the kids away for a surprise getaway weekend. Wil and Trish were at their son's, and Thomas was in Pittsburgh at his new condo. I'd called him earlier, asking if he wanted to have dinner or something, but he had an appointment with the interior decorator. Or so he said. And tomorrow he was going to the Pirates game. I'd mentioned that I loved baseball, but he didn't take the hint.

"Nothing special," I told her. "Why?"

She paused. "I want you to come to church with us."

I took a breath. "Jasmine—"

"Come on, Mom. It's Mother's Day. We have a potluck dinner planned for after the service in the fellowship hall."

"Jasmine, honey, I can't go."

"For heaven's sake, why not?"

I told her about being stripped of my music, all because I'd left Brian. "I haven't set foot in a church since."

"I'm sorry, Mom. I didn't know. After all you did for that church too."

I swallowed the lump in my throat. "Thank you for understanding."

"But you've never been to *our* church. Trust me, Mom, you'll like it."

Jasmine and Josh had started attending Katie and Jon's church after they'd tried—unsuccessfully—to start a family. *After three miscarriages in two years, you'd think she'd give up on that prayer stuff. I sure have.*

"Will you come tomorrow?" she asked. "Please?" The shyness in her voice surprised me.

"Honey, it's too far."

"The weather's supposed to be beautiful. No snow. No ice. And you're all alone."

"Maybe I like being alone."

She paused. "You can't mean that."

I glanced out the window. The sun was just slipping below the horizon, the sky aflame with a copper-red glow.

"I think I do—I mean, I do and I don't." How to explain? I loved being responsible for only myself. No one complaining that the food was too hot or too spicy or too whatever. But it sure got lonely sometimes. One day I found myself talking to the peanut butter jar. And the nights— occasionally I coaxed Glenda's well-trained dogs to sleep on top of the covers. I kept a jar of treats on the nightstand for that purpose. Their furry bodies kept me warm, and their panting and snorting were a comforting reminder that I wasn't alone. *Oh, quit it!* The vase of flowers on the coffee table blurred.

"I won't take no for an answer," she said. A lot less shyly.

"Why don't we meet at a restaurant halfway between here and your place? What time will the service be over?"

"No can do," she said.

"And why not?"

"Because I have a ride all set up for you."

Oh, no.

"Dad will pick you up at nine-thirty." Her tone was the one I so often used when she was a headstrong teenager.

"No."

"I already told him you agreed."

"Jasmine! That was a lie! And you call yourself a Christian."

"I didn't lie. I gave a true answer before the fact."

And so, a little before nine the next morning, I sat at the kitchen table in my robe, sipping my coffee and reading the sports page—the Pirates were playing in Colorado—when a car pulled up under the portico. *A half an hour early.* Of course I wasn't ready. *Well, he'll just have to wait.* I headed to the door. The dogs followed me, tails wagging away.

Brian stood there in the blue shirt I loved, a silk tie I didn't recognize, and black dress pants, clutching a bouquet of flowers. I opened the door.

"Here," he muttered, shoving them in my hands and stepping past me. "Happy Mother's Day."

"And a good morning to you, too." I followed him to the kitchen, where I put the flowers on the counter by the sink and began cleaning up my breakfast dishes. The dogs nuzzled their noses in Brian's hands. *My, they took to him fast.*

"I'll do the dishes," he said, scratching both dogs behind the ears, then taking the plate and mug I had in my hands. He eyed my robe. "You don't have much more to do to get ready, do you?"

My face grew warm as I clutched the lapels of my robe together. Silly. We'd been married for thirty-two years. He'd seen a lot more than a little cleavage on me.

"Just give me fifteen minutes. Want some coffee? There might be a cup left."

He sniffed. "If it's that flavored stuff, no thanks."

I unplugged the coffeemaker and nodded toward the flowers. "There's a vase under the sink."

I brushed my teeth and put on my makeup, taking more time than usual—not to be difficult, but because my hands were trembling. Why was I so flustered? It had taken me an hour last night to pick which dress to wear. After I'd hung up with Jasmine, I'd tried on just about everything in my closet, finally settling on the emerald green silk number that I'd bought last week in celebration of meeting my goal weight. I slipped the gold necklace Brian had gotten me for our last anniversary around my neck and put on the matching earrings, which he'd gotten me the year before.

Brian stood staring out the window when I waltzed into the kitchen. He held my coat. He turned and took me in from head to foot. For an instant something flashed in his eyes.

He let out a low whistle. "Bet that cost a pretty penny."

I snatched my coat and thrust my arms in the sleeves. "I got it on sale—40 percent off."

*****

"Is it always this crowded?" I whispered to Jasmine before the service started. True to form, she'd made sure Brian and I sat beside each other. She nodded, sliding closer to me to let another person in our pew, which practically put me in Brian's lap.

I leaned and put my lips to her ear. "Don't try to be cute."

She rolled her eyes and opened her hymnal. But I saw that sly little grin.

To my surprise, I enjoyed the service, especially the music, a nice blend of the newer gospel songs with a few old hymns, sung the old-fashioned way, not with a silly, newfangled beat no one could follow.

I had taken an instant liking to Wes Hunt that night at the hospital when he prayed with us. And he preached the same way he prayed—down to earth.

"A good wife who can find?" he began, quoting that well-worn proverb usually used for Mother's Day. Pausing for effect, he scanned over the congregation and deadpanned, "We're still looking."

Even I grinned. As Rev. Hunt continued, I glanced at Brian, hoping he was listening. That particular portion of scripture was a familiar one. The wife is more precious than jewels. She works hard from sunup to sundown and is everything to everyone. Maybe hearing it from the pulpit would help him to realize all he'd lost. But Wes Hunt surprised me.

"If you have your Bibles, open them to First Corinthians chapter eleven, verse nine. You're probably going to say I'm old-fashioned—and you'd be right. But I base my life on this—" He waved his open Bible in the air above his head. "I call it the manufacturer's handbook. When something goes wrong—whether in a relationship or circumstances—you can count on this Book to help you figure out what's wrong and how to fix it." He slipped on a pair of glasses and began reading. "For man did not come from woman, but woman from man; neither was man created for woman, but woman for man."

I squirmed.

"Did you get that? The woman was made for the man. If you don't believe me, go back and read the creation account in Genesis. Now, before you men start nudging your wives, turn to Ephesians five, twenty-three."

Here we go. The all-important submissive, wimpy wife. Why did I ever agree to come?

"The husband is the head of the wife—" He paused. "But, as I heard in a movie I saw recently, the wife is the neck, which turns the head." Laughter and guffaws filled the sanctuary.

"Too often this verse is misquoted so as to make a woman feel as though she is somehow inferior to the man and must submit to him because she's too stupid to do anything else. Aaliya is far from stupid." He smiled at his wife, who sat in the first pew. "I don't know what I'd do without her."

I liked this guy more and more.

"Let's read further to some verses that are conveniently left out. 'Husbands, love your wives, just as Christ loved the church and gave himself up for her.' Men, the best thing you can do for your children is to love their mother. And don't let a day go by without showing her how much you love and cherish her."

Brian, are you listening? I snuck a sideways glance at this man I'd spent thirty-two years with. *That's what I tried to tell you.*

Then I remembered the long hours Brian had worked at construction, then came home and worked on the house. Was that "giving himself up for her?"

*****

On the way home, we talked about the kids—in particular, Danny. He'd done better this semester, but too many semesters of sub-par grades meant he couldn't graduate until at least December. He'd have to repeat some courses—and he was balking.

"I wouldn't worry too much about Danny," I said. "He's still young. He'll come around."

"I just don't want him to end up like me. I've always regretted not finishing college."

"His failures are not your failures, Brian. Because he fails doesn't mean you've failed. And you can't live his life for him or dream his dreams for him. He's twenty-two—an adult now."

I stared at the yellow line on the road ahead. "Besides, if he does flunk out, what's the worst that can happen? Don't you remember when you were that age? Give the kid some slack."

Brian gripped the leather-covered steering wheel.

"Let it go, Brian. He'll survive."

"Then you talk to him. He always listens to you."

"He doesn't want to disappoint you, Brian, and he knows he let you down when his grades were too bad to play baseball this semester." I sighed. "You know, you're a hard man to live with sometimes."

Brian's cell phone rang. He fished it out of his shirt pocket and glanced at the screen. I turned my head, watching the guide rails whiz by as Brian took the call.

"I'm sorry to hear that, Sam. Is there anything I can do?...Take as much time as you need."

He disconnected and slipped the phone back in his pocket. The muscles in his cheek twitched.

"That was Sam. Goldie died today."

CHAPTER TWENTY-NINE

When the alarm went off at five the next morning, I hit the snooze button three times before the dogs' wet noses nudged through the covers and found my face.

"All right, all right," I mumbled, kicking the quilt off my legs. They bounded around the room, tails wagging with more energy than I'd have all day, I was sure. Groaning, I rolled out of bed and shuffled to the mudroom door, let them out, and headed for the bathroom.

Extra concealer, I thought, squinting at my reflection in the mirror. Dark circles under my eyes gave away my sleep-deprived night. I'd wrestled with the covers and with the words from yesterday's sermon and argued with an absent Brian until three a.m. *I gave up my career to raise our kids. Didn't you recognize me in the Proverbs 31 woman?*

My body ached all over, and I had to face a full day on two hours of sleep. Work at the newspaper all morning, then give piano lessons all afternoon. *Maybe I'll call Thomas and see what he's doing for dinner.*

In the kitchen I flicked on the light over the sink then made coffee. No decaf today. I had to be in the newsroom at seven to write the obits. Obituaries were not my favorite kind of writing, but every little bit of income helped. I let the dogs in, poured coffee into the biggest mug I could find, and headed for the shower.

*****

Before the clock struck noon, I was in hotter water than my morning shower. I hadn't even settled in my chair when Rick, the managing editor, stopped at my desk.

"Linda, I need to talk to you when you're done with the obits," he said.

Rick never asked to speak with staffers unless he had a big assignment for them or they were in trouble. I highly doubted he had an assignment for me. I shuffled through the obits and groaned. Double digits! I'd need help getting ten obits done by deadline.

"Hey, Lin, fax for you," someone hollered.

"Not another obit!" I muttered and made my way back to the fax machine. I lifted the paper from the tray and scanned the name. Goldie Calhoun.

Two hours later Chas, the editor who checked the obits after I wrote them, hollered across the newsroom.

"Hey, Lin, check the name of that funeral home for the Calhoun obit, would you?"

I opened the file and read through the obit, checking it against the information on the fax. Uh-oh. I'd mixed up two letters in the name of the funeral home. Which was a little mistake compared to the one I got called on the carpet for.

After we put the day's paper to bed, I stopped at Rick's desk.

"You wanted to see me?" I tugged the straps of my purse over my shoulder.

"Yes." He removed his glasses and pushed his chair back. The wheels screeched on the hard plastic mat, stopping suddenly at a section where a chunk of plastic was missing. "Let's go to the conference room."

Yep. I was in trouble, all right.

"Linda, do you know the difference between market value and assessed value of real estate?" he began once the door was shut and we'd settled in the scratched pine chairs.

"No, why?"

"Because we could have had a crisis on our hands if we'd printed that story you wrote last week on the proposed budget for the school district."

"I'm sorry," I said, confused. "I'm not following you. I used the information I was given."

"Yes, but whoever gave it to you apparently wasn't aware you were clueless about what he was talking about. Property owners would have rioted had we printed that their taxes were going up that high. Good thing we checked the figures and changed them before the story hit print."

"Oh." I squirmed in the hard chair. "I'm sorry, but I thought you knew I wasn't experienced covering school board meetings when you assigned me to cover the meeting."

"Good reporters check their facts. Double check. Triple check. And ask questions if they don't understand something."

I could tell he was trying to control the volume of his voice. Even so, everyone in the newsroom, I was sure, could hear through the thick paneled door.

"And that's not all." Rick fiddled with his wedding ring. I remembered Brian wore his yesterday. Maybe, like me, he couldn't get it off.

"Do you remember the story we printed about the old lady who turned a hundred?" Rick said.

How could I forget that one? She'd gushed over me, excited that an actual reporter had visited her home, and gave me brownies. To eat there *and* take home.

"Do you remember her sister Sarabelle, who, according to what you wrote, died in infancy?"

I nodded slowly.

"Well, Sarabelle called on Saturday." He paused, apparently to allow the meaning of his words to sink in.

"Oh."

"She was crying, wailing into the phone, 'It's bad enough that I died, but to think I'd never even lived!' "

I stifled the urge to giggle. "Don't you think she was overreacting, Rick?"

He shrugged. "That doesn't matter. What does matter is that this newspaper takes pride in providing accurate information. That's two strikes against you, Linda."

I stood. "Three."

He looked puzzled.

"I typed 'Macaroni' Funeral Home today instead of 'Maraconi.' Chas caught it." I stepped to the door. "Rick, consider this my two weeks' notice."

Surprise registered on his face. "Oh, Linda, I didn't mean for you to quit. I wasn't going to fire you. I just want you to be more careful."

I smiled. "Rick, I've loved working with the staff, but writing obits, covering school board meetings, and putting up with people who aren't happy with the way I typed up their daughter's engagement announcement just isn't for me."

It turned out I didn't need to serve my two-week sentence. A journalism major from the local university had just been hired as a summer intern. Relief filled me as I headed for the community center. Sure, I'd miss that paycheck, but my piano lesson schedule was full, and I had a waiting list. I'd be just fine.

*****

I called Thomas right before lunch.

"Hey," I said, unwrapping my tuna-on-wheat sandwich. "What's up?"

"Who's this?" he asked.

I swallowed. "Linda. Linda Laverly." *You know—Lulu? Lana?*

"Who? Oh, sorry. I just got up. How's it going, babe?"

I explained about Goldie and asked him if he'd accompany me to the funeral home that evening after we'd had dinner—my treat. *Please say yes.* I desperately needed to end this horrible day on a positive note.

"Sorry, hon." I heard him yawn. "I don't do funeral homes."

Well, I thought, disconnecting, *that takes care of that.*

The afternoon dragged on. I kept hoping one of my students would cancel so I could lie down on the love seat and take a nap. I really wanted to cancel all my lessons and go home and sleep, but I needed the money. My cell phone rang as I pulled out of the community center parking lot. *Maybe Thomas changed his mind.* But it was Diane, one of the reporters at the paper.

"Hey, Lin. Sorry to hear you quit. We're going to miss you around here. Especially that laugh. Rick can be a real jerk sometimes."

"It's not his fault," I said, checking my surroundings to make sure there were no cops around. I'd heard they'd really been clamping down on drivers using cell phones. "But thanks anyway."

"Are you coming to ladies' night out tonight? You didn't forget, did you?"

Actually, I *had* forgotten. The girls at the paper met the second Monday evening of the month in one of the local lounges, a different one each month.

"Wouldn't miss it," I told Diane. "Where is it?"

"Paddy's. Oh, I'm so glad you're coming. The band is supposed to be really great."

*****

I skipped supper—I wasn't hungry, anyway—to lie down before I got ready for the evening. I chose ebony slacks that, I thought, made me look thinner and a midnight blue silk blouse. After slipping into black dress sandals, I checked myself out in the full-length mirror before I left.

Not bad, I thought, twirling my keys around my index finger.

First I went to the funeral home, which was packed. I joined Wil and Trish in the line that snaked out the door and spilled out onto the covered porch. I shouldn't have been surprised. Sam and Goldie were well-loved. Their big hearts and generous spirits had touched a lot of lives.

I didn't see Brian until I reached the second door inside. He was about fifty people in front of me. I stood on my tiptoes and arched my neck to see if he was alone. He wasn't. Kelly was with him. Some emotion must have registered on my face because Wil put his arm around me and leaned over so his lips touched my ear.

"She can't hold a candle to you, Linda Sue."

"That's not it," I stammered. But it was. Kelly, with no children to ferry around, fight with, and fret about, had taken good care of herself over the years, frequenting spas, hiring her own personal trainer, never missing a hair appointment. At fifty-seven, she looked like a woman twenty years younger.

By the time we'd moved up to the third inside door and into the room where Goldie lay in a yellow chiffon-lined casket, I wanted to turn around and leave. It killed me to see Brian with Kelly.

"What's your brother been up to?" I asked Wil. Ever since the night at the hospital, it seemed as though Thomas had been keeping his distance. I'd called him several times, but either he said he was too busy to talk or I got his voice mail. He didn't return my calls.

"Getting settled in his new place," Wil said. He looked around then leaned over to me. "Listen, Linda Sue, Thomas is—how do I want to say this—Thomas isn't the kind of man you need."

I arched my eyebrows. "Oh?"

"He's like a bird that flits and swoops but never lands. You need a man you can count on." He jerked his thumb towards the line in front of us. "Like that one."

"In case you haven't noticed, Wil, that one is taken."

"No, he's not. Well, not by the woman who's with him, anyway. I can't tell you much more, Linda Sue, except things aren't what they appear to be."

After I gave Sam a hug and shook hands down the line, I edged my way to the door. Somewhere in the crowd I heard someone say, "That's Brian Laverly, the man who gave our Sammy a job after the college let him go. Wonderful man. And that pretty blond with him must be Mrs. Laverly."

I elbowed my way out as fast as I could, ignoring the surprised and angry looks I got. *Aw, phooey with them,* I thought, getting into my car. *Phooey with them all. I hate Kelly! I hate Brian!*

I arrived at Paddy's a little after nine. The girls waved me over to the table—two tables pushed together. I plopped in a chair and ordered water.

"Water!" Diane shrieked. "After today, you need something stronger." She turned to the waitress. "A shot of tequila for my friend."

A half an hour later I was still feeling the effects of the shot when a nice-looking guy who looked to be in his early sixties asked me to dance. We sashayed around the floor for a slow set then sat in a booth and exchanged lies.

"What are you drinking?" he asked, loosening his tie.

"Water with a slice of lemon."

He ordered a bottle of the house wine. To be nice, I accepted a glass and sipped it slowly while we chatted about our jobs. I told him I was a writer. He told me he was the CEO of some big corporation, but his slightly wrinkled suit told me differently. *How stupid do these guys think we are?*

Reaching across the table he grabbed my left hand and tapped my wedding ring. "Married?"

I pulled my hand away, pretending that I needed it to hold my glass. "In the process of getting a divorce."

"I see."

The next slow set, he pulled me to the dance floor. Didn't even ask, just winked at me and tilted his head towards the band. This time the gentleman—John, I think he said his name was, which was probably a lie—wasn't such a gentleman. His hands were on my behind before the end of the first stanza.

"Don't do that."

He moved his hands up my back. "Don't do what, honey?"

"You know what."

In the middle of the second stanza his hands were back on my behind and his smelly breath in my face.

I removed his hands. "I said, don't do that."

"What? I can't hear you." He planted a sloppy kiss on my lips. I wanted to spit.

"I said," nearly shouting over the music, "don't do that!"

"Aw, come on, honey." He tried to kiss me again. I shoved him away.

"Get lost."

I made my way to the table. Only Diane and Cindy were there, deep in conversation. I grabbed my purse and jacket.

"I'm calling it a day," I told them, suddenly feeling the effects of two hours of sleep, eating nothing all day but a tuna sandwich, getting canned for the second time in six months, and seeing Kelly fawn all over Brian at the funeral home. They smiled and waved me off, then went back to their conversation.

Somehow I made it home without running the car into a ditch or telephone pole. I turned into the driveway and pulled up to the garage door....*Garage door?...Wait a minute. The McCormick House doesn't have*....I went to push the brake, but my foot slipped off the pedal. The front bumper thumped against the door. *Oh, no!* I shoved the gearshift in park and cut the engine.

In my exhausted state, I'd driven not to the McCormick House, but home.

CHAPTER THIRTY

I didn't know whether to laugh or cry. I was too tired to turn around and head back to the McCormick House. Brian's truck was parked in the driveway. I glanced at the clock on the dash. Eleven thirty. If he was home, he'd be asleep in his chair. *I could probably slip in quietly, and—* Suddenly a glaring light flooded my car. *Well, so much for subterfuge.* I checked my makeup in the rearview mirror and grabbed my purse.

"Well, well, this *is* a surprise," Brian said when he opened the front door.

You're telling me. "May I come in?"

He looked at me for a second or two before stepping back. I didn't know what to say, where to begin, so I decided to simply tell the truth.

"I need to stay here tonight."

He looked puzzled.

"It's been a long day," I said. "I got only two hours of sleep last night, and I'm dead on my feet. And, quite honestly, I hadn't planned to come here tonight. It was like my car drove itself here."

He scratched his head then shrugged. He still wore the white dress shirt and black Dockers I'd seen him in earlier.

"Sure," he said, shutting the door and locking it. "Do you want the guest room or our room?"

*****

I awoke the next morning in my own bed, alone, on sheets that felt fresh and clean. I suspected Jasmine wasn't pulling my leg when she told me Brian hadn't slept in here since I'd left. The window shades were pulled down. I rolled on my side to check the time. Eight ten. For an instant I almost panicked, thinking I was late for work. Then I remembered. No more seven a.m. obit duty. No more newspaper duty period. I smiled. Maybe yesterday wasn't so bad after all. I reached for my old flannel robe and slipped it on over Brian's oversized T-shirt.

In the kitchen the morning sun sparkled through the window. I filled the kettle and put it on to boil. Then I noticed a large, thick, white envelope lying on the counter. I picked it up. It was addressed to "Mr. and Mrs. Brian A. Laverly." Inside was another white envelope addressed to "Brian and Linda." I pulled out the wedding invitation.

Brian's niece was getting married in July. I'd forgotten all about it. Brian was giving her away. SueEllen's own father had been killed in a car accident shortly after she was born, leaving Bethany, Brian's younger sister, to raise SueEllen alone. She never remarried. The reply card slipped out onto the counter. I picked it up. It was blank. I grabbed a pen from the penholder. "Number attending." Well, definitely Brian. And Danny. And me. I loved SueEllen. I wouldn't miss her wedding for the world.

Would Brian take Kelly? I suddenly felt I had no business filling out this response card. I found a sticky notepad—bright pink so Brian wouldn't miss it—and wrote a message, "B., Count me in. L." and stuck it to the reply card. I'd check with Bethany closer to the wedding to see if I could bring a guest.

After I finished my toast and tea, I decided maybe it would be a good time to start sorting through stuff to decide what I was going to take. But where to start? My eyes fell on the window seat, where I kept the pictures I hadn't gotten into albums yet. *Oh, the albums!* I groaned. How many did we have? And how many pictures?

I sank to the plush brown carpet and started pulling out the boxes. An hour later snapshots and scrapbooks were scattered all around me, and I hadn't decided a thing. I'd spent the entire time giggling and smiling and sniffling. Jasmine all dressed up in a blue net tutu for her first ballet performance. Jasmine in her orange softball uniform, smiling big, oblivious to the braces that glinted in the photographer's flash. Danny's first baseball team. How old was he? Five? Danny all dressed up in white tails and a top hat for his senior prom. A grinning Brian dressed in camo, walking toward the camera with his shotgun in one hand and a dead turkey—his first—in the other. Brian and I holding baby Lexie between us on our laps. I held that snapshot a bit longer than the others.

I ran my finger over his grinning, proud-Poppa face. Something akin to longing tugged at my heart. Katie's engagement picture. Kelly holding Katie at her first birthday party. That snapshot took me aback. Kelly looked so *happy*. When, I wondered, did the happiness begin to fade?

The phone rang. I started to get up to answer it but changed my mind. Only one person knew I was here. I let the machine pick up.

"Lin?" Brian's voice boomed across the room after the beep. "I was just calling to see how you were feeling. But you're probably gone by now anyway." He paused. "Oh, if you *are* there, nice job on the garage door."

The garage door? Then I remembered. And winced. I didn't hit it *that* hard, did I?

When I checked as I was leaving a half an hour later, all I saw was a little dent. But Brian would never let me forget it.

Back at the McCormick House, I'd just gotten out of the shower when my cell phone rang. It was Aunt Retta, wanting to know if I could do lunch. I checked my appointment book. My first lesson was scheduled for two. I glanced at the clock.

"Where?" I asked her.

"Let's go to Anna's Place," she said. "They've got great food and an elegant, but homey atmosphere. Would an hour from now work for you?"

*****

"Bring me up to date on you and Brian," she said when we settled in our nook and had given our orders. "I see you're still wearing your wedding ring. Does that mean that the divorce is off?"

I hadn't seen or spoken to Aunt Retta since the end of February, right after I'd found Jasmine's thong in Brian's and my bed and thought it was Kelly's. She and Uncle Ray had taken off on one of their spontaneous jaunts.

The waitress brought us our salads.

"No." I squeezed thick ranch dressing out of the little paper cup onto my salad. "Things just aren't happening very fast."

"What's the holdup?" She peered over her glasses at me. "Or should I ask *who* is the holdup?"

"To tell you the truth, we haven't really talked about it. I've had two appointments with my lawyer, and she wanted a list of all our assets. I simply haven't had the time to get all that information together."

"Haven't had the time or won't take the time?"

I thought for a moment. "A little bit of both, I think. This morning I spent a couple of hours at the house, going through pictures, thinking that I could separate them into two piles, one for me and one for Brian, but all I accomplished was a trip down memory lane. It's not as simple as I thought it would be." I stared out the window, watching green leaves waver in the wind. "I ended up putting all the pictures back."

"What about—what's her name? Your friend who you thought was carrying on with Brian. You found her underpants in your bed."

I grinned. Here I was, a fifty-four-year-old grandmother, discussing sexy underwear with my seventy-five-year-old aunt in a restaurant.

"I was wrong. The thong wasn't Kelly's. It was Jasmine's."

"I'm not surprised."

"But I'm still not sure what's going on between Brian and Kelly. Every time I turn around, there they are, together."

I told her about the night at the hospital. I told her about the funeral home.

"Why is it that Brian doesn't have any trouble finding someone else, and I, who want love in the worst way, can't find someone to love me the way I want to be loved?"

"Have you met any men?"

I told her about Thomas and about Mr. Roman Hands last night at Paddy's.

"You know, Linda, men sense when a woman's heart is taken."

"What do you mean?"

"Is it the men you meet who are holding back—or you?"

The waitress brought our sandwiches—tuna melt for me and a steak and cheese for Aunt Retta.

I thought about "John" last night. I was hardly encouraging, even before he started groping me. Maybe I did hold back. And Thomas, well, the night everything changed between us was the night at the hospital. No, it was before the hospital. On the hilltop. He'd asked me why I still wore my wedding ring. When I told him it was stuck, he suggested I have it cut off.

"But I could never do that," I said absently.

"Never do what?" Aunt Retta asked.

"Never have my wedding ring cut from finger." I told her what Thomas said. "And it bothered me that he was a draft dodger and here Brian signed up to go."

"So you are comparing every man you meet to Brian, and every man you meet comes up short." She pointed to my left hand. "And why, Linda Sue, if you want to fall in love again—with another man—why *are* you still wearing your wedding ring?"

"It's stuck. See?" I tugged at it to show her just how stuck it was. To my surprise, it slipped off my finger.

"Well, now, isn't that interesting," Aunt Retta said with a sly smile. "It looks like you're not stuck anymore. You've lost enough weight to take your ring off—for good."

I glanced down at my hand. A white indentation was the only indication of a gold band that had announced to the world for thirty-two years that I belonged to someone. My finger felt bare, incomplete. *I* felt incomplete. I looked up at Aunt Retta, but her face was blurry. Opening my palm, I stared at my wedding ring. I looked at my purse, then back at my ring. Then, swallowing back tears, I slipped it back on my finger.

Aunt Retta smiled and nodded once. "Well," she whispered, "I guess that answers that."

"Yes." I opened my napkin and blew my nose, "I guess it does."

I signaled the waitress for another cup of tea. She brought it along with a plate of cookies.

"But what now? There's still Kelly."

Aunt Retta clucked her tongue. "Does he look and act like a man in love with her?"

"No." Something clicked in my mind. "It's always been her. She's the one that's been hanging all over him. I just wish Brian would tell her to get lost."

"Maybe he's not ready to."

"What do you mean?"

She winked at me. "She hasn't served her purpose yet."

I was aghast. "But you once told me Brian was true blue, that he'd never be unfaithful."

She plucked a cookie from the plate and dipped it in her cup. "I don't mean that, Linda Sue. Let me ask you this: Are you jealous when you see her with him?"

"No." I shot back.

She laughed softly. "You answered that way too fast for it to be the truth."

I reached out and took a cookie and bit into it. I hated to admit it, but, yes, I was jealous. I nodded.

"Then she's serving her purpose. Let him know how you feel—how you really feel about him—and she'll be history."

I thought for a minute then shook my head. "I don't know how he feels about me, after all that's happened."

"Well," she said, looking me straight in the eye, "there's only one way to find out."

"What's that?"

"Ask him."

*****

I almost had my chance a month later at the Father's Day cookout at Katie's. Brian and I were sitting on the gently swaying swing after we'd eaten, sipping iced tea, and enjoying the balmy afternoon. We weren't talking, but not because we were angry or upset. It was just a nice comfortable silence. For once the battle lines had disappeared.

"Brian," I began. I felt like a schoolgirl asking a guy to the Sadie Hawkins dance. He turned his head to look at me.

"I've had a lot of time to think about things these past six months."

He nodded. "Yeah, me too."

"I'm sorry for some of the things I said. Some of the things I did. I was just...." I shook my head. This wasn't coming out right. I took a deep breath.

"Brian, I—"

"Hey, Poppa!" Lexie appeared out of nowhere, climbed up in Brian's lap, and shoved a blue envelope in his face.

"Happy Poppa's Day, Poppa!"

The rest of the crew gathered round. Why did I sense they were in cahoots about something?

"Aren't you going to open it?" Jasmine asked, pointing to the envelope.

Putting down his glass, Brian used his index finger to tear open the envelope and pull out the card. He opened it carefully. I leaned over to see what the kids were all giggling about. I inhaled sharply. They'd gotten him—us—a gift certificate for two nights at Perfect Paradise, a romantic bed and breakfast in the Poconos. Was that a blush spreading across his cheeks to his ears?

"Thanks. I think," he said with a shy grin. I had no doubt this was all Jasmine's idea.

"We figured a getaway weekend was in order," she said.

Just then Kelly stepped around the corner of the house, carrying a sheet cake. In the commotion I hadn't heard her car pulling in the driveway or even the car door shutting. Brian shoved the gift certificate into his shirt pocket.

I wanted to scream. What was she doing here? This was a family get-together. She wasn't family. I got up from the swing and excused myself. On my way to the bathroom, I glanced at the cake. She'd decorated it with a fishing theme. *How appropriate. Hook, line, and sinker.* "Happy Father's Day" was written in blue icing across the middle. In the bathroom, I washed my hands three times, trying to calm down. When I returned to the party, Kelly was beside Brian on the swing, her arm through his, laughing softly. I wanted to hurl that stupid cake at her—at them.

Instead I picked up a paper plate and pretended to study the food on the table. I was close enough to the swing to hear Kelly and Brian—mostly Kelly—talking.

Jasmine sidled up next to me. "Who invited *her*?" she whispered.

I shrugged, helping myself to a more-than-healthy serving of pasta salad—a big no-no on my eating plan. But I didn't care. I put my finger to my lips discreetly, hoping Jasmine would get the message. She did. So we both stood at the table, plates in hand, eavesdropping. What I heard next almost made me drop my plate.

"So when's this wedding, Brian?" Kelly said in a syrupy voice—for my benefit, I was sure.

"Two weeks."

"Oh, great," she gushed, loud enough for me to hear. "Plenty of time to find a new dress."

I dumped my plate in the trash can on the way to my car.

On the way home, I did two things: I ripped the ring from my finger and tossed it in my purse. Then I pulled out my cell phone and punched the speed dial. Somehow, some way, Thomas was going to be my date for the wedding.

CHAPTER THIRTY-ONE

Thomas picked me up for the wedding in his Mustang. I don't know which looked more impressive—the gleaming red convertible with soft white leather seats or the man driving it. Thomas's white linen suit showed off his tanned face. The close-cut jacket hugged his broad shoulders, and dress pants draped casually from his hips. A white silk tie shimmered against a black silk shirt.

"Nice," he said with a low whistle when I answered the door.

I'd splurged and bought a new dress, along with matching shoes—low sling-back heels—and a small handbag. I was in a fourteen now, so when I spied the backless, shimmery dress—emerald green, of course—with just a touch of sparkle in the store window, I didn't hesitate.

He'd surprised me when I'd called him two weeks earlier and asked him if he'd want to come to the wedding with me. I couldn't reach him Sunday. Or Monday. Or Tuesday.

"When is it?" he'd asked when I finally reached him Wednesday.

I gave him the date and the time.

"You got yourself a date," he'd told me.

I could never figure him out. At first he seemed interested in me. Then, after the hilltop-hospital incident, he seemed to avoid me. I'd been prepared for a haggling session when I called about the wedding. Now here he was, looking like the dream man I'd been longing for.

He opened the car door for me, and I slid in, adjusting a white sheer scarf on my head. I silently wished he'd ask if I wanted the top up. I'd spent at least a half an hour on my hair, and I didn't want to arrive at the wedding looking like I'd just fought my way through a wind tunnel.

Coming around and sliding into the driver's seat, Thomas slipped the key in the ignition then turned to me. *He's going to kiss me.* I was ready. I wasn't wearing my wedding ring. I hadn't touched it since Father's Day. It was still in my purse.

He noticed, I thought, feeling a stir of excitement. I leaned toward him.

"What are you doing with two purses?" he asked.

"This," I said, holding up the spangled evening bag that matched my dress, "is mostly for appearance. All it holds is my compact, lipstick, driver's license, a small packet of tissues, and my cell phone.

"And this" —I held up my oversized purse— "is my portable file cabinet. In it I have everything I need that I can't fit into the evening bag."

"Don't you think you'll ruin the effect carrying two purses? Especially that ugly monstrosity."

I laughed. "I'm only taking the evening bag, silly. We'll put the 'monstrosity' in the trunk."

He drove more slowly than usual, and when he dropped me off in the front of the church, I still felt put together.

"Mom, you look sensational!" Jasmine, in a lavender bridesmaid's dress, appeared next to me. "Wait 'til Dad sees you."

I scanned the crowd.

"He's inside, doing his father-of-the-bride thing."

Thomas's hand pressed lightly in the small of my back. "Ready to go inside?" he asked, ignoring Jasmine, who glared at him.

"Talk to you later, sweetheart," I said, pecking her cheek.

Inside, I laid my hand in the crook of Danny's offered arm as he escorted me to a pew down front—right behind where Bethany would sit. Where would Brian sit after he walked SueEllen down the aisle? Next to Bethany, probably.

Stepping into the pew, I glanced around. The church was filling up quickly. I was sure everyone was wondering who this drop-dead handsome man was sitting next to me with his arm draped across the back of the pew behind me, so close his thigh brushed against mine. I opened the program and scanned the names of the bridal party. I wondered where Kelly was.

I didn't have to wonder long. Wearing a yellow satin gown that clung to her in all the right places, my former best friend glided down the aisle on my son's arm, head high, a soft smile—or was it a smirk—playing on her lips. Pearl drop earrings dangled in rhythm with her graceful step. I caught a whiff of her Chanel as she swept past. They stopped beside the pew in front of us. Just before she sat down, she turned and nodded to me, then smiled sweetly at Thomas, who removed his arm from the back of the pew and sat straighter.

Weddings are emotional for me—even when I barely know the bride or groom. But when I saw Brian walking SueEllen down the aisle, I got more choked up than usual. My eyes were drawn to them. SueEllen beaming at the man waiting at the altar for her; Brian, solemn, covering her small, dainty hand protectively with his big, work-worn one. If my heart did a flip flop when I saw Thomas, it was doing somersaults now. Dabbing my eyes with a wadded tissue, I swallowed and turned my attention to the groom. Marty's eyes shone, love pouring out, as though reaching out and drawing her to him. Brian had looked at me like that.

*****

"What makes absolutely no sense to me," Thomas said at the reception while we waited for the wedding party, "is why the guests have to sit here for—what—an hour or more, waiting for the bridal party."

I shrugged. "That's just how it is. I'm getting another iced tea. Do you want me to bring you anything?"

"Nah. I'm good."

I pushed my chair out, stood—and bumped into Mark, Kelly's ex-husband. How long had he been standing there?

"Hey, Lin," he said. His breath reeked of whiskey. "How are things? Heard you left Brian."

I stared at him.

"You shouldn't have done that." His black eyes pierced mine. His words slurred together. How many drinks had he had? I shifted, suddenly uncomfortable. I'd never seen this side of him.

"She always had a thing for him," he sneered. "You know that, don't you?"

"How do you know the groom?" I said, changing the subject.

"His father's one of my clients. Well, look who's here. If it isn't my ex and your soon-to-be ex."

The wedding party had arrived. At the head of the line waiting outside the door to be announced was Brian—with Kelly on his arm. I thought of going to the restroom, but everyone would see if I left. I sat back down.

"First, the uncle of the bride, Brian Laverly, and his friend, Kelly Windsor," the DJ said. There was scattered applause and a couple of hoots. Behind me, Mark snorted. I put my purse on the chair next to me—the only empty chair at our table. It wouldn't do for Mark to plop himself down beside me. I was worked up enough. Fortunately, he disappeared after the newlyweds were announced.

Following the buffet dinner, the tables were moved back to make room on the dance floor, A disco ball sprinkled shards of colors as the celebration kicked into high gear. Thomas was a good dancer, and we swung around the parquet floor more than once. I even did the electric slide. He stopped, however, at my favorite—a polka. I scanned the room for a partner.

"Uh-oh."

Thomas followed my gaze to the bar, where Mark had just stepped in line behind Kelly. He grabbed her arm and swung her around. Surprise flashed in her eyes, then anger. Prying his fingers off her arm, she stepped back. I gasped as his hand swung up, and she flinched, a shadow of fear flickering across her face for just an instant. Quickly he looked around and lowered his arm. He bent toward Kelly, his face next to hers. She shoved him away, turned, and disappeared in the crowd.

"Jerk," Thomas muttered.

I was stunned. Why didn't she ever tell me?

"I had no idea," I said when we were settled in our seats. "All those years. And I thought we were so close."

Thomas looked angry. "They're ashamed. They think it's their fault. Abusers are good at that—making their victims feel guilty, like they deserve the beating they got."

"If that's the case—"

"It is. Trust me."

"—it explains a lot of things. Why Kelly would drop off the radar for weeks at a time. The fading bruises she'd blame on her clumsiness." Aaliya's words that night in the hospital waiting room came back to me: "Hurting people hurt people."

Thomas shoved his chair back. "Be right back."

Lost in thought and still reeling from what I'd just seen, I nodded. Maybe I should go talk to her. But what would I say?

I got up to get myself another iced tea. Where was Thomas? It had been almost fifteen minutes since he excused himself. Maybe he went out to check on his car. You never know what a bunch of drunks would do. I got my iced tea and returned to my seat. I didn't see Thomas anywhere.

I was thinking about joining the dancers doing the Macarena when he appeared.

"I'm taking Kelly home," he said. Or that's what I thought he said. The music was so loud it was hard to understand him,

"What did you say? I didn't understand you. The music is—"

He put his lips to my ear. "I'm taking Kelly home. She's upset about that jerk of an ex-husband and doesn't want to stay if he's here. Her date is busy with his wedding duties. So I'm taking her home."

After they left, I watched the dancers whirl around the floor. I wanted to go home, too. Then it hit me: my ride had left—and said nothing about coming back.

Now how am I going to get home? I'll ask Danny. Or Jasmine. Katie and Jon had already left. The room darkened and the DJ's voice broke into my worry. "We're going to slow things down now with a special request—The Righteous Brothers and 'Unchained Melody.'"

A lump rose in my throat. I closed my eyes against the tide of emotion rushing through me. Our song....Maybe I should leave now. Call a taxi. Were there such things as taxis anymore?

I opened my eyes, and through my blurry vision saw a calloused hand open in front of my face. I raised my head. Brian.

"May I have this dance?"

How could I not say yes? I nodded and stood. He clasped my hand and led me to the dance floor. I put my left hand on his shoulder—not behind his neck as I used to—and my right hand rested in his—out to the side. Brut filled my senses and me with longing.

I tried to shut out the words of the song. Shut down the feelings. I felt Brian's lips brush my ear. "You look...you *are*...beautiful." They were words I'd longed to hear for years, but were they too late in coming?

*I need your love....*His hand tightened on my back, gently pulling me closer. We moved together in rhythm with the music. We didn't even have to think about it. It was just so natural.

When the song ended, my head rested on his shoulder, my left hand was behind his neck, and my right rested inside his, on his chest. It felt right. It was where I belonged. I knew that now.

We danced the entire slow set. At one point someone bumped into us. I opened my eyes. Jasmine.

"Hey, Mom." She grinned wickedly. "I hear your ride took Kelly home. How are *you* going to get home?"

With that she twirled away. I sighed. That girl.

"I'll take you home, Lin," Brian whispered hoarsely.

CHAPTER THIRTY-TWO

"Nice truck," I said, settling in by the door and clicking my seatbelt as Brian pulled himself up into the cab and slid effortlessly behind the wheel. Leave it to Brian to show up at his niece's wedding dressed to the nines and driving a redneck truck. But this was no ordinary work truck. This baby was a monster—high and huge and new. Brand spanking new. The glossy black hood sparkled in the moonlight. The truck was too high for me with my short legs, and, since running boards were conspicuously absent, Brian boosted me up into the cab. My skin still tingled where his hands had touched me. I ran my fingers across the soft leather.

"I'm glad to see you're doing well enough to afford a new truck." I twisted around to scan the plush seats in the rear of the extended cab.

Tossing his tux jacket into the back, Brian turned the key, and the engine roared to life.

"It was time," he said, turning to look out the rear window. "The old girl was—what—fifteen years old?"

"I'm impressed," I said grinning. "With the truck *and* with the man. What's your gas mileage on this thing, anyway?"

He gave me a lop-sided grin. "You don't want to know."

My neck whipped back, then forward as he shifted gears and gunned onto the main road.

"Easy! I'm not as young as I used to be, you know."

He shifted again, easier this time. "Neither am I."

"Do you miss it?" I asked, allowing my body to lean toward him as we turned onto a country road.

"Miss what?"

"Being young. Having energy and drive." *And passion*, I wanted to say.

"Sometimes. Like when I get home at night. I'm so beat I don't feel like fixing myself something to eat."

We rode in silence for a while. I had the urge to reach across the seat and touch his forearm, run my fingers lightly through the graying hairs. Heck—I wanted to flip the middle console up, unbuckle my seatbelt, and slide across the seat, right up next to him.

"What happened to us, Lin?" he asked softly.

I shook my head. "I don't want to go there, Brian. Not tonight."

He slowed, pulled over to the side of the road, and shut off the engine.

"Why'd you stop?"

He turned to face me. "Because I want to talk to you."

I looked around. I didn't recognize the surroundings. "Where are we, anyway?"

"On a shortcut to the house you're staying in."

The air in the cab was getting close. I pushed the window button. Nothing. I pushed again. Brian turned the key. The window slid down with a soft whir. The scent of pine wafted on the breeze that sang with the chorus of a million crickets.

"Oh," I murmured.

"What?"

"It's such a beautiful night. Let's get out and walk."

"Good idea," he said, whirring the windows up again and reaching in the back for his jacket.

"Wait a second," I said after he'd hopped out of the cab. I hurriedly kicked off my heels and peeled off my pantyhose. It was a night for bare-footing. Shoving my evening bag under the seat, I pushed the door open.

Brian stood there, holding out his hand. I took it. On my way down, my face brushed against his bristly chin. Once my feet touched the ground, though, I pulled my hand out of his.

"Where to?" He looked around. Soft moonlight filtered through a sparse forest that lined the side of the road. Across the road an overgrown field stretched to a grassy hill.

"There." I pointed to the top of the knoll, where the almost-full moon hung in a star-studded sky. "Let's climb that hill."

"Hold on."

Bending over, he yanked off his shiny black wedding shoes and pulled off his socks. Shoving the socks inside the shoes, he opened my door, tossed them in, and slammed the door shut. Grabbing my hand, he pushed the button to lock the truck and pulled me across the road. Feeling like a giddy schoolgirl, I giggled and stepped behind him, placing my size sixes in his size twelve footprints while he trampled the high grass.

By the time we reached the summit, we were gasping for breath and laughing like a couple of teenagers who'd just snuck out. Spreading his jacket on the ground, he motioned for me to sit. I peered at him in the moonlight. Was this ol' stick-in-the-mud Brian—who could never, ever, do anything spontaneous? Who had to plan every single detail before he moved even one big toe forward? I plopped down on the satin lining of the jacket. He eased himself down beside me.

We sat under a canopy of winking stars, catching our breath, drinking in the summer night. He stretched back, his hands beneath his head. I curled up my legs beneath me, savoring the moment.

"Remember that old nursery rhyme you used to sing to the kids?" Brian asked. "Star light, star bright—"

I smiled into the night. "First star I see tonight—"

We finished together, our voices in tandem "—I wish I may, I wish I might, have the wish I wish tonight."

He rolled over on his side facing me, propped up on his elbow. "What would you wish for?"

"Oh, Brian, I'm too old for wishes. They don't come true, anyway."

"Come on, Lin, what would you wish for?"

There was only one thing I wanted. A wispy cloud floated across the face of the moon. A sweet sadness stirred my soul. I shook my head.

"You wouldn't understand," I said softly, plucking the grass beside me and laying it in a pile.

He reached across and grasped my hand, stopping me in mid-pluck. "Let me try."

"It's a woman thing. You'll laugh at me."

Pulling my hand away, I stared at the meadow spread out below. Lightning bugs flickered and flashed in the moonlight. The night breeze teased through my hair. I shook my bangs out of my eyes. But it wasn't the wind in my hair—it was Brian's fingers.

I gently pushed his hand away. "Don't."

"I won't laugh at you."

Should I tell him? Why not? I took a deep breath. "To fall in love again."

His sweet gaze turned into bewilderment, his features screwed up in his clueless look.

"You want to fall in love again?"

"Yes. I want to be swept off my feet, head-over-heels, with that I-can't-live-a-moment-without-you feeling." I sighed. "Just one more time."

Somewhere an owl hooted. Tree frogs sang their night song. *At least he's not laughing. Maybe just this once....*

"I didn't realize you stopped feeling that way."

"Oh, Brian. We got too busy. Life blindsided us. All the worries and hurries choked what love we had."

"Speak for yourself." His voice was a hoarse whisper. "I never stopped feeling that way."

"Then why didn't you show it, Brian?"

He sat up abruptly, pulled his knees to his chest, and crossed his arms around his knees. He stared at the meadow below.

"Lin, I'm no good with words. You know that. But what do you think I was saying when I hauled myself out of bed every morning at five to go to work for twelve, fourteen hours? When I worked all day and came home and built you a house? When I tried to give you everything you wanted?"

I stood and brushed my dress. "Let's go. It's getting late."

He got up slowly and looked me in the eyes. "Is that why you left me? To fall in love with someone else? Or because there already was someone else?"

"Yes...No!"

"What is it, yes or no?"

"Yes, I left you because I wanted to fall in love again. And no because there wasn't anyone else when I left."

"There is now though." It was a statement, not a question.

I had wanted to fall in love with Thomas. He was everything Brian was not. Thomas sizzled, but my feelings for him fizzled. I realized that all I felt, or thought I felt, for Thomas had been forced. Was I that desperate? That pitiful?

"I don't have to answer that," I said, turning and striding off down the hill.

"Stubborn woman," he muttered, snatching up his jacket and hurrying after me. I stepped faster, not wanting him to catch up to me. With his long legs, though, he had the advantage. I broke into a run. I was doing pretty good for an old lady when my foot slipped into a groundhog hole. I fell forward, my arms flailing in front of me. Somehow my foot jerked back out of the hole, my ankle cracked, and I tumbled the rest of the way down the hill.

At the bottom, I just lay there, wanting the ground to open up and swallow me. My right ankle hurt something fierce. But my pride hurt more. Brian stood over me, doubled over in a fit of laughter.

"It's not funny," I said, panting.

"Yes, it is. It's the funniest thing I've seen in a long time." He wiped his eyes. "If you wanted to roll around in the hay that bad, though, you should have told me."

"Shut up." I tried to move my ankle. Pain shot up my leg. Great. Now what? If I couldn't walk, I could crawl. Rolling over on my stomach and pushing myself to my knees, I began to creep toward the truck.

"What are you doing, woman?"

"What does it look like I'm doing? I'm going to the truck. And you're going to take me home. And without much more ado, thank you."

"Your knees will be raw and bleeding by the time you even get to the road."

"So?"

He bent over and swooped me in his arms. "You want to be swept off your feet, huh? How's this?"

"Oh, yeah, go ahead. Make fun of my deepest dreams and desires. Like always."

I tried to fold my arms in front me, avoiding having to put them around his neck, but that made us off balance. A strange mixture of pain and pleasure coursed through me. I had the urge to nuzzle my face in his neck, but that would give him the wrong idea. He hoisted me to the truck and plopped me on the front seat.

"Where are we headed?" I asked a few minutes later. We weren't on the country road to the house. We were on the main highway to town.

"To the hospital. I heard that ankle crack."

I shook my head vigorously. "No! Take me home."

"Why?"

"Because."

"Why because?"

"Just because."

He ignored me and drove on into the night, turning into the hospital parking lot and gunning up to the ER entrance.

"I'm not going in," I said, trying to keep the pain out of my voice.

Brian turned and poked his finger at my face. "You're going in."

"But—"

"No buts. Let's go."

"I don't have to listen to you."

"Didn't you listen to the sermon on Mother's Day?"

"What does that have to do with this?"

"I quote: 'The husband is head of the wife.' And," he said, shoving open his door, "you're still my wife."

CHAPTER THIRTY-THREE

Fortunately, my ankle wasn't broken, just badly sprained. Unfortunately, that meant staying off my feet for twenty-four to forty-eight hours—and using crutches when I absolutely had to get around. I had a full schedule of piano students Monday and an appointment with the divorce lawyer after that.

"How's the ankle?" Brian asked on the way home. I was sitting sideways on the bench seat in the back of his pickup, my injured ankle propped up, fighting a drug-induced drowsiness.

"I nearly broke my ankle trying to get away from you, ruined my new dress—"

"Which looks very nice on you, by the way."

"—and am probably going to be laid up for longer than I can afford. My butt hurts, thanks to a nurse who doesn't know the difference between a hypodermic needle and a dart. I can't walk, can't drive—Why couldn't it have been my left ankle?"

"You've got crutches, you know."

I snorted. "Yeah, right. Can't you just see klutzy me getting around on those things? Why couldn't they have given me a wheelchair instead?"

"You don't need a wheelchair."

He flicked on the turn signal, shifted gears, and turned in to the driveway. But it wasn't the driveway of the McCormick House. It was home. Real home.

"What are we doing here? If you think I'm staying—Brian, I can't. I have to feed the dogs."

The truck gently slid to a stop in front of the garage door. Brian cut the engine and twisted around.

"The dogs. Right. And how—" he eyed my swollen, mummy-wrapped extremity "—are you going to manage that? I don't see why you can't stay here tonight. Those dogs are not going to starve."

"They need let out."

He stared at me with an incredulous look. "You left them in?"

"They're inside dogs. Brian, we don't have the time to argue. The dogs, the house—they're my responsibility. Look, it's two in the morning, and I just want to get to bed. Take me home."

"You are home."

"Home to the McCormick House."

"That's not your home."

"It is now. Brian—please!"

He released a long sigh. "Oh, all right. Just let me get some things. You'll need some help for a while."

The truck door slammed. I didn't feel like arguing. I fact, I kind of liked the idea of Brian being around for a couple of days. I laid my head on the back of the seat and closed my eyes.

When I awoke, I was snuggled in my bed at the McCormick House—alone. My ankle throbbed and I had to go to the bathroom. From the way the sunlight angled on the drawn window shade, I figured it was around seven. I turned my head to check the bedside clock. And smiled. There, beside a bottle of water and a straw, was a brass hand bell with a note propped up against it: "Ring if you need me." I rang.

Breakfast was oatmeal, toast, and coffee on the sun porch.

"I would have gotten a dozen doughnuts, but I didn't want to leave you alone," Brian said, draining his second cup of coffee.

I glanced at him, an unusual shyness filling me. "Thank you."

"You don't have to thank me." He reached for the Sunday paper.

Love is patient. Love is kind. Where did that come from?

"Yes I do," I murmured, enjoying this feeling of being pampered. "I do."

After breakfast, I showered and then Brian rewrapped my ankle.

"Hey," I said after he fastened the little pin. "Pretty good."

"I," he said, standing up and holding his hands out to me, "am a man of many talents."

"I can see that." I placed my hands in his. "And I thought, after three-plus decades, I'd seen all of them."

"What now?" he asked, pulling me up.

I yawned. "Bed and a nap. I'm so sleepy. Must be the pain medication."

Using Brian as my crutch, I hopped to the bedroom, where he once again tucked me in.

"If you need anything—"

"I know—ring the bell."

We grinned at each other, and a warmth—a jingle—coursed through me.

"Have a good nap," he said, closing the door.

Lunch was tuna sandwiches and macaroni and cheese. It was the best Sunday I'd had in a long time. Brian took care of the meals and the dogs and me. Oh, how he took care of me.

Supper was spaghetti, garlic bread, and salad—once again on the sun porch. He even baked brownies.

"I'm impressed," I said, biting into a moist square slathered with milk chocolate icing and topped with chopped walnuts. "Where'd you learn how to do all this?"

His cheeks reddened. "It was nothing. Really. Canned sauce, and, hey, even an idiot could boil spaghetti. The salad came in a bag, the brownies from a boxed mix, and I found the icing and walnuts in the cupboard."

I sipped my iced tea. "Well, I appreciate it. I don't know what I'm going to do tomorrow when you go to work."

He shifted in his wicker chair. "I took the week off."

I stared at him. "The whole week? Why?"

"Because you need me."

"Oh, no."

"What?"

"I forgot to call my piano students and cancel tomorrow's lessons." I struggled to get up.

"What do you think you're doing?"

"My cell phone." I looked around. "Where's my purse?"

Uh-oh. It was still locked in Thomas's trunk.

"Sit back down," he said, pushing himself up from his chair. "I'll get it."

"It's in my evening bag," I called to him. "On the dresser. I think."

By the time he returned, I'd stacked all the dinner dishes and silverware on the tray.

"Thanks," I said, pulling out my cell phone. "Oh, great."

"Now what?"

"The battery's dead, and I lost the charger. I was going to get a new one Monday. I'm just going to have to go ahead with the lessons."

Brian reached into his shirt pocket and tossed me his cell. "Here. Use mine."

"No can do."

"Why not?"

"Because all the numbers are on my phone."

He stared at me. "Don't you have their numbers written down anywhere?"

I shook my head.

"Some businesswoman," he muttered, lifting the tray from the glass table top. "What time's your first lesson?"

*****

The next morning my ankle still hurt but not as bad. Brian had gone out before breakfast and bought me a new charger. While my phone charged up, I used the landline and called Thomas, leaving a message on his voice mail about my purse. After scrambled eggs and turkey bacon, and a session in a nice, hot shower, I grabbed my music bag and hopped out to my car, which I insisted on taking instead of the truck. It was easier getting into and out of.

Brian drove to the community center, ensconced me in my second-floor classroom, and was fussing over my propped-up leg when the first student of the day appeared in the doorway.

I smiled. "Good morning, Amy."

Amy, a cute ten-year-old with blonde ringlets and Precious-Moments blue eyes, stared at my still swollen, wrapped ankle as she took her seat on the piano bench.

"What happened, Mrs. Laverly?"

"I was, uh, jogging in the country and twisted my ankle," I said, opening the book to the day's lesson.

Amy pointed to Brian. "Who's that?"

"That's Brian. He's helping me get around today."

She smiled sweetly at him. "Hi, Brian. Are you staying for my lesson?"

He grinned at her and held out his hand, which she took. "Amy, nice to meet you. Yes, I'm staying for the lesson. Mrs. Laverly has to stay off her feet. Doctor's orders."

She nodded. "Are you a doctor?"

He laughed. "No."

"A nurse?"

"Not by profession."

"Are you her boyfriend?"

Brian's eyes twinkled. "No, I'm her—"

I shifted uneasily on the padded bench. "Let's get started, Amy. We don't want to waste any more time."

I had set up my teaching schedule so that I taught half-hour lessons all morning and afternoon, with an hour for lunch. The community center was in the middle of the downtown, which was blessed with several restaurants. Brian spent the morning with his laptop, leaving the room occasionally to make phone calls, then left to get us some lunch, arriving with several bags from KFC just as the last student of the morning was leaving.

We ate at the desk.

"Are you going to change your name?" he asked suddenly, breaking the silence.

I shrugged. "I really hadn't thought about it. Why?"

He fished a paper napkin out of one of the bags and wiped his fingers. "Just wondered."

My cell phone rang. I'd left it on the piano, so Brian crossed the room and picked it up. Glancing down at the caller ID, he pressed his lips together and tossed the phone to me.

"It's your boyfriend."

I glanced at the screen. Thomas.

"He's not my boyfriend," I mouthed as I pressed the phone to my ear. "Hello?"

"Hey, Lin." Thomas's thundering voice echoed in the classroom. In my haste, I'd accidentally pushed the button for the speaker phone. "I got what you asked for, babe. When do you want it?"

Brian was quiet after Thomas's call. Too quiet. I knew he misunderstood. I hadn't told him I'd left my purse in Thomas's car. But the afternoon's full slate of students didn't give me any time to explain.

By the time my last student left, my ankle was throbbing, my head felt as though it was being squeezed by giant rubber band wrapped around it, and my stomach was threatening to empty itself in the wastebasket. I'd taken only half the pain medication I was supposed to at breakfast. It wouldn't do to fall asleep at the keyboard. Brian took our things to the car at the beginning of the last lesson. My student left. No Brian. I checked my watch. It had been at least forty-five minutes since he'd left. Where was he? I had an appointment with Elizabeth Morgan-Shuster in half an hour. I planned to tell her to hold off on the divorce for now. I didn't know why; it just felt right.

I was getting ready to call him when he appeared in the doorway, puffing.

"Where were you?" I grabbed my music bag. Then I saw what he was pushing—a wheelchair. "What's that for?"

"You. Since you refuse to use your crutches."

I was aghast. "I don't need a wheelchair."

"I'm going back to work tomorrow."

My heart sank. Lunch, bitter and bile-tasting, rose to my throat. "I thought you said you took a week off."

He pushed the wheelchair to me. "Sit."

"No."

"Why do you have to be so contrary, woman? You said you wanted a wheelchair. I got you a wheelchair. Now you don't want it?"

"No."

"Well, too late. You've got it. So sit."

"No. And who's being contrary now? You told me you'd taken a week off to take care of me. Why the sudden change of plans? Was it Thomas? Are you jealous?"

"Jealous? Of that muscle shirt without a brain?"

"That," I sputtered, pulling the straps of my bag over my shoulder, "is not even worth a response."

I started hopping to the door. Suddenly strong hands lifted me and plopped me in the wheelchair. It was then I lost my lunch.

"Lin, Lin, I'm sorry," Brian murmured, stroking my hair as I sat there in that awful wheelchair and alternated between heaving into the wastebasket and sobbing. His touch made me cry harder—and the more I blubbered, the more I heaved.

"Lin, what can I say? I'm stupid." Brian's voice dripped with concern. I didn't trust myself to look at him.

"You got that right," I sniffled, checking my watch. "I have an appointment in ten minutes. I'm going to the restroom to clean myself up."

Brian took in the mess on the floor and sighed. "I'll clean up here."

Twenty minutes later we pulled into my lawyer's parking lot. As I hopped into her office, Brian's arm around me, Elizabeth Morgan-Shuster gave me a wry smile, then watched with interest as he settled me in one of the two chairs, plopped down in the other, and gently placed my swollen, wrapped ankle on his knee.

"Elizabeth Morgan," she said, holding out her hand to Brian. "And you are…?"

Ignoring her proffered hand, he leaned forward.

"I'm Brian," he said, steel in his voice. "Linda's husband. Where do I sign?"

CHAPTER THIRTY-FOUR

"Mr. Laverly," Elizabeth said smoothly, "there are no papers to sign yet."

"Why not?"

"Brian—" I twisted to face him, and my throbbing ankle reminded me I'd forgotten to take my pain pill. "Brian, there's nothing to sign because you wouldn't talk to me. Every time I tried, you had some lame excuse."

"Those weren't excuses," he muttered.

"Mr. Laverly, since you're here now, perhaps we can discuss the divorce settlement."

Brian stood abruptly, and my ankle slid off his knee and hit the floor with a jolt. Searing pain shot up my leg. Biting my lip, I held in the scream and blinked back the sudden tears.

"What's there to discuss?" Brian turned to me with a defiant look. "She can have her divorce if she wants it. She can have whatever she wants."

I bent down and rubbed my leg, avoiding his eyes. Something was wrong here, but I couldn't figure out what. Brian had just agreed to a divorce. This was what I'd wanted, wasn't it? I'd won. But if this was victory, it felt hollow.

"Mr. Laverly," Elizabeth began, "let's not rush this. You'll need to discuss this with Linda and with your attorney."

I straightened up in my chair and reached for my music bag. My pain pills were in there somewhere.

"I told you, there's nothing to discuss," he said, still glaring at me. "Didn't you hear me? I said she can have it all."

"Everything?" Elizabeth's voice had a note of caution. "Mr. Laverly, you really need to discuss this with your attorney."

Brian shifted his weight from one foot to the other and ran his fingers through this hair. "Well, maybe not *everything*. I want my work truck, tools, fishing boat, fishing and hunting stuff, and everything in my shop. Oh, yeah, and the hunting camp. She can have everything else."

"I understand you have a construction business, Mr. Laverly," Elizabeth said, slipping on her glasses and leafing through a file of papers. "You and Linda need to decide how you're going to handle that. It would be so much simpler if you two could sit down and discuss this first."

Hell hath no fury like the rage I saw in Brian's eyes—rage and pain so deep I felt it, too.

"Brian—" I reached out to him. "I don't want your business. You built it up yourself—"

He pushed my hand away. "I'll be in the car." He spat the words at me.

"Brian, wait—"

He spun around, strode to the polished mahogany door, yanked it open, and slammed it behind him. I swear all the books on the shelves jumped. In the silent wake of his departure, I sat there, stunned. Shame washed over me like a dirty flood. And guilt. I hadn't really thought this through. I'd rushed into it, thinking we could just simply split everything down the middle. But I hadn't taken the time to realize what "everything" meant. It wasn't as simple as I'd thought.

I found the pills. I fished out two and slipped them in my mouth, using saliva to help them go down.

"Oh, well," Elizabeth said, unruffled. Apparently she'd dealt with angry soon-to-be ex-husbands before. "Why don't we give this some time to cool? Then, when everybody's ready, and Mr. Laverly has his attorney, we can—"

I shook my head. "I don't think so."

She cocked her coiffed head to the side, watching, waiting for me to continue.

"I changed my mind," I said, unsure of what I was about to say. I mean, I was sure it was what I wanted. I just wasn't sure how it was going to play out.

"I don't want a divorce, after all."

She closed the file and set it on the desk.

"Is that my file?" I asked.

"Yes, it is."

"I'd like to see it, please."

I leaned over, lifted the file from her desk, and flipped it open. I took the sheaf of papers and, with trembling fingers, tore them in half, then in half again. Then I dumped the shredded remains in the gold-rimmed wastebasket by her desk. I pushed myself up, standing on my good foot.

"Elizabeth," I said, "thank you for your time. But I won't need your services anymore."

"All right, Linda. You're the client. I'll mail you my final bill. But I'm curious," she said, looking at me with a hint of a smile. "Why did you change your mind?"

Suddenly everything became clear.

"Because," I said, smiling, "I still love him."

*****

"That was quick," Brian said when I all but tumbled into the car.

"It didn't take long to do what I had to do," I said, buckling my seatbelt.

He snorted then went to turn the key. I reached out and stopped him. Thunder rumbled in the distance.

"Brian, I fired her."

He leaned forward and peered out the windshield at the darkening sky.

"Looks like a storm coming. We'd best get going. I'll take you home, then—" he took a breath—"I'm going home. I'm sure you'll be fine. You and Theodore have *plans*."

He turned the key, put my car in gear, and eased out of the parking lot.

"Didn't you hear me? I said I fired her. I'm not going through with the divorce."

The muscles in his cheeks twitched, but he said nothing.

"And *Thomas* and I don't have *plans*. If you'd had stayed in the room instead of stomping out when he called at lunchtime, you would have realized he was referring to my purse. My *purse,* you silly man—which I left in his car Saturday night. I called him this morning and left a message about it."

He acted as though he hadn't heard me. We rode in silence, angry, roiling black clouds following us. When we turned in the driveway, the wind was whipping the trees, bending them almost in half. Brian pulled under the portico and stopped.

"You go on in," he said in a voice that sounded like someone was strangling him. "I'll take care of the dogs before I go."

I turned to him. "Brian, we need to talk."

He shook his head and turned to me. The sadness in his eyes scared me.

"Lin, it's over. You won."

"No, Brian, it's not over. Didn't you hear me? I said—"

A crackling sound whizzed close by, followed by a thunderous boom that shook the car.

"Get in the house, Lin. Now."

"I'm going, I'm going." I hobbled up the steps, an angry gale tearing at my clothes. Brian reached around me to unlock the door. I leaned back slightly against him. He stiffened then leaned back away from me. We stepped into the mud room just as the first pellets of hail hit the windows.

I hopped to the kitchen and flipped the switch to turn on the overhead light. Nothing. I flipped the switch off, then on again. Nothing. I glanced at the microwave. No blue lighted numbers telling me the time.

"I think the electric's out," I said.

"Obviously."

"Guess we should have gotten takeout."

"Don't worry about it. Listen, I'll stay until the storm's over. Too dangerous to drive in this, anyway. Too many nuts on the road."

I dropped my music bag on the kitchen table and hopped to the refrigerator.

"I can throw some sandwiches together."

He shook his head. "I'm not hungry."

I shut the fridge door and plopped down on the closest kitchen chair.

"Me neither. But I could go for a nice, hot cup of tea."

The dogs were jumping on me, whining. I knew they wanted out, but they'd just have to wait until the storm was past. It was only seven o'clock, but it looked—and felt—like it was midnight, it was so dark. I scanned the room for a candle. Brian stepped to the door and lifted the leashes from the hook. Jonathan and David bounded to him.

"What are you doing? Are you crazy? Brian, they can wait."

"I'm just taking them outside the door, under the portico."

While Brian was outside, I rooted through my music bag and found my pain pills—a brand new bottle. Brian must have filled the prescription when he went to get us some lunch. Thankfully, it wasn't a childproof bottle. I flipped open the cap, shook out two pills, and popped them in my mouth, washing them down with a gulp of water from my water bottle.

All I wanted was a hot bath, a cup of tea, bed—and Brian. All I'd get, though, was bed. I pushed myself to my feet and hopped to the bedroom, dropping down on top of the covers, and allowed myself to succumb to the strange buzzing in my head.

CHAPTER THIRTY-FIVE

"Lin? Lin! Wake up."

Buzzing—loud—in my ears. In my head. The voice sounded like it was coming from a long, hollow tunnel. *No. I don't want to wake up. Leave me alone.*

"Lin!" Someone was shaking me gently. "Linda Sue! Do you hear me? Wake up, honey. Please."

I felt my upper body being lifted, strong arms around me. Felt a cold glass rim against my lips, water running down my throat. I sputtered, water went up my nose.

"Stop." I coughed. "I'm awake. I'm awake."

I blinked open my eyes. Where was I? The room was dark, except for a kerosene lantern on the dresser, throwing flickering shadows on the wallpaper. Oh, yes. The McCormick House. The glass on my lips again.

"No."

"Yes. Just a little sip. Here."

I sipped. Swallowed. I felt weak, shaky. What happened? What day was it?

"Lin, how many pills did you take?"

"Pills?" I mumbled. "I didn't take any pills."

My whole body felt heavy. I could barely move. All I wanted to do was go back to sleep. "Leave me alone. Let me sleep," I mumbled, pushing him away. Brian. That's who was holding me. What was Brian doing here?

"Not until you tell me how many pills you took."

"Just give me a minute."

A cool, wet washrag brushed my forehead, my cheeks. More sips of water. Something rough brushing across the top of my hand. I blinked my eyes open. The dogs. A faint thunder echoed in the distance. The storm. Yes, it was coming back now. Brian. Thomas. The lawyer. I had to make him understand.

"Help me sit up."

I leaned against the headboard, trying to pull my foggy, scattered thoughts together. I remembered now. I'd taken two pills before I fell asleep.

"Two," I said.

"Two pills? That's all?" He sounded relieved.

I nodded. Something niggled in my memory. What was it? *Uh-oh.* I'd taken two pills in Elizabeth's office, too.

"No. Four."

"*Four?* Aw, Lin. You were only supposed to take one every six hours—and this sticker says 'not on an empty stomach.' And your stomach, my love, was most definitely empty."

"Oh."

"Do you have any ipecac syrup around?"

"Why?"

"I have some in the first aid kit in my truck. Be right back." He strode out of the room. I closed my eyes. The next thing I knew he was forcing some awful smelling stuff past my lips.

"No!" I pushed his hand away.

"Honey, drink it. We have to get those pills out of your stomach."

"Oh," I moaned, "I don't want to puke again."

I gulped the last of what was in the medicine cup.

"Here." He held the water glass to my lips. "Drink."

He made me empty the glass. Then he sat on the side of the bed and held me and rocked me, running his fingers over my hair. After about ten minutes I pushed him away.

"I have to throw up," I said, gagging.

A wastebasket appeared under my chin. And for the second time that day, I emptied my stomach. When I was done, I lay back on the pillow in a cold sweat, breathless and limp. The cool washrag made a pass over my face again.

"I—my ankle— hurt so bad. I only took one pill this morning. Didn't want to be sleepy during lessons. Wasn't the dosage two?"

"Yes, but this—" he shook the new bottle in front of my face "—is a different prescription than what they gave you in the ER. It's stronger. You were only supposed to take one every six hours."

"Oh. I took two in Elizabeth's office, then two more when we got back—while you were out with the dogs. I forgot about taking the two earlier. I feel so stupid."

"Lin, listen to me. Can you hear me all right?"

I nodded.

"Listen, honey. Your cousin Rand called on your cell."

Rand? Why would Rand call? "Are they home? Maybe Aunt Retta can come over now, and you can go home."

His rough hands held my face. His eyes, so sad, gazed into mine.

"What? What's wrong?" I asked.

"Sweetheart, it's Aunt Retta." He took a deep breath. "She's dead, honey."

Dead? My beautiful aunt, so full of life and love?

"What happened?" I whispered. Hot tears—and I thought I'd cried the well dry today—rolled down my cheeks.

"They were on their way home in the storm. Some idiot driving without lights crossed the centerline. Ray swerved, trying to avoid a head-on, but the other car smashed into the passenger door. Honey, it was instantaneous."

"Uncle Ray?"

"Just shaken up. His airbag deployed. Hers did, too, but the impact was on the side."

I cried. Hard. Long. For Aunt Retta. For Uncle Ray. For me. For the unfairness of life. For what I'd had and lost through my own stupidity. Brian held me close, soft kisses on my hair, gently running his fingers up and down my back.

Wait a minute. I pushed him away. "What did you call me?"

"When?"

"Just now."

He pulled me to him again. His arms felt good around me.

"Did I hear the words 'honey' and 'sweetheart'?"

"Yes," he whispered, "and 'my love.'"

"But I thought you didn't love me anymore."

"I could never stop loving you."

"Then why did you act like such a jerk today? Storming out of the room when Thomas called at lunchtime, then again at the lawyer's office?"

"Because—" He hung his head. "Because I was jealous," he whispered.

"I'm sorry."

"For what?"

"For everything. For leaving you. For thinking you didn't love me. For looking for love in all the wrong places."

He squeezed me tighter and kissed my nose. "Oh, Lin. You were so right."

I shook my head.

"I took you for granted. I thought you'd always be there. I forgot your needs. I thought a house, a family, the kids and grandkids, and then freeing you to pursue a career were what you needed." His voice shook.

"Oh, Brian," I whispered, nuzzling my nose at the bottom of his neck.

"I—I wrote you a song."

A song. It had been so long. Too long.

"Sing it to me." I nodded to the corner. "My guitar is over there by the rocking chair."

I watched him as he strummed a chord then tuned each string. My heart, like my eyes, was overflowing. He played through a series of chords then began to sing. I'd forgotten what a rich voice he had. I closed my eyes and leaned back against the headboard.

"Days go by, and I forget to tell you I love you;
Nights go by, and I'm much too tired to hold you;
But that doesn't mean that I don't love you so.
Dreams ago, we made a vow to each other,
To have and to hold, from that day on, 'til forever;
And I just supposed one promise was enough.

I just thought you knew, my love, each day I live for you, my love,
Without me telling you so.
I just thought you'd see through me, and all you've come to mean to me,
And you would always know.

*So when I get busy and seem to ignore you,
Know that I, I need you and I adore you,
But words don't come that easy for me."*

The last chord faded. I opened my eyes. Brian sat in the rocking chair, his head bent over the guitar, his shoulders shaking. I slipped out of bed and, because I still couldn't put weight on my ankle, crawled over to him. Putting the guitar down, he pulled me up in his lap.

"Oh, Brian," I whispered, slipping my arms around his neck. "That was beautiful. Thank you."

He held my face close to his. I could see the fire—the passion—in his eyes. "I love you so much, Lin."

And the passion ignited in my soul.

"And I love you, Brian."

"Lin?"

"Yes?"

"Will you marry me—again?"

CHAPTER THIRTY-SIX

Brian stayed the night, but on the sofa in the den. I'd wanted him to sleep with me—after all, we were still married. His half of the bed had been empty too long.

"I don't want to rush things," he'd told me when he tucked me in, a shy smile spreading across his face.

"With your permission, Linda Sue Laverly, I'd like to court you."

I smiled back. "Permission granted."

Sleep came softly and deeply and quickly.

Now, in the morning light, it all seemed like a dream. Had he meant what he'd said the night before? Or had he just wanted to comfort me? I put down my mug of tea and stared out the window, elbow propped on the table, chin in hand.

The rising sun peeked through the wispy pines at the eastern edge of the yard. Yesterday's ugly haze was gone, swept away by last night's storm. The world, washed clean, was fresh and new and bright. Drops of moisture—whether it was dew or rain, I couldn't tell—clung to blades of grass, sparkling in the morning sun. *Acres of diamonds,* I thought, remembering the short story from a long ago high school lit class. *Search the world over for the treasure of a lifetime and come home to find it in your backyard.*

"A penny for your thoughts."

I turned my gaze to the man across the table. The neckline and shoulders of his white T-shirt sagged. *He's lost weight.* Lines had seemingly creased themselves into his rugged face overnight. And was that more gray I saw running through his hair or a quirk of the morning light?

Brian pointed to my cinnamon toast with his fork.

"Aren't you going to eat? After I slaved all morning over a hot stove?"

I smiled. "I'm not hungry."

"You've got a long day. You'd better get something in your stomach. When do you want to go to Uncle Ray's?"

They'd kept Uncle Ray in the hospital overnight for observation. The boys, Rand and Reggie, were to pick him up when the doctor discharged him. From there, they'd go to the funeral home to make arrangements.

"After work. I'll call them first. Oh, Brian, I can't believe she's gone."

He reached across the table and squeezed my hand. On the counter behind me, Brian's cell phone rang.

"Get that for me, will you, Lin?"

I reached around and checked the caller ID. Kelly. I hesitated. Brian looked up at me, eyebrows raised.

"It's Kelly," I said, wanting to roll my eyes. Instead I gave him the sweetest smile I could muster.

His eyes twinkled. A mischievous grin spread across his face. "Well, answer it, woman."

A sunbeam flickered through the window. I grinned, feeling delightfully wicked.

"Hello?"

"Who's this?"

"It's Linda."

She paused. "What are—Is Brian around?"

"Yes, he is," I said. And waited.

She clucked her tongue. "Don't be cute. Put him on."

Wordlessly, I held out the phone to Brian, who was wiping the over-easy egg from his plate with a folded slice of bread. He took a swig of coffee then held out his hand. I slapped the phone in his palm and shoved my chair away from the table. Brian held his hand up. *Don't go,* he mouthed.

"I can't, Kelly," Brian said. "Not today....Tomorrow?" He shifted uneasily in his chair. "Maybe. I'll call you."

I didn't want to hear any more. I hopped out of the kitchen.

"Why did you leave before I hung up?" Brian asked me on the way to the community center. I'd wanted to cancel my lessons for the rest of the week, but I couldn't afford to. Losing one day—the day of the funeral—would be hard enough on my budget.

"I had to get in the shower," I lied, watching the crisp, freshly washed greenery roll by. "Does she always call you that early in the morning?"

"Lin, look at me."

I shook my head. I didn't want him to see the tears that threatened to wreck a path through my makeup. Would I ever stop crying? For two years, I couldn't. Now the dam had disintegrated, and the floods came relentlessly.

"Lin, she's just a friend."

"She doesn't think so," I mumbled over the lump in my throat.

"Honey, I love you. I thought I made that clear last night." He flicked on the turn signal, and with one deft twist of the wheel, glided around the pokey car in front of us.

"You were high school sweethearts, Brian. I read what you wrote in her yearbook."

"Whatever we had was over long ago." He eased back into the right lane.

"Brian, what exactly has been going on with you and Kelly for the past seven months?"

He glanced at me, a look of uncertainty—or fear—flashing across his features. The muscle in his cheek twitched.

"I don't know," he said, running his fingers through his hair. "She kind of latched on to me. Told me all these stories about Mark. I felt sorry for her."

"Did you—do you—have any feelings for her?"

He drove in silence for what seemed like an eternity.

"Lin, when you left, I was so messed up."

Well, that answered that.

"Did you sleep with her?"

"I wasn't that messed up."

"What about your feelings for her? You never answered that question."

"You mean did I love her? No. How could you even ask that?"

"I can ask because every time I saw you two together, you were fawning over her. What else was I to think?"

"I was trying to make you jealous."

Ah, so Aunt Retta was right. "Then you don't love her?"

"No."

"You *never* slept with her?"

"After I married you, no."

"I'm not sure I like that answer."

"I'm not going to lie to you, Lin. That was a long time ago. Once I met you, Kelly was history."

"Did you—in the past seven months—ever kiss her?"

He was quiet for a few moments.

"She kissed me, so yes."

Why did I ask?

"But nothing happened. It was like—it's hard to explain. It felt like…like flat pop—no fizz at all." He reached over and caressed my cheek. "Nothing like when I kiss you."

I leaned into his hand, enjoying the feel of his flesh against mine.

"Well," I said as we turned into the community center parking lot, "I'm glad we got that settled."

*****

It was a long day. Supper was takeout from the Italian deli. We ate in the den. Well, Brian ate. I nibbled. My appetite was taking a long vacation. I was in the bedroom changing when I heard the motorcycle outside. I glanced out the window. Thomas. *Oh, that's right. My purse.* I hobbled out to the kitchen. Thomas leaned against the door frame, my purse in hand. The dogs growled at him, their hackles raised. Brian, a dish towel thrown over his shoulder, held them back by their collars.

Thomas tossed me the purse. "Here you go."

I caught it. "Thanks."

Somehow Brian got the dogs somewhat settled. They lay on the floor, still growling at Thomas. But Brian didn't have to hold them back.

"Hey, Lin," Thomas said, winking at me. "I brought the Harley. D'you want to go for a ride?"

"No," Brian said, "she doesn't."

"I asked her." Thomas jerked his head toward the door. "What do you say, gorgeous?"

Why is he acting like this? He's not interested in me.

"Thomas, may I talk to you—outside?" I limped to the doorway.

"Why are you walking funny?" Then he noticed my wrapped ankle. "What happened? Country girl fall in a groundhog hole?"

"Yes, as a matter of fact, I did."

"As a matter of fact," Brian said, grabbing my arm and helping me across the kitchen, "she turned her ankle while we were having a tumble in the hay the other night."

"Brian! That's not exactly true."

He grinned then glared at Thomas. "Close enough. Here we are." He stopped in front of Thomas and planted a noisy kiss on my lips. "Don't be too long. The hay calls."

"Brian!"

I hobbled out to the swing, Thomas following me slowly.

"What's with him?" he asked, jerking his thumb towards the house, when we settled onto the wooden seat.

"What's with *you*?" I said. "When I first met you in January, you acted like you were interested in me. Then, three months later, you don't even remember me or that you drove me home. Then you take me to a hilltop to watch a sunset, and I think you're going to kiss me, but you back away. And then you avoid me for two months until I ask you to a wedding, to which you quickly accept. You are one confusing man." *Or confused.*

He shifted uncomfortably. I remembered what Wil told me—that Thomas was like a bird that flit and swooped, but never landed. And I felt bad. It wasn't all his fault. I had a hand in this mess, too. I had chased him like a lovesick teenager.

I took a deep breath. "Thomas, so much has happened—I hardly know where to begin."

"You're back with your husband." It was a statement, not a question.

"Yes."

"I'm not surprised."

"Why not?"

"I knew your heart belonged to him—it never left him."

"How?"

He laughed softly and tapped my bare ring finger. "Your wedding ring. Why don't you have it on now?"

"It's in my purse. I took it off when I got mad at him on Father's Day. Long story."

"Ah," he said, nodding, "so that's why your voice sounded so urgent when you left me the message."

He stood. "Well, Linda Sue, you've got your purse, your ring, and your husband back."

I watched him walk away, swing his leg over his hog, and ride into the crimson sunset. Then I hobbled to the house, straight to the kitchen table, and rummaged through my purse. For a panicked instant I couldn't find it. Then my fingers felt the solid, smooth circle. I pulled it out and slipped it on my finger. Brian stood at the doorway, watching me. I limped to him.

"In case I haven't told you today," I said as I wrapped my arms around his neck. "I love you, Brian Laverly. And don't you ever doubt it."

CHAPTER THIRTY-SEVEN

Aunt Retta's funeral was held Thursday, a clear, balmy day, not hot and humid like July days can be. God love her, she'd planned the entire thing, right down to the song she wanted Brian and me to sing—"I Know Who Holds Tomorrow," her favorite hymn. It was all I could do not to break down right there. But Brian's strong tenor carried me as he accompanied us on his guitar.

Aunt Retta's service, though, was not a funeral—it was more of a celebration of her life and a testimony to the faithfulness of the God she loved. *Aunt Retta,* I thought as though she could hear me, *I wish I had your faith.* My ankle was strong enough now for me to play the organ—almost obsolete anymore, but Aunt Retta had loved organ music, so when I found out the church had one—albeit hidden in the back of the sanctuary, up in the choir loft, the organ it was.

My fingers flew through "Mansion over the Hilltop," "Where the Roses Never Fade," "Suppertime," "I'll Fly Away," and "I'll Meet You in the Morning"—all hymns she loved—while my mind skipped through the years, remembering the aunt I loved more than my own mother. I was glad the organ was hidden where it was—so no one could see the tears streaming down my face.

After I was done, I repaired my makeup, then limped down the aisle and slipped into the pew beside Brian, Katie, who snuggled a sleeping B. J. on her shoulder, and Danny, who'd cut his beach trip short when he got the news. Jasmine, in Japan on business, had sent a lovely bouquet of daisies, Aunt Retta's favorite flower. "They're such a happy flower," she'd always say.

I was pretty certain Katie suspected something was up between Brian and me. He'd hadn't been home all week. Brian would have told her where he'd be. And what Katie knew, Jasmine knew, and what Jasmine knew, Danny knew.

Poor Uncle Ray looked lost, like he'd aged ten years overnight. He sat erect between his two sons, who weren't ashamed to shed a few tears. The church was packed, and I was amazed at the crowd of people who joined the funeral procession to the cemetery.

The funeral dinner was held at the church's fellowship hall and catered by the Italian deli. I'd just returned from the rest room and was headed to my seat with Katie when I saw her. Wearing a white silk blouse and short black skirt that showed off her curvy hips, Kelly stood in front of Brian, her fingers playing with his tie. They appeared to be deep in conversation.

"What's *she* doing here?" I muttered.

"Cool it, Mom," Katie said. "She works for the caterer."

"Wait," I told Katie, grabbing the back of the nearest chair. "I need to give my ankle a rest."

My ankle ached, yes, but my heart lurched when I saw Kelly and Brian together. In spite of all he said, all he'd done this week—he'd been treating me like a queen—I was suddenly unsure of myself. I couldn't be what he wanted. I was short, klutzy, and, still a bit on the dumpy side—even after months of demanding exercise sessions and eating so many salads I felt as though I was turning into a rabbit. Kelly, on the other hand, was slender, blond, athletic, and graceful. And she knew how to make a man desire her. Maybe that's why Brian wouldn't sleep with me. He had no desire for me.

"Let it go, Mom," Katie said, nodding toward where Brian and Kelly stood talking. "You don't have anything to worry about. Trust me."

From where we stood, I couldn't see Brian's face, but I imagined his expression to be what every man's was when he saw Kelly—hungry and fawning. I wanted to march right up between them, yank those willowy fingers off my husband's tie, and tell her to get lost. But the ache in my ankle was getting worse. I'd overdone it and needed a pain pill.

I took a deep breath. "I'm ready. Let's go."

Katie kept pace with me as I limped across the room, each step more painful than the last.

"I feel like a *stara baba*," I groaned.

Katie giggled. "I haven't heard you use that term in a long time. Well, you don't look like an old hag. Mom, you look terrific. How much did you lose, anyway?"

I watched as Kelly smiled sweetly up at Brian. "Not enough," I said, trying not to limp as we made our way to the table. Brian held the baby, who was awake now and surveying his surroundings with interest. Seeing Brian with B. J. infused me with courage.

I stepped up to Brian and slipped my arm through his. "Why, hello, Kelly," I said sweetly.

"Hey," she said, her eyes shooting daggers at me.

I smiled demurely and batted by eyelashes. "Don't you have work to do—pour water or something?"

Brian coughed. Kelly snorted then spun around.

"Well," I muttered, watching her hips sway as she made her way through the tables, "that takes care of that."

Brian grinned. "I guess so." He pecked me on the cheek. "Thanks."

"Don't mention it."

He was pulling out a chair for me when my cell phone rang. I eased into the chair and fished the phone from my purse.

"Hey, Mom," a voice from the other side of the world said. "I hear you and Dad are back together."

"What are you doing, calling from Japan? Isn't it expensive?" I said, gingerly resting my aching ankle on the chair Brian had pulled out for that purpose. Needing a pain pill, I fumbled through my purse for the prescription bottle.

"The company's paying for my personal calls, too."

"Sweet." The chatter in the background was getting louder. Where did all these people come from? Brian's face brushed up against my cheek, his lips on my ear.

"I'm going to the restroom," he whispered, planting a soft kiss on my ear. "Be right back."

He sure goes to the bathroom a lot. Didn't he just go when we got here? Come to think of it, over the past week, it seemed as though he was wearing a path to the loo. I returned my attention to the magpie chattering away in my good ear.

"...and we can have the reception..."

"Whoa, hold your horses, girl. What reception?"

"Oh, Mom, didn't you hear a word I said?"

"No. Slow down and tell me again."

"I think you and Dad should have a wedding—renewing your vows, you know? Eloping like you did, you never had a real wedding."

"We didn't elope."

"You call that little slam-bam-thank-you-ma'am ceremony in front of a JP a wedding?"

"Judge," I corrected her. "It was a judge."

"Right. And how many people were there? Three?"

"Five. Me, Dad, the judge, the best man, and—" I winced. "—the maid of honor."

"Who were the best man and the maid of honor? We'll ask them to do it again."

In her headlong rush of excitement, Jasmine had forgotten who my maid of honor had been.

"That won't work," I said.

"Why not?"

"Because the best man died ten years ago, and the maid of honor I don't think would be willing."

"Can't you ask her?"

"No."

"Oh, come on, Mom, don't be so difficult. It'll be so romantic."

"Jasmine," I said, lowering my voice, "the maid of honor was Kelly."

"Oh. That's right. I forgot."

The room around me suddenly got quiet. Someone nudged me. I glanced around. Heads were bowed.

"Sweetie," I whispered, "I have to go, They're saying the blessing."

"All right, then. We'll pull it all together when I get back."

*****

"What did Jasmine want?" Brian asked on the way home. My hand rested in his. Ah, what I'd missed!

"She wants us to have a wedding," I said, with a laugh.

He glanced at me and grinned. "That's not such a bad idea."

I stared at him. "You're kidding, aren't you?"

"I think I shortchanged you."

"Shortchanged me? How?"

"You were a beautiful bride, honey, but..." he paused, like he was searching for the right words. "...but I've always wondered what you would look like in a wedding gown and veil."

I slipped my hand out of his and twirled my fingers through the soft curls that touched his shirt collar in the back. "I've never regretted it, Brian. I had exactly the kind of wedding I wanted." Then a thought hit me. "Didn't you?"

He looked at me, sadness in his features. "It didn't matter. I had you."

I was floored. All these years, and I never dreamed he'd wanted a big wedding. I'd just plunged on, making plans. I'd never even asked him what he wanted. I just assumed he wanted what I did. I turned to the window, blinking back sudden tears.

"I'm sorry," I whispered. "I didn't know. Why didn't you say something?"

"Because if you were happy, I was happy. Nothing else mattered."

We rode in silence the rest of the way home.

After we changed, we headed for the swing.

"If we do this," I began, nestling myself under his arm, "we'll do it your way this time."

His fingers caressed my arm. "Great. So I get to make all the plans?"

"Yup," I grinned. "Just tell me when and where. Like I did to you thirty-three years ago."

"Ah, yes," he murmured, gazing at the cloudless sky. "Do unto others —"

"Oh, no."

He turned to me. "Now what?"

"We want a traditional wedding, right?"

"Yes."

"And a traditional wedding is held where?"

"In a church?"

"Bingo. I stopped going to church right after I left you. I refuse to set foot in another church again."

"Hmm," he said, tapping the armrest. "That could be a problem."

"Brian, the church is filled with hypocrites—a bunch of judgmental, self-righteous bigots who condemn you without even listening to your side of the story. Whatever happened to love and mercy?"

"Whoa," he said, pulling his arm away and grasping my shoulders. The swing stopped.

"Where did this all come from? And here you were the piano player and music leader for how many years at Community Church?"

I snorted. The bitterness was like bile. "Twenty-five years. And don't forget women's Bible study leader, VBS, children's Bible club, Christmas and Easter programs, and whatever else they shanghaied me into doing."

He looked puzzled. "I thought you loved it."

"I did, Brian. It gave my life purpose. I was someone—not just Brian's wife or Katie's, Jasmine's, and Danny's mother."

He leaned back and let out a long sigh. A honeybee buzzed by in search of nectar. On a branch by the birdfeeder two blue jays squawked. Above us a squirrel hopped onto a branch, showering us with pine needles. Brian's voice came in a whisper I could barely hear.

"And I thought—all those years—you were such a good Christian."

"But I was," I stammered. "I am."

He shook his head sadly.

"I've gone to church all my life." Cold fingers of fear clutched at my heart. "The only time I didn't go was when I was sick or one of the kids was sick. And, of course, these past few months."

"But you're not a Christian, are you?"

"Didn't you hear me? I've gone to church all—what's the matter? Stop shaking your head at me!"

"Lin, going to church doesn't make you a Christian. Neither does doing all those things, good as they are."

Something niggled in the back of my mind—something Aunt Retta had told me once. What was it? "Too many people play at being Christians without the foggiest idea of what a Christian really is."

"And what, exactly, is a Christian?" I asked.

"A Christian," he said clearly and confidently, "is someone Christ lives in."

"Nice answer, Brian. You get an A-plus," I said with more sarcasm that I'd planned. "But what does whether or not I'm a Christian have to do with us?"

He leaned against the back of the swing and sighed.

"Oh, Brian, I'm sorry. I didn't mean for it to come out like that."

"I understand, Lin. Katie told me what Deacon Dudley and Pastor Frank said to you."

"And did she tell you how they stripped me of my music duties without giving me a chance to tell my side of the story?"

"That was wrong."

I tapped my good foot against the dirt under the swing. "I wonder if there's any such thing as a true Christian."

"You're looking at one."

"Huh?"

He shifted, turning to me. "Lin, when you left, I was messed up. And mad at God. Then Katie almost died having B. J. I sat in that hospital waiting room and prayed. 'God, if you're real, show me. Don't take my little girl.'" His voice broke. "Then Jasmine's pastor walked in. There was something different about him. He wasn't pushy. He was...loving."

I nodded. "I thought so, too. And I liked his wife."

"So I started going to church there. Joined a men's Bible study. Went to a Promise Keepers conference."

"Promise Keepers—isn't that a men's movement or something?"

"Yes, but much more. I gave my life to Jesus Christ and asked him to be my Savior and Lord of my life."

"Whoa, this is heavy."

Brian's eyes searched mine. "Honey, it's more than 'heavy.' It's real. I'm a different man."

He *was* different. And he treated me differently. I'd felt loved and pampered and cherished all week.

"Honey," he continued, "the Bible says not to be yoked with unbelievers. You, my love, are an unbeliever."

"Hey, I'm not a pagan or a heathen or anything."

"Are you a believer?"

"Of course."

"And what do you believe?"

I realized at that moment that all my life I believed whatever I'd been told to believe. I'd never dug deep enough to find out for myself. What was it that Aunt Retta had said? "You'll know the truth, and the truth will set you free." Maybe it was time to find that truth.

"Does that mean," I asked him, "that you won't marry me now?"

"Honey," he said, taking my hands in his, "I'm already married to you."

"But I don't want to lose you again."

"And I don't want to lose you again."

"Then I'll become a Christian for you."

He shook his head.

"*Now* why are you shaking your head? Will you stop doing that?"

"Because, my sweet, you don't become a Christian for any reason other than realizing your need for Jesus Christ as your Savior."

I wondered how long that would take.

CHAPTER THIRTY-EIGHT

Friday evening Brian decided to go back home, since I was getting around well now and my ankle was healing up nicely.

"Besides," he said, rubbing the back of his neck, "I can't take another night on that sofa."

Smiling seductively, I glanced toward the bedroom and raised my eyebrows. But Brian shook his head. Placing his duffel bag on the floor, he pulled me in his arms. "Not yet."

I stomped my good foot. "Why 'not yet'? We're still married." I ran my fingers up his back. "I've missed you so much."

His lips were warm on mine. "I've missed you, too."

"Please?"

"Lin, this week has been great. Let's not argue."

I didn't understand, but I didn't want to push it either. I kissed him goodbye.

"Hurry back," I murmured.

He kissed my nose. "You bet."

He hopped up in his truck, and I watched him drive out the lane, wishing I could go with him.

*****

The rest of July flew by. My days were taken up with piano lessons. Brian came by most evenings. We spent every weekend together, even going to a couples' Bible study on Saturday mornings.

One Friday after work, he walked in carrying a pizza in one hand and single red rose in the other. I checked the calendar hanging on the wall by the phone.

"Did I miss something?" I asked. "Is today something special?"

He placed the pizza on the table and the rose in my hand. "Yes. Today is something special."

I was confused. It was the beginning of August. We had no special dates in August. I was the one who ran the calendar and sent all the cards to the relatives and made special dinners for the anniversaries of the day we met, our first date, and our wedding. What did I miss?

"I give up," I said, holding the soft petals under my nose. "What's so special about today?"

He grinned. "I get to see you."

I peered at him suspiciously. "Who are you and what have you done with my husband?"

He pecked me on the nose, then swept the pizza off the table and headed for the den. I followed, carrying a tray with paper plates, napkins, glasses, an ice bucket, and two bottles of soda that I'd had ready. I put it down on the coffee table. Brian was tearing the wrap off a new DVD.

"What movie did you bring?" I asked, pouring caffeine-free cola into his glass.

He grinned. "Wild Hogs."

The movie must have triggered a mid-life crisis because on Sunday I heard a rumbling in the driveway. *What's Thomas doing here?* I peeked out the window. It wasn't Thomas. It was Brian. I threw on my robe—I'd been getting ready for the annual Laverly family reunion—and rushed out the door.

"Brian Andrew Laverly! What did you do?" I gasped, circling the bike. It was nicer than Thomas's.

"Well?" If he grinned any wider, his face would have split in two. "What do you think?"

I stroked the shiny gas tank, the soft black leather seat. "Is this brand new?"

"It's a year old. Only five thousand miles. I bought it from a guy who was getting a divorce, so I got a great deal. So, what do you think?"

I knew he wanted me to love it as much as he did.

"It's big, it's blue, and it's beautiful," I said, pressing down on the seat. "How comfortable is this?"

"It's a touring bike, Lin. Made to be comfortable. But I could get a wider seat for you if you wanted."

"Thanks."

"Oh, I didn't mean—Oh, Lin, I'm sorry. I did it again, didn't I? Stuck my foot in my mouth."

At one time I would have gotten angry and given him the silent treatment for a day or two. But this was a Brian who was new to me. This Brian made me feel cherished. This was a Brian whom I was falling in love with more every day.

"Sweetheart," I said, putting my arms around his neck. "A wider seat would be just wonderful."

He checked his wristwatch. "Are you ready?"

I pointed to my robe. "Does it look like I'm ready? What time is it, anyhow?"

"It's almost noon," he said, using his sleeve to polish the gleaming handlebars.

"But the reunion doesn't start until one. Didn't you say you were going to pick me up at twelve-thirty?"

He grinned, his blue eyes twinkling away. "I thought maybe you'd like to go for a ride first."

So off we went, leaving the tuna noodle casserole I'd made back home on the table. The sky was cloudless, the breeze soft, and the heat unbearable, which made the rush of wind on my face feel good. After about fifteen minutes, Brian pulled over and cut the engine. The countryside looked vaguely familiar, especially the hill to the left.

"Where are we?" I asked, pulling off my helmet.

He grinned. "Don't you recognize your favorite hayfield? But I guess it does look different in the daylight."

I stared at the overgrown meadow, then it hit me. It was the same hill I'd tumbled down the night of the wedding. Brian grabbed my hand.

"Come on," he said, pulling me behind him. "The view from the top is spectacular."

We trudged up the hill. There, at the summit, a blanket was spread. On it was a vase of wildflowers, with an envelope propped up against it. My name was scrawled on the envelope—in Brian's chicken scratch.

"Go ahead." Brian's hand pressed the small of my back. "Open it."

Sinking to my knees, I lifted the envelope and, with trembling fingers, carefully tore it open. Inside were two tickets for an Alaskan cruise. I gasped and looked up, but Brian wasn't standing over me anymore. He was kneeling beside me, holding a small, silver-wrapped box with a white bow, which he placed in my palm. "Here. This is what I wanted to give you thirty-three years ago."

With shaking fingers, I tugged the bow off then slowly pulled off the wrapping paper. A black velvet jewelry box. I pushed the lid back. There, nestled against deep blue velvet, was the most beautiful diamond ring I'd ever seen, sparkling in the noonday sun. My vision blurred. Brian pulled the ring out and slipped it on my finger.

"Linda Sue," he said, holding my face with his hands and wiping my tears with his thumbs, "I want to spend the rest of my life with you, if you'll have me."

*****

Once Jasmine spied the ring, there was no stopping her. A week after the reunion, she'd already scheduled the church and the fellowship hall for December 15th, our anniversary. And she bugged me for a guest list.

"Oh, I don't know," I said over lunch one day. "Family. Don't have a whole lot of friends anymore."

"What about your Bible study group? And your small group?"

I sipped my lemon water. "They hardly know us. What would they care? I want folks who've known us for thirty-three years."

"Well then, you can expect a dozen people." She sighed impatiently. "How many of those people are even around anymore?"

"I'll think about it, talk to Dad, and get back to you, all right?"

She grabbed the check and pointed it at me. "Friday. That gives you a week. No later."

I smiled, my heart filling with love for this headstrong daughter of mine. "Yes, dear."

*****

I knew something was wrong as soon as he stepped into the kitchen the first Friday in October.

"Lin, we need to talk," he said, avoiding my eyes.

With a sick feeling in the pit of my stomach, I followed him into the den. He nodded for me to sit. I sank onto the love seat. Brian eased himself down beside me, running his fingers, which were shaking, through his hair. After a few wordless minutes, he sighed.

"Lin, honey, we might have to put those wedding plans on hold."

Fear, raw and ugly and bleeding, stabbed me.

"I have prostate cancer."

CHAPTER THIRTY-NINE

"No."

Suddenly my insides felt so very cold. I wanted to say something—anything—but it was like someone had shot me in the head.

"Tell me it isn't true," I begged, searching his face for hope. I saw only sadness.

"Lin, the biopsy came back positive."

"Maybe there's been a mistake," I said. "Maybe they got your test results mixed up with someone else's."

"Sweetheart—"

"But it's possible."

"Possible. But hardly probable."

I looked away—out the window, into deepening dusk. I couldn't breathe. It was as though a giant hand were pressing down on my chest. I buried my face in Brian's flannel shirt, savoring the sweet feel of his lips against my hair, the familiar scent of his aftershave, the comforting sound of the beat of his heart. The clock on the mantle chimed the hour. Time, I thought, is the biggest liar of all—it fools you into thinking it's passing by slowly, but all the while it's rushing, rushing forward. Oh, how I wished I could turn it back—a month, a year. I leaned my head back and looked up at this man whom I'd fallen in love with twice. His cheeks, like mine, were streaked with tears.

How long had he known something was wrong? Anger, tinged with guilt, surged through me.

"Why didn't you tell me?" I choked out.

"I didn't want you to worry. I thought—"

"Don't I have a right to worry? I love you!" My fists pounded his chest. He pulled me close and held me tight.

"I'm sorry," he murmured. "I'm sorry."

I pulled away and looked into his eyes. "What did the doctor say?" I wished I would have gone with him, heard the report, gotten the prognosis firsthand—been there for him.

"It's all in here." He lifted a file folder from the coffee table and shoved it in my trembling hands. "Brian Laverly" was typed neatly on a label on the tab. Shivering, I flipped it open.

Brian stood. "I'll start a fire," he said, avoiding my eyes.

I consumed the copies of test results and other information the doctor had given him.

"Brian," I said when he sat beside me again, "did you do any research online?"

Pulling the file from my hands, he leafed through the papers. "Here." He tapped the top page. "But it's not much more than what Dr. McCullough told me."

I scanned the page hungrily. I wanted to know that everything was going to be all right. That we had another thirty-three years together. The words blurred. The fire crackled. I couldn't stop shivering. Reaching back, I pulled the quilt from the back of the love seat and draped it around me.

I began reading aloud. "In general, the earlier the cancer is caught, the more likely it is for the patient to remain disease-free." I looked up. "You caught it early, didn't you?"

"I think so, but we won't know how early until he goes in."

"Has the surgery been scheduled yet?"

"Next month."

"Next *month*?" Rage flared again. This was ridiculous. Tell a man he has cancer, that it has to come out then make him wait a month. I imagined squiggly, squirmy cancer cells spreading throughout Brian's body while we waited. I wanted to get on the phone, call that idiot of a doctor, and tell him a thing or two. "Why do we have to wait so long?"

"It's slow-growing."

"Can't you make them schedule it any sooner—like next week?"

"It's all right, Lin." He pointed to the file I held. "It's all in there—all different kinds of treatments, even nutrition. Sometimes they don't do anything except wait and see."

I turned my attention back to the paper in front of me and continued reading. "Oh, Brian, listen to this: Because approximately 90 percent of all prostate cancers are detected in the local and regional stages, the cure rate for prostate cancer is very high—nearly *100 percent* of men diagnosed at this stage will be disease-free after five years."

I put the paper down. "Sweetheart, we've got a good chance to beat this thing."

But he didn't seem to share my excitement. Raking his fingers through his hair, he stared into the fire.

"Lin, even with the best-case scenario, I'll be impotent for up to a year after the surgery."

"I can wait."

"Worst-case scenario: I won't be much of a man any more."

"Oh, Brian." I grabbed his hand. "Let's not think about the worst-case scenario. Let's be positive. We're going to be in each other's hair for the next fifty years."

"Honey," he sighed, running his thumb lightly over the top of my hand. "This is cancer. The big C. I'll be looking over my shoulder for the rest of my life."

I hurled the file across the room, toward the fireplace. Papers scattered.

"It's not fair!" I raged. "Why you? Why now, just when—How can God allow this to happen?"

Brian turned me to face him. "Lin, don't," he said in a choked voice. "I figure I've got a choice: either trust Him or not. I choose to trust Him." He took a deep breath. "And right now I need Him more than ever."

*****

Sleep, of course, was out of the question. My exhausted body couldn't settle in a comfortable position. *Is this my punishment, God, for leaving him?* Beside me, Brian stirred. I tried to lie still so he could doze off, but if the pillow wasn't flat, the blanket was twisted or the mattress lumpy. It must have been an hour before I heard him snoring softly. *How much longer will I hear this beautiful, sweet sound.* I rolled on my side, snuggling next to him, spoon-fashion. In his sleep, he wrapped his arm around me. *Oh, God, heal him, please. I'll never complain about anything he says or does ever again.* I sniffled. Would I ever run out of tears? Where was that box of tissues? *Oh, drat.* I took it out to the kitchen this afternoon.

Carefully lifting his arm, I eased out of bed, grabbed my robe and slippers, and tiptoed to the kitchen.

We'd spent three hours online before bed, searching and scrolling and clicking and printing until it all blurred together. My mind still whirled with the information overload. Maybe a cup of chamomile tea would calm me down.

When the kettle boiled, I poured my tea and headed for the den. The dogs padded beside me and dropped down on the carpet in front of the hearth with a soft thud-thud. The embers from the dying fire glowed, spitting little sparks up the chimney. A faint scent of wood smoke rode the draft across the room. I put my cup on the end table, accidentally knocking a plaque to the floor, and knelt before the fireplace.

Leaning back on my heels, I rolled up a newspaper and lay it on the coals, then placed a few twigs on top. Brian had taught me how to build a fire. I smiled, remembering our camping days. We could never agree on the fire. I liked a fire that was hot and high and hungry—a bonfire, really.

"But what good is it?" Brian would say. "You can't get too close for too long or you'll get burned."

Brian preferred a fire that was slower to start, took more time to build, but was sure and steady, with a cozy heat that lasted far longer and let you sit up close.

How like love, I thought. Youthful passion was instant heat, fast and furious—and over before you knew it. Mature love might have a slower start but was sure and steady—and lasted much, much longer.

Like Brian's love. I thought of all the times over the years I was too tired, too busy, too whatever. What I wouldn't give now to have those moments back. I'd never push him away again. The ironies of life.

As I watched the flames dance up the chimney, I remembered Brian packing his lunch so I could sleep in, rolling out of bed in the middle of the night to change a crying baby, bringing home pizza when I had night classes, folding laundry when I had a paper due or a test to study for. And I'd complained because I had to clean the bathrooms. I saw a woman who perceived herself a martyr because she gave up her dreams of a career to raise a family—a silly woman who acted as though motherhood and wifehood was second rate, who thought only of what she wanted.

Shame filled me. *I've been so blind.* I couldn't go back and undo the damage, and I didn't know how much time we had left.

I crawled to the love seat. On the floor by the end table was the plaque I'd knocked off earlier. I picked it up. And read the words of First Corinthian thirteen. Again. This time, the love chapter had a whole new meaning.

Love is patient, love is kind....Brian is patient, Brian is kind. He does not envy, he does not boast, he is not proud.

I swallowed, remembering all the times I wanted things done right away, but he took the time to do them right, ignoring my complaining and criticizing. And he always let me have my own way, never even mentioning what he wanted. Like our first wedding. Dabbing my eyes with the sleeve of my robe, I read on.

Brian is not rude, Brian is not self-seeking, he is not easily angered.

I smiled, remembering the times I'd tried to start a fight, but he just ignored me. And he'd supported every decision I ever made—even the one to go back to school, even though it meant taking up the slack when it came to the housework.

Brian keeps no record of wrongs.

Which is why we didn't get divorced years ago. But I was always harping about his shortcomings—criticizing him when he didn't get a project done as fast as I wanted him to.

Brian does not delight in evil, but rejoices with the truth. Brian always protects, always trusts, always hopes, always perseveres.

"Oh, God, I've been so selfish!" I cried, hugging the plaque to me and sobbing. "I don't want to be this way anymore. Help me."

I couldn't stop crying. Strangely, the more I cried, the cleaner I felt, until spent, I couldn't cry anymore. I crawled up onto the love seat, still clutching the plaque to my heart.

A warmth coursed through me. I leaned my head against the wing of the love seat and closed my eyes.

*****

Someone was gently shaking me.

"Lin. Lin. Wake up."

The aroma of coffee reached my nostrils. I blinked. Brian stood in front of me.

"Coffee or tea?" he asked.

I pushed myself to a sitting position, tossing the quilt back. Quilt? I frowned. I didn't remember covering myself with the quilt. The plaque stood upright on the coffee table.

"Tea," I mumbled, stretching my arms over my head and arching my back, feeling the kinks of a night spent on the love seat. "What time is it?"

"Eight o'clock," he called from the kitchen. "I have to leave in half an hour."

"Why?" I stepped into the kitchen and sat at the table.

"Saturday morning Bible study—remember?" He placed a mug in front of me, dropped in a tea bag, and poured the boiling water.

"Oh, right." I swirled the tea bag through the hot water so it would brew faster. "But why are you leaving so early? It doesn't start until ten."

"I have to stop by the house. I forgot my Bible."

"I'm coming with you."

He looked surprised.

"I know," I said, dumping three teaspoons of sugar in my cup and pouring in creamer. The concoction overflowed. I grinned. "My cup just runneth over."

"I thought, after last night, after what you said...."

I wiped the spill with a dish towel. "Let's just say I've had a change of heart."

An hour later we pulled up to our house. While Brian went in search of his Bible, I waited in the game room downstairs. It was a mess. An opened potato chip bag lay wrinkled on the floor beside Brian's recliner, crumbs spilling out onto the carpet. An empty plastic pop bottle lay on its side on the end table. DVDs littered the carpet. I bent over and shuffled through them. All romances. What was Brian doing with love movies? Suspicious, I grabbed the remote and flicked on the TV. *Oh, no.* The station that came on was WE—the women's romance channel.

"Got it," Brian said, stepping into the room. "Ready?"

I faced him, holding up *You've Got Mail.* "What is this?"

He shrugged. "What does it look like? A movie."

"Yes, I know it's a movie. But it's what *kind* of movie that bothers me. And what—" I pointed to the TV— "is *that* doing on?"

He grinned sheepishly, his ears turning redder than I'd ever seen them.

"Brian, what is going on here? Besides ball games, the only shows you ever watch are those infernal hunting and fishing shows. And, oh, yes, that one with Tim Allen, *Tool Time.*"

"*Home Improvement.*"

"What?"

"*Home Improvement.* That's the name of Tim Allen's show."

"Whatever. But what, pray tell—" I swooped my hand over the scattered DVDs—"is all this about?"

"I was, uh, taking a crash course."

"A crash course in *what*?"

"Romance."

I stared at him, speechless.

"Aw, Lin, you wanted romance, and, let's face it, I'm just not wired that way. Every time I tried to say something romantic, I'd end up saying something stupid."

"And so you started watching romantic movies." I didn't know whether to feel disappointed or relieved or mad.

"Actually, it was Jasmine's idea."

"Jasmine!" I dropped onto the sofa. "So, all those sweet things you said and did—it was all an act."

Putting his Bible down, Brian strode across the room and knelt in front of me, his hands on my knees.

"Aw, Lin. I had to get you back. I didn't know what else to do. Especially when Theodore showed up."

"Thomas."

"Whatever."

Suddenly I started giggling, which escalated into full-scale laughter. Brian joined in, and we howled until my sides hurt.

"Oh, Brian," I said, wiping tears from my eyes and clasping my hands around his neck. "My very own Tim-the-tool-man. What else did you learn from those movies?"

We didn't make it to Bible study.

CHAPTER FORTY

I stand on my tiptoes and peer out my kitchen window. The sky this early May evening promises a beautiful day tomorrow. Not a wisp of a cloud speckles its depthless face.

He is working in the yard. His step is slower than it used to be, his back slightly hunched over, a result of arthritis which seems to get us all in one place or another. His limp is more pronounced, a result of too much radiation so close to his hip. He jokes about it—says he's beginning to walk like his great-grandfather, whose bad hip eventually made a cane a permanent appendage. His beard, which he grew at my suggestion, came in gray. I say it makes him look even more sexy. His beautiful black wavy hair is much thinner and straighter than it used to be. Chemo does that, you know. He's thinner, too. It's been a hard battle he's waged. And it's not over yet. Well, that battle anyway.

He comes to the patio door. "When's supper, love?" His voice wafts through the screen. His blue eyes twinkle. I feel a nameless thrill in my soul.

"Soon," I say. "I'll call you. Go back to your yard work." I want to watch him just a little bit more. When he doesn't know I'm watching.

Aunt Retta, God rest her soul, was right. Love the second time around is much, much sweeter. You've ironed out all the kinks. You've tasted the honey of forgiveness. You've poured it on your wounds and others'. You've learned the secret of accepting and adapting. And you've discovered courage you never knew you had.

We celebrated my fifty-fifth birthday in Brian's hospital room, a week after his surgery. His stay was only supposed to be a couple of days, but complications extended it. Just the family was there. A small but loud party. The nurse had to warn us to settle down. But, hey, we had a lot to celebrate.

I'd gotten through the year without dying. And I'd found what I set out to find. Knock-your-socks-off, I-can't-live-without-you, romantic love. All the bells and whistles. I'd been swept off my feet.

We had our wedding, too—on our thirty-third anniversary—with all the hoopla and hype we didn't have the first time. Jasmine helped Brian plan everything. All I had to do was show up. I wore a white velvet gown and lace veil. Danny gave me away—and performed duties of best man. Jasmine and Katie were my matrons of honor. Lexie was the flower girl. She jumped up and down on the church platform and threw rose petals in the air during our vows and stole the show. B. J. wailed the entire time. I loved it. It was perfect.

The look in Brian's eyes as I walked down the aisle made me feel like a young bride. I'd gained some of my weight back, but he didn't care. He looked at me like he did when I was the girl in the picture in his wallet.

I step onto the patio. "Brian, supper's ready."

"Be right there," he calls. "Just let me finish fixing this—"

I smile. "Take your time," I say. "I can wait."

I have all the time in the world.